CHRISTINE POPE

DRAGON ROSE

ISBN: 978-0615718521

Published by Dark Valentine Press

Cover design by Ravven
Book layout by Indie Author Services



To learn more about this author, go to
www.christinepope.com.

*To Ilan of the Visions Fine Art Gallery in Sedona, Arizona, and to Manuel Nunez, the incredible artist who provided the original inspiration*

# Chapter One

My mother shut the front door and looked over at me. I waited on the bottom step of the staircase at the far end of the foyer, wishing I could flee and knowing all too well how that sort of behavior would be rewarded.

"Well?" she asked.

I hesitated. For the briefest second I contemplated the sort of prevaricating non-reply that might allow me to make my escape without having to give her the truth, but I knew better than that. My mother could sniff out a lie at twenty paces. I told her, "He's forty-five if he's a day, and his breath stinks of onions."

"Rhianne." My name on her lips was barely a sigh...albeit a sigh that spoke volumes. "You are in no position to be so choosy. When you are the eldest of four daughters—"

"—it's your responsibility to get yourself married off and out of the way," I finished for her. I knew the tale all too well by then, but that did not make me any happier to hear it once more. "I assure you, I know what is expected of me, but really, Mother—could you find no better prospects than Liat Marenson?"

"He is one of the richest men in Lirinsholme. He trades his wool all across the continent. And with the new factory he is building, he will only increase his wealth."

She spoke simply, as if reciting facts I had never heard before, but of course I knew them already. A town the size of Lirinsholme, with roughly five thousand souls within its walls and a little more than half that number living on its outskirts, did not have many secrets. I knew how many sheep Liat Marenson owned, knew that he had just spent a goodly sum to refurbish his large house on Lampwell Square. His first wife had died a year before, in childbed, and apparently he thought enough time had passed that he could go looking for a new one without causing too many tongues to wag.

I also knew that I could never, ever marry Liat Marenson. A fine house and gowns of Keshiaari silk were not inducement enough to lie down with a man old enough to be my father.

"I am sure Master Marenson will make a fine husband for some lucky girl," I said, since it was clear my mother expected some sort of reply. "But not me."

Her lips pressed together, and her dark eyes narrowed slightly. It was the only sign of anger she would allow herself. In all my almost twenty years, I had never once seen her lose her temper.

The gods only knew I had given her reason enough on more than one occasion.

Voice even, she said, "If you married him, you would be safe."

That again? In less than two months, I would not have to worry one way or another. I would have turned twenty, and therefore be too old to be selected as the Dragon's Bride. My mother and I both knew that, and we also both knew that her pressing me to marry someone so unappealing had far less to do with my supposed peril at the Dragon's hands...or talons, I suppose...and far more to do with the understanding that once I was Master Marenson's wife, his wealth could help to improve my younger sisters' prospects immensely.

Because that thought was uppermost in my mind, I found it easy enough to reply in flippant tones, "I think I would rather be married to the Dragon than to that paunchy, smelly old man!" as I gathered my skirts and hurried away up the stairs before my mother could remonstrate with me. As it was, I heard the shocked intake of her breath at my words, and I wondered if I had gone too far.

After all, marriage to an overweight, balding wool merchant was not a certain sentence of death...unlike marriage to Theran Blackmoor, the Dragon of Black's Keep.

The curse had been part of our lives for so long that we accepted it as part of the natural course of things, like the color of the sky or the phases of the moons. But of course there was nothing natural at all about a dragon who used to be a man.

How exactly such a thing had come to pass, no one could say, and the Dragon kept his own counsel. Legend had it that in ages past, when magic still existed in the world, Theran

Blackmoor was cursed by a mighty sorcerer. What Lord Blackmoor had originally done to so upset a sorcerer was now shrouded by the passage of time. A few tried to argue that he had never been a man at all, but had been born in his monstrous dragon form, although that theory was not widely supported. Whatever the case, the Dragon had cast his shadow, both literally and figuratively, over Lirinsholme for more than five hundred years…and he had been claiming his Brides for just as long.

All young women between the ages of sixteen and twenty lived under that shadow. We never knew precisely when the summons would come, for apparently it pleased the Dragon to vary his schedule to keep us off balance. Seven years might pass before the ominous banner of red silk would be hoisted above Black's Keep, or it might be as short a span as three or four. My grandmother told me once that in her grandmother's grandmother's time, there was a period of almost twenty years where the Dragon was not heard from, and people thought perhaps he had finally died and released the town from its peculiar bondage. But then fierce storms swept down on Lirinsholme from the mountainside where Black's Keep stood, ravaging the town. The earth itself shook, leveling houses and injuring many. Soon after, a bright red gash appeared against the sky, signaling the doom of one of the town's daughters, but at least once she had been sent, the town itself suffered no further catastrophe.

Whether these incidents were connected, my grandmother could not or would not say.

One might think we should appeal to the king, so he could send his knights and warriors against the Dragon.

This happened once, even longer ago than the storms and the quakes. The ruins still stood to the north of Lirinsholme, where the original town square stood before the wall was built. The scorched bricks and scattered stones were left as a warning, I think, and in any case, no other king dared raise his hand against the beast that dwelled just within the farthest northern borders of his kingdom. The sacrifice of one young woman every once in a while did not seem too great a price in order to avoid any further destruction. And besides, the Dragon always compensated the families of his Brides well. One thousand gold crowns in exchange for a daughter. Some might say it was a fair price.

Because of all this, Lirinsholme was left to manage its own peculiar curse.

My father was a potter, and quite a successful one, as such things are measured. On his own, he probably would not have done so well, but my mother managed him just as capably as she managed her daughters, and if he had had a son to carry on the family business, all would have been well.

Of late, however, his eyes had begun to fail, and for the last few years I'd taken over the fine painting on the most expensive pieces, those items destined for the houses of rich merchants such as Liat Marenson and his ilk. I had drawn since I could remember, using up the precious lead pencils intended for my sums and penmanship studies to instead draw the mountains surrounding the town, the faces of my sisters, the horses tied in front of the shops and taverns—anything save the occupations for which those pencils had actually been intended.

Because of my skills in this area, it seemed logical for me to perform the one task I could do to help keep the household going. And although I would rather have been sketching landscapes, at the very least painting flowers on a pitcher or tracing out the intricate Sirlendian twistwork that had lately come into vogue on a platter or serving tray seemed vastly preferable to helping my mother in the kitchen.

We told no one what I was doing, of course. People paid for Barne Menyon's work, not his daughter's. Luckily, my father's workshop was at the back of the house, in an area where no one could spy on what I was doing, and so it was easy to conceal the deception. It seemed harmless enough, after all, and I suppose I hoped in the back of my mind that my utility with a paintbrush might serve as a means to keep me at home longer, and out of a marriage I definitely did not want.

The meeting with Master Marenson had perhaps not dashed those hopes, but it certainly made them seem rather naïve and foolish. And when he sent a fine necklace of garnets the following day, I realized he was not one to be dissuaded quite so easily. I wished I could send the jewels back. My mother would have none of it, though, and instead had me pen a stilted little note of thanks, which she dispatched by means of our one servant, Janney, who was glad to escape the kitchen for a little while to deliver it.

"Perhaps I should run off with the next caravan of Keshiaari merchants," I remarked to my friend Lilianth, who had accompanied me to market the next morning.

"As if you would!" she laughed, but her expression sobered. "At any rate, you know that sort of thing never turns out well."

I paused at the stand of one of the vegetable vendors, pretending to measure the relative merits of one bunch of carrots over the other, but really, I was considering her words. Whether it was a quirk of the curse or just spectacular bad luck, whenever a young woman tried to leave Lirinsholme, she either ended up right back in the town after a series of misadventures, or suffered some ill fate on the road. We learned it was not wise to leave—at least not until we reached the magical age of twenty.

"I suppose not," I replied, and nodded toward Alina, who managed the vegetable stall my mother preferred. Alina handed me the indicated bunch of carrots, and I gave her a copper piece before tucking the vegetables into my basket, already heavy with my other purchases.

"It is rather dreadful," Lilianth said, after we stepped away from Alina's stall and wandered a few paces, going in the direction of Mertyn Pike's cheese shop. "If only you could meet someone like Adain!"

Adain Sweeton had been besotted with Lilianth since she had taken her hair out of braids, and she loved him just as fiercely. He'd had a domineering mother who wished for no rival at her hearth, but since she had obligingly passed away from a sudden heart spasm, the way seemed to have been cleared for Lilianth and her beau to marry, and soon. And since she was six months younger than I, Lilianth had more of a reason to marry as soon as seemed proper.

There was no one in town who caught my eye, and I was not one of those girls who would snatch up someone—anyone—just to avoid the Dragon's curse. Those marriages, more often than not, seemed to result in years of misery, a poor trade for the small chance that one's name might be drawn by the city elders as the Bride. After all, there were at least a hundred young women of the correct age at any given time. Those odds didn't seem to be that poor.

"Have you chosen a date yet?" I asked, not bothering to reply to Lilianth's remark. I guessed it would be easy enough to distract her from a conversation about my own conspicuous lack of appealing suitors.

As I had thought, she did not seem to notice the redirection. "Yes, just yesterday evening. We did not want it to seem to be too soon, because of Mistress Sweeton. But we thought the fifteenth of Sevendre should be far enough off."

Making it a little more than two months from now. Some might still think that too short an interval, but I was sure it felt like an eternity to Lilianth. "And your gown?"

"Oh, well, I don't want anything too grand..."

And she was off on a spirited discourse on the fabrics she was contemplating, and whether or not to make the sleeves slashed in the new fashion that had come all the way from Sirlende, and whether I should wear blue or green. All of this I listened to with only half an ear, my gaze caught instead by the mountains that surrounded us on all sides. The bright midsummer sun brought out all sorts of shades of purple and indigo on their heights, and my fingers itched for a paintbrush, even if all I could afford were some watercolors and not the far more expensive pigments used for oils.

We had one true painter in town, a man called Lindell—he used no other name—who had come to us after a stint in Lystare, the capital city of our kingdom of Farendon. Apparently Lindell had made the mistake of painting an unflattering portrait of the Duke of Tralion, and had to make himself scarce. Why Lindell escaped to Lirinsholme, and not some other better-situated location, he would not say, although I suppose the town had the advantage of remoteness. At any rate, it was he who showed me how to mix the pigments he had brought with him from the capital, and how to stretch a canvas, and how to work the heavy paints with a palette knife as well as a brush.

All this was done in brief stolen bursts, for of course that sort of painting was not considered proper for a young lady. I'd heard that accomplished young women of noble families lately had been allowed to create pencil sketches and watercolors, but even those would have earned me some sidelong looks here in Lirinsholme, had anyone else known of my obsession. Lindell tutored me in those techniques as well, and I enjoyed using them, but there was something about the strength and nuances of the oils that spoke to me. I knew better than to broach the subject at home, for even if my mother would have allowed such a thing...which I very much doubted...we could not have managed the cost of the supplies.

At any rate, I knew there would be no time for watercolors when I got home. It would be back to my father's workshop, and yet another in a long series of trailing vines painted on the edge of a plate, or scrolled ribbon shapes winding themselves around the neck of a pitcher.

Lilianth and I chatted a bit more, finished our purchases, and went our respective ways. I guessed her afternoon would be more enjoyable than mine, since fittings for her wedding gown were to commence as soon as she returned home. I, on the other hand, had to get back to the seemingly endless dish set that Elder Macon had ordered.

Ah, well, at least it helped to put food on our table.

My mother was ominously silent on the subject of Liat Marenson for the next few days, which meant she had to be plotting something. What, I wasn't quite sure, as the days when daughters were dragged kicking and screaming to the altar were mercifully behind us—unless one counted the unfortunate few who ended up as the Dragon's Bride. But I had the impression that she was planning something, using that sharp mind of hers to try to convince me that marrying the portly merchant was the only right thing to do.

Whatever her plan exactly was, I never discovered it. Disaster struck before then.

I did know that she had invited him for dinner, at which revelation I groaned inwardly but kept my silence. But still, with both my parents present and my three sisters to act as something of a buffer, I thought I could survive the evening without too much trouble. It seemed a poor use of the household's resources, when I had no intention of accepting Master Marenson's suit, but so be it.

That afternoon she had me dress far sooner than was strictly necessary, and I protested, for I had a mind to finish up the rest of Elder Macon's dish set. Only a few pieces remained.

"Oh, tut," my mother said, pulling the full sleeve of my chemise out slightly so it puffed between the shoulder of my gown and the lace-on sleeves that went with it. "Just wear one of your aprons, and be careful. And make sure you put everything away by half-past five, for Master Marenson is due to arrive at six."

I nodded, only listening with half an ear. It wouldn't be the first time I had painted in one of my better gowns. I knew her careful fussing with my sleeves was wasted effort, however, since I'd take off the lace-on bits and roll up my chemise sleeves to give myself adequate room to work. No use in mentioning it, though. I'd just have to readjust as best I could when the fated hour drew near.

My father was not in his workroom when I descended the stairs and took up my normal spot at the table by the window. I needed the light for my work, while he claimed that much of what he did was purely by feel. That I could believe, for many times I had seen him bending over his potter's wheel, grey-streaked dark hair falling into his face, his eyes shut as his hands found the shapes hidden within the fluid clay.

Where he had gone, I didn't know. What I did know was that the more bustle my mother created in the house—and there was much bustling in advance of Master Marenson's visit—the more reason my father found to go elsewhere. He liked to gather his own clay, from secret spots only he knew along the banks of the River Theer, and it seemed he discovered a pressing need for fresh supplies whenever things got too chaotic at home.

So I took little note of his absence, save for a wistful desire to be out with the wind and the sky instead of cooped up in the workshop, which always seemed stuffy and over-warm. And since we were at the peak of the summer's heat, it seemed sultrier than ever. I grimly rolled up my sleeves and pulled a set of bone hairpins from my pocket, fixing my hair in a messy knot at the back of my head and no doubt ruining the careful curls that had been achieved by means of sleeping with my hair up in rags the night before.

The pieces awaiting paint before their final firing sat on a shelf next to my worktable. I picked up a bowl, sat down with my back to the door so I wouldn't block any of the light, and got to work.

The challenge for me, as always, was not to faithfully reproduce the pattern of ivy and forget-me-nots that Elder Macon had prescribed for his new dishes, but rather to keep that pattern consistent from piece to piece. I would much rather have altered each one, not hugely, but enough to give the dinnerware some interesting visual variation. But variation was not what the Elder wanted, so instead I made myself concentrate on churning out uniform leaf after uniform leaf, consistent flower after consistent flower.

When I worked, I paid very little attention to what was going on around me. My father sometimes joked that I wouldn't even notice if the house caught fire, if I happened to have a paintbrush in my hand at the time. I'm not sure how true that really was, but I did tend to let the world close down to only me, the brush, and the surface I was painting, whether it was a piece of stoneware or a leaf of paper.

So I vaguely half-heard a door somewhere slamming, and feet rushing across the wooden floors, but since no one came in to see me, I paid those sounds very little mind. The light coming in the window also did little to inform me of the passage of time, as at that season of the year, full dark didn't set in until very late. Six o'clock in the evening was just as bright as three, or four, or five.

It wasn't until I heard Master Marenson's shocked tones exclaiming, "My lady Rhianne!" that I realized something was amiss.

I started and dropped my paintbrush—luckily not on the plate that was my current project, but on the stained wooden tabletop. Then I realized his was the absolutely last voice I should be hearing in my father's workshop.

Although at the moment I wished I could simply flee out the back door, I knew that escape was not feasible. So I slipped off the stool and turned, one hand going up to pull the pins out of the hasty knot at the back of my head.

By some miracle, my voice sounded almost calm. "Master Marenson. Is it six o'clock already?"

His face had flushed an unbecoming dark red, doubly unattractive, as it clashed horribly with the maroon doublet of heavy linen he wore. "Past six, Miss Rhianne, and no one to greet me at the door but a scullery maid and some chit not old enough to leave the schoolroom, let alone allow visitors into her house!"

By "chit" I assumed he meant my youngest sister Darlynne, who had just turned eleven at midsummer. Where everyone else was, I had no idea. "My apologies, Master Marenson. I'm sure this can all be explained. Perhaps there was some emergency that called my mother and other sisters out of the house."

His eyes, small already, seemed to almost disappear as he scowled down at me from the top step. "And what 'emergency' is it, Miss Rhianne, that has you engaged in such an unseemly enterprise?"

For the first time I realized I stood there in a paint-stained apron, my current occupation abundantly clear, not just through those telltale paint spatters, but also from the stoneware ranged around my spot at the worktable. Oh, dear.

Although there was no way to deny what I had been doing, I thought perhaps if I made light of it, or even ignored it, he would do the same. Essaying a smile, I reached up to untie the apron from the back of my neck and then discarded it on my abandoned stool. At least my gown seemed to have escaped relatively unscathed.

"Why don't we go up to the sitting room?" I suggested. "I'm sure there is an explanation for my parents' absence—they were so very much looking forward to dining with you—but in the meantime I can have Janney bring you some porter or a glass of wine while we wait."

For a second or two I thought he might actually acquiesce. But then I saw him straighten and cast a jaundiced eye around my father's workroom.

"If you think, Miss Rhianne, that I am going to accept hospitality from those who have purposely lied to me, then you have quite an incorrect idea of my character."

"I hardly know you, Master Marenson, and therefore I feel I am not qualified to have yet formed any idea of your character."

His face reddened further. "Impertinence! I count myself glad that I discovered this now, before it was too late!"

"Discovered my impertinence?" I asked innocently.

"Discovered that you are engaged in trade, young woman—that you are doing your father's work for him, as no properly brought-up young lady should."

"And so the 'proper' thing to do would have been to let our livelihood dwindle along with my father's eyesight?"

"The proper thing is to be truthful, Miss Rhianne. Your father is selling work that is not his."

My mother would have known to guard her tongue, to find the soft tone of voice that might placate an angry man. But I had not her skills, and I found I enjoyed giving in to the anger that flared in me at this preposterous man's misplaced indignation.

"What difference does it make?" I snapped. "If the work is good, and our patrons are satisfied, who should care whether it was my father's hand or mine that painted those flowers, those leaves? Are they any less pleasing to look at because they came from a woman and not a man?"

"A very great difference," Liat Marenson said, and his fleshy lips thinned a little. "A very great difference." With a kind of vindictive satisfaction he added, "And you may find that I am not the only one who feels this way."

With that he replaced his velvet cap on his thinning hair and stalked out.

After he had gone, I realized my hands were shaking. Not so much because I had been discovered, but because of Master Marenson's not-so-subtle threat to reveal my family's secret to the rest of the town. Such a revelation could ruin us.

More pressing, however, was the mystery of my parents' absence. What could have possibly happened to prevent them from being at home for such an important guest?

I found out soon enough. My father had gone to gather clay, as I had guessed. What I hadn't guessed was that he would suffer a heart spasm while hauling the heavy barrow of clay homeward.

Luckily, a cowherd found him sprawled across the path and had taken him to his cottage, only a quarter-mile away. Word came to the house, and my mother and two of my sisters had left immediately. It would take something of that magnitude for my mother to forget Liat Marenson and her plans for him, and in summoning the doctor and waiting through the examination that followed, she had quite lost track of the time.

It was falling dark by the time she returned, looking drawn and preoccupied and not at all her usual poised self. She reassured me that Father was fine, but that he shouldn't be moved for at least a day or so more.

"And what of Master Marenson?" she asked, casting a worried glance around the dining room, where the unused table settings still awaited a guest who would never use them. Darlynne and Janney and I had cleaned up the uneaten food and stored it in the larder several hours past.

The truth would only upset my mother further, and besides, I had no idea whether Liat Marenson actually planned to make good on his threats. "I made our apologies," I said. "He understood that some emergency must have occurred, and so returned home." Well, that was at least half true.

She nodded and, after making a quick inspection of the kitchens, told me that it was time for bed. I wasn't about to argue; the day felt as if it had dragged on quite long enough.

Perhaps I wouldn't have been so eager to sleep if I had known what awaited me on the morrow.

They began to appear at as early an hour as was considered half-way civil—Elder Macon, the Widow Mallin, everyone who had placed an order with my father in the last few months. My mother met them at the door and tried to explain that Barne Menyon was very ill and not even at home. They cared little for that. They only wanted their money back.

Somehow she got rid of them and came to see me where I sat in the schoolroom, looking down at the street from my second-story window. The plumes on the Widow Mallin's hat bobbed indignantly as she strode away, and I thought the sight reminded me of nothing more than an outraged barnyard fowl.

"What happened, Rhianne?" my mother asked, standing in the doorway with her arms crossed. The shadows under her eyes seemed very pronounced in the bright sunlight streaming through the windows.

"I fear Master Marenson discovered me painting the last of Elder Macon's dish set yesterday afternoon."

"And you waited until now to tell me?"

"You had more pressing things to worry about yesterday evening."

She was silent, mouth tight as she contemplated my words. I knew she wouldn't explode—not my mother—but that didn't mean she couldn't say some very cutting things when pressed. Perhaps she would tell me that I should have made up some plausible lie, or that I should have noticed the passage of time and been safely out of the workroom long before Liat Marenson appeared on our doorstep.

I held my breath, waiting.

At length she said, "We will wait and see if this blows over. I have some money set by, and we needn't worry. Not yet."

Relief course through my veins, even as I wondered at her words. Oh, there had been money on her side of the family—her father, though he had died before I was born, had been a successful tinsmith, and it was his house that we lived in now, the house my mother inherited when my grandmother died. I had been a small child then, barely five years, and I remembered very little of my maternal grandmother. She had been a wispy pale little woman who seemed content to let her daughter rule things. I guessed there had been very little argument when my mother took it into her head to marry a young potter with barely a copper *graut* to his name.

However, I'd never heard a whisper of any savings, and indeed, with the way my mother talked about the household finances, I had always assumed that we lived from month to month, with only my father's earnings to keep us afloat. Now those earnings were threatened, but perhaps it didn't matter quite as much as I had thought.

"*Some* money," she repeated, giving me a warning look. "Certainly not enough to permanently replace your father's income, or even keep this house going for more than a month... possibly two, if we are very careful. So do not look quite so relieved, Rhianne."

Since there was very little else I could say, I merely bowed my head. I wouldn't let myself become too discouraged.

After all, a great deal could happen in a month's time.

# Chapter Two

My father came home three days later, riding in the back of the cart his savior shepherd used to bring wool to town. We all clustered around him, exclaiming over his return, but he was uncharacteristically quiet, a grimness that couldn't be completely attributed to his condition somehow clinging to him. My mother shushed Darlynne and Maeganne, saying that their father needed his rest, and bustled him up to the room my parents shared.

Down in the entry hall, my sister Therella and I exchanged wary glances. I had not spoken of what passed between Liat Marenson and myself, and neither had my mother said anything, but news gets around in a town the size of Lirinsholme. More than once I had seen Therella give me grudging looks, as if she blamed me for our current situation. Ridiculous, of course—it was not my fault that Liat Marenson was such a narrow-minded prig, nor that the world carried such prejudices against women engaging in trade. Or, to be more precise, women engaging in trades reserved for men. It was all very well for Alina to sell her vegetables in the market, or for the Widow Lanson to sew clothing for those who did not wish to make their own, but the potter's trade—along with that of the tinsmith, the glass blower, the ironmonger, and all those others who made up the Craftsmen's Guild—was the sole province of men. In their eyes, I had far overstepped my bounds and intruded where I had no right.

Finally, Therella said, "I hope you're happy."

"I?" I repeated. "I am happy Father is home, if that is what you mean."

She made an impatient gesture. "I always knew it was a bad idea, you helping Father is his workroom. Now look where we are! No one has placed an order for days, and I saw Mother giving money back to the Widow Mallin. What are we going to do now?"

"Wait for Father to get better," I replied, trying to keep the bite out of my words. Truly, I understood my sister's fear, even if I found her blame to be entirely misplaced. But she was seventeen, old enough to want to be grown up while at the same time lacking the life experience to achieve such a state. She could not—or would not—understand that we were all victims here. It wasn't as if I had asked to help out in the workroom. My parents had decided on the matter together, knowing the risks.

"And that will help exactly how?"

"At least then he will be able to go back to work. If people see him working—while I am far away from his workshop—then perhaps things will begin to mend. But fretting isn't going to do anyone any good."

She made a derisive noise but did not argue, instead turning from me and going upstairs to the room we shared. This was her own form of revenge, for our bedroom was not large, and with one of us occupying it, the other was effectively locked out.

I sighed and moved on to the little sitting room off the kitchen, where I had left some of my hated embroidery. At least no one could accuse me of painting while my hands were occupied with a needle and silk floss.

Days passed, and my father slowly mended, although he could not or would not return to his workroom. My mother seemed to turn paler and more silent with each passing day, and one night I chanced upon her as she sat at the kitchen table, a meager-looking stack of silver coins in front of her and a paper covered with figures set off to one side, as if she had pushed it away. Her head drooped, and I heard her weeping.

I stopped then, and crept away. I knew she would not want me to see her weakness.

That night I dreamed.

I saw the dark granite bulk of Black's Keep silhouetted against the night sky. And from its highest tower I saw a black shape move off into the wind, the shadow of its wings blotting out the stars. With the night wind came a high, keening cry, like that of a diving hawk, yet a thousand times stronger, filling the cold air with the echoes of its pain. Darkness seemed to flow out from it, running up the hills and down the valleys between the Keep and the town of Lirinsholme, swallowing everything in its path, as if some god had poured ink from the heavens to paint the entire world black. And we all stood in the town square and watched the shadow approach, fear rooting us in place, until the black tide rushed up and over us, drowning us all.

Then I sat up in bed, gasping, cold sweat trickling down my back even though the night air coming in the open window was sweet and warm. I grasped the linen of my bedsheets, softened by countless washings, and made myself remember where I was. From across the chamber I heard my sister's soft snores. I was home. I was safe.

Once I might have discounted such a thing as merely a nightmare, simply fragments of the day's worries recast into a dream shape. But a year earlier I had dreamed of my cousin Clary giving birth to her son in the night, and when I awoke the next morning, news came to us that she had indeed borne a healthy boy that night. I might have thought nothing of it—after all, Clary's impending childbed had been on all our minds—save that another night, only two months later, I dreamed that my Granny Menyon had fallen and broken her hip. So she had, as she'd gotten up in the darkness to fetch herself a cup of water.

I spoke of the dream to her several days later, as I was taking my turn in watching over her, and she smiled. "It's a true Seeing, child. Nothing to fear."

"'Nothing to fear'?" I echoed. "But isn't it...magic?"

I had lowered my voice on that last word, for even in these latter days magic is something mistrusted and even reviled, an unquiet relic from an age when sorcerers ruled the land. No one much believed in it anymore, at least not in the world at large. Here in Lirinsholme, however, we had the Dragon as a constant reminder that magic wasn't quite as dead as the rest of the world seemed to think it was.

Granny Menyon only smiled again and shook her head. "Not magic…at least not the way people think of it nowadays. It's only your heart seeing the important things, and telling your head. Nothing to fear. It's a gift, such as the way you can make a few strokes of paint look like a forget-me-not."

Her words made me look at her in surprise. I had thought I was being so careful about hiding my unconventional avocation.

The smile didn't waver. Despite her years, she still had teeth as white and straight as a twenty-year-old's. "Your father is proud of you, proud of your talents. He shares things with me…as he should. Any road, 'tis only that you have a way of seeing things, and sometimes you see them with your heart first. Tell yourself that, child, and it won't seem so strange."

At the time I had been comforted, and since I hadn't had a true dream like that for some time, I had almost forgotten my so-called gift, pushed it off to some corner of my mind where I could forget it.

But now…

I pushed back my bedclothes and stood, then went to the window and looked out over the town. A half-moon hung low in the east, its twin barely visible above the horizon. To the north all was dark, although in the town itself the streets in their orderly grids were picked out here and there by flickering torchlight. All calm, all quiet. Perhaps my dream had been only that, a dream. Never mind that I could still hear the echoes of that wailing cry in my ears, still feel the cold air freezing my very marrow. In the past my Seeing had been of things taking place the same time I saw them, and yet nothing in my world seemed to have been disturbed.

Why, then, could I not forget that image of darkness rising to swallow us all?

Lilianth came by the next morning, as she wanted me to accompany her to the shop of Willem the cloth merchant to help make the final choice of fabric for her wedding gown. I was glad enough of the diversion, even though I knew I would have to tell my friend soon enough that I could afford no fabric of my own for a new gown.

But it was good to be free from the brooding atmosphere in my house, where things had once been bright and merry. Oh, we had not been abandoned entirely—several of those who counted themselves friends of the family had made sure to purchase some pieces from us—but these small gestures could not begin to replace the income we had lost from our wealthier clients.

Even now some people stared as I passed them in the street, but I affected not to notice, and Lilianth was so caught up in her chatter about the upcoming nuptials that of course she didn't detect any frostiness on the part of the passers-by. We spent a good hour in Willem's shop, and although she had protested earlier that she meant for it to be a very quiet affair, her choice in fabric seemed to bely that description, for she ended up walking out with a length of marvelously supple sky-blue cloth that Willem said was a new weave of linen and silk, providing strength and sheen at the same time. It was truly lovely, I had to admit, but I blanched a little at the number of coins Lilianth counted out to the merchant in exchange for the material.

We emerged into the bright noonday sun and blinked. Certainly nothing could be more different from my black dream of the night before than the clear sky above and the reflected green of the hills all around us.

At first I didn't even realize I had seen it. A flash of red, just a glimmer of crimson above the dark shoulders of Black's Keep. And then I heard the murmur of the people around me grow into a roar, as Lilianth's fingers dug into my arm and people began pointing northward. Yes, there it was, a red silk banner snapping in the breeze above the Dragon's castle.

I swallowed, and realized my dream had been a true one after all. Not with darkness, perhaps, but nevertheless, doom had come to Lirinsholme.

"A month," my mother said, staring at me in some despair. "One month more, and you would have been safe."

"It's better this way," I said stoutly, and gave Therella's hand an encouraging squeeze. "At least we can go as sisters, and stand together."

My mother swallowed and shot a despairing glance at my father. He was pale but composed, although I noticed his hand shook a little as he grasped the cane he'd been using ever since his heart spasm.

"It will be all right," he said. "There are many eligible, and they choose only one. We'll be back for supper and laughing, knowing that the Dragon will not choose another Bride until after both girls are old enough to be safe."

That was true enough, but it didn't secure the safety of my two younger sisters, thirteen and eleven. Still, suffice the day's evil, as they say, and the odds of two girls being chosen from the same household were probably about the same as being struck by lightning. Or worse, maybe, as we all knew old dazed Janson, who had been hit by a bolt in his youth and had never been the same since. On the other hand, there were no records of sisters ever having been the Dragon's Bride.

Therella and I stood in the entry hall, having put on our best gowns. That was always the way of it—the daughters of the town would assemble in the main square, all wearing their finest, and the elders would gather on the wide balcony that topped the entrance to Lirinsholme's town hall. The name was drawn from a large silver urn into which small pieces of paper with the candidates' name written on them had been dropped. Maintaining the list of names was part of the elders' duty, as was sitting up the night before the Bride was selected and writing out all the names on those scraps of paper.

It had not been a good night for any of us, of course. My sister had muttered and cried out in her sleep, and I was restless as well, shifting seemingly every quarter-hour so I could find a more comfortable position. What sleep I did manage was untouched by any dream, true or otherwise. This halfway disappointed me, for while I was not overly eager to learn my fate, at least if I'd had some inkling of what I faced on the morrow, I might have been better equipped to face it.

The sun shone through the stained-glass windows on either side of the front door, tracing elegant patterns in blue and green and red on the gleaming wood floor beneath. The air smelt of the beeswax we rubbed into the molding to make it shine. I glanced around me, and wondered if this might be the last time I ever stood here.

But I knew better than to speak such words aloud.

The town square was not large enough to accommodate all of Lirinsholme's citizens; the candidates had first priority, of course, and stood closest to Brecken Hall and the balcony where even now the three elders stood, the silver urn containing all our names sitting on a small table off to one side. Ranged beyond the uneasy crowd of young women were their families, and beyond that the merely curious, the onlookers who wanted to see firsthand the Dragon's doom fall on yet another unlucky candidate.

My sister Therella did not seem overly concerned with sisterly fellowship and left my side almost as soon as we joined the throng. From a few paces away I had spied her friend Gilly's bright red hair and guessed her destination was the other girl's side. At another time I might have been offended by her desertion, but almost at once I saw Lilianth pushing through the crowd to join me. Her face was white with worry, the usual pretty pink in her cheeks having deserted her this morning.

At once I reached out and took her hand, and she grasped mine with such force she might have been a drowning woman grabbing for a rescuer's outstretched fingers. "Oh, gods," she said, blue eyes apparently locked on the silver urn that held all our names. "How can this be happening? Why now? I am supposed to marry Adain!"

"And you will," I told her, in what I hoped were soothing tones. Despite the size of the crowd, it was oddly quiet, everyone speaking in low murmurs or whispers...or not at all. The young women, their faces as known to me as my own, stood silent, watching the balcony with its ominous urn. "There must be at least a hundred of us here. What are the chances that they'll pull your name?"

This didn't seem to reassure her as I had hoped it would. Instead, she only clenched my hand more tightly and bit her lip. Despite the warm late-morning sun—far too strong for my good blue gown of heavy damask linen—her fingers were ice-cold against mine, fragile as tatting needles.

And truly, though my words had been measured enough, I felt her doubt and fear almost as if they were my own. It wasn't fair. Why should she—or any of the young women standing around us—have to put her life at risk, merely to serve the whim of some unseen monster?

I knew better than to ask...not that anyone would have been willing to inquire. It seemed the time for questions was long gone, because a stir went through the crowd as the first of the three elders, Elder Macon, appeared, followed by Elder Drewson and Elder Dahlish. My own heart began to beat a little faster, despite my resolution to stay calm, no matter what happened. I had already done enough to draw attention to myself.

The three elders clustered around the urn and cast disapproving glances at one another. Even though they more or less ruled Lirinsholme, they all distrusted one another mightily. I suppose in a way that was good, as it reduced the risk of any two of them colluding against the other. On the other hand, it did make for some highly contentious town meetings, or so my father said.

Elder Drewson stepped forward and cleared his throat. Despite his title, he was not so elderly at all, a little more than two-score years. If he had been the one paying suit to my parents, rather than Liat Marenson, I might not have protested so strongly, as Marr Drewson was a well-looking enough man, with a fine chin and heavy dark hair. However, as he was not looking for a wife, despite being a widower of more than five years, his personal charms did not matter much.

"The Dragon has spoken," Elder Drewson said, with a brief flicker of his gaze over his left shoulder, toward Black's Keep and the baleful red pennant that flew from its highest battlements. "One will go to him to be his Bride, to keep Lirinsholme safe. She has our gratitude, whoever she is."

He sounded almost sincere, unlike Elder Macon, who had performed this task last. He had spoken the ritual words in a dry tone that made it sound as if he were reciting off a list for the butcher.

Elder Drewson nodded. "Elder Dahlish?"

The third elder stepped forward. He was quite old, having held his post for longer than I had been alive. His hand shook a little as he reached into the urn, but whether that was from nerves or some sort of palsy, I couldn't be sure.

Lilianth's fingers tightened around mine, pushing the silver band I wore on the middle finger of my right hand uncomfortably into the flesh on either side. I did not bother to move my hand, or tell her to stop. It would be over soon enough, and then we could both relax.

Elder Dahlish withdrew a narrow piece of paper, looked at it, and seemed to shake his head slightly. Then he handed it over to Elder Macon.

The third elder squinted at the words on the paper, then said, "Lilianth Fortens."

My entire body went cold, even though I could feel sweat trickling down the back of my neck from the warm midsummer sun. Lilianth let out a little cry, the crushing pressure on my fingers abruptly ceasing as she lifted both hands to her mouth. From behind them I could hear her saying, "No, no, no, no..."

The girls who surrounded us stepped back a few paces, their faces bright with relief, although in a few I also saw pity. Lilianth's love for Adain was well-known.

It was the custom for the chosen Bride to walk to the steps of the town hall and wait there for the elders to descend to her. After that she would be brought inside, and taken away to Black's Keep. No time for farewells, no chance to say goodbye or even pack a few belongings. She always went wearing only the dress—her finest—on her back.

Somehow I knew Lilianth could not make that walk unassisted. And I had already thumbed my nose at tradition, so what difference did it make if I broke one more rule in giving her the only succor I could?

"Come, Lilianth," I said, and placed one arm around her slender waist. She sagged against me, and I thought she would have collapsed if I hadn't held her up. "I'll go with you."

"You can't," she breathed.

"I don't see anyone stopping me. Come along."

And so we began the long walk to the front steps of Brecken Hall. We had been standing toward the back of the crowd, and so it seemed as if we traversed the long road from Lystare to Mellinshall, the capital of Purth, rather than the hundred yards or so it was in actuality. The crowd parted before us, but I did not try to hasten Lilianth's footsteps, rather, slowing my own. She would be lost to us soon enough. What difference did a minute or two make?

From somewhere behind us I heard a young man cry out, "Lilianth!" and knew it was Adain who called her name. She stiffened, and paused, but then continued her slow walk forward. A muffled commotion ensued, and I guessed Adain had tried to press forward but had been detained. He could not save her.

No one could.

As we walked a slow fury began to build in me. No, it was not fair that Lilianth should have to throw away her life thus, not when she had everything that was bright and good ahead of her. And all for some monster's whim, his cruel notion to take a Bride when the mood suited him. Why couldn't Elder Dahlish have chosen some other name...any other name?

*My name.*

At that thought a tremor went through me, but Lilianth seemed not to notice. We put one foot in front of the other, in a movement as slow and inexorable as the incoming tide. But as we walked my mind began to race, even as a new and terrible thought took hold.

My family would mourn, but I could help them no longer. There was not even the prospect of a good marriage awaiting me, as most men seemed disinclined to take a wife so eager to flout tradition as I. Lilianth was an only child, whereas I had three younger sisters.

And the Dragon always gave a thousand crowns to the family of the woman he took as his Bride.

It would be enough to see them through comfortably for many, many years. Enough that my mother would not have to count her last silver coins. Enough that my sisters would have good dowries.

Enough that all their lives would be made easy.

I knew then what I must do, and although the resolve strengthened in me with every step, still I could feel my heart beating faster and faster, the snug-fitting bodice of my gown seeming to keep me from gathering enough breath to fill my lungs. By the time we reached the steps of the hall, I could not tell any longer whether I was the one holding up Lilianth, or whether she supported my suddenly shaky frame.

The three elders had descended from the balcony and stood waiting on the steps. From the waspish expression on Elder Dahlish's and Elder Macon's faces, I gathered they were not overly pleased by my act of friendly support in assisting Lilianth on her walk to the hall. Elder Drewson looked somewhat surprised, but at least he wasn't frowning.

I had a feeling his pleasant expression would not last much longer.

Elder Macon stepped forward. "Lilianth Fortens, you have been chosen as the Dragon's Bride. From here on out you have no family, no connections, no ties to anything but the Lord of Black's Keep. Do you understand?"

She hesitated, and I knew I must speak up then or let events continue on their own inexorable path.

I cleared my throat. "Excuse me."

All three of the elders stared down at me, Elder Macon and Elder Dahlish frowning in a manner that would have once intimidated me. Now I felt as if I had very little left to lose.

"Rhianne Menyon," said Elder Macon, in tones that should have been quelling, "you have rendered your service to your friend. It is time now to step aside and let her meet her destiny."

"As to that," I replied, meeting his cold blue gaze as directly as I could, "why does it have to be her?"

At this question, all three of the elders exchanged glances that seemed to communicate either extreme annoyance or possible concern that I might have gone mad. "Her name was drawn out of the urn," Elder Dahlish said, in his wispy dried-paper voice.

"But you drew it out. It isn't as if the Dragon came here and chose it himself."

"Watch your tongue, young woman, and guard against speaking of things of which you know nothing," Elder Macon snapped.

"It is said that the will of the Dragon guides the elder's hand as he makes the selection," Elder Drewson put in.

"You don't really believe that, do you?"

At that question even Lilianth stared at me as if I had lost my mind. "We do not question these things," she murmured.

"Perhaps we should." I set my hands on my hips and gazed up at the three elders. "The Dragon requires a Bride, that much is true, but I do not see why it should be poor Lilianth here, not when she has a betrothed and has already bought the cloth for her wedding gown. I have no betrothed, and my family will still have three daughters left when I am gone. Let me be the Dragon's Bride in Lilianth's stead."

Elders Macon and Dahlish gasped, and Lilianth turned to me at once, saying, "You cannot think of such a thing, Rhianne! You mustn't! I would never ask such a thing—"

"You didn't ask," I interrupted. "I offered. It only remains to be seen if the elders will allow me to take your place."

"Such a thing has never happened before—" Elder Dahlish began.

"—which does not mean it cannot happen now." I took a step forward and stared up at them, willing them to understand why this was the only right and true thing to do. "I'm begging you. Please let me save my friend."

"A moment," Elder Drewson said, and the three men turned away from Lilianth and me and began whispering furiously.

"You cannot mean such a thing," Lilianth said. Her eyes were bright with tears. "I cannot allow you to sacrifice yourself."

"I do mean it, and it isn't a question of allowing—that's up to the elders. I only want you to be happy."

She began to weep then, tears running down her cheeks and leaving damp spots on the frilled edge of her chemise where it peeked out from beneath her sapphire-colored gown. Truly I did not want to cause her pain, but I also knew she would make no further protest.

The elders turned back to us, and Elder Macon stepped forward. "You assert that you do this by your own choice, and with no coercion?"

"No coercion," I said wearily. "You've made it quite clear, Elder Macon, what my standing is in Lirinsholme, the damage I have done to my family. Is it not better that I should go forth thus? At least then you can say I have served some useful purpose."

His lips thinned, but he did not bother to contradict me. "We elders have agreed that you, Rhianne Menyon, may take Lilianth Fortens' place as the Dragon's Bride. From here on out, you have no family, no—"

"I heard it the first time." And as Elder Macon spluttered, I turned to Lilianth. "Go, my dear. Go and be happy."

"But Rhianne—"

"Be with Adain." My throat seemed to tighten, and I added, "If you have a daughter, perhaps you could name her after me?"

Tears shone bright on her cheeks in the morning sun. "It would be my honor."

She turned then and began to walk down the steps. The watching crowds in the square had been silent throughout this exchange, but as Lilianth moved away from the town hall, a murmur began to rise, one that soon swelled into an outright clamor as everyone seemed to take in what had just transpired on the building's steps. I thought I heard a despairing cry from somewhere far off to the left, one which I fancied could have come from my mother's throat, but I told myself that was a foolish notion. There was no way I could have heard one person's voice above such a noisy throng.

In silence the elders led me into the hall.

"You have brought nothing with you?" asked Elder Drewson, who looked somewhat troubled, as if he were not altogether happy with this turn of events.

I spread my hands wide to show I carried nothing. The silver ring on my finger gleamed as I did so, and Elder Macon said immediately, "The ring. And the earrings."

Truly, I'd almost forgotten that I wore the little garnet and silver drops that had been my name-day present when I turned seventeen. With a pang I removed them from my ears and dropped them into Elder Macon's outstretched hand, followed by the silver band I wore on my third finger. Why the Dragon should care whether I possessed such modest pieces of jewelry puzzled me, but I knew now was not the time to protest.

"Can you see that they're given to my family?"

Elder Macon gave a grudging nod and slipped them into the pouch he wore at his belt. "Now we must be off. The horses await."

Neither of those pronouncements did much to hearten me. I supposed it would have been too much to ask that they would delay my departure—the Brides were always immediately whisked away. And while I certainly did not dislike horses, I had very little experience of them. In Lirinsholme I walked everywhere, and my family did not own a single horse. One time when my father traveled to the capital in Lystare, he had borrowed a mount from Tylin, the goldsmith, but of course I hadn't been allowed near the animal.

I let out a small sigh and told myself that it wasn't that far to Black's Keep. Four miles, five at the most. Of course, the last part of the journey would be up a twisting mountain path. But perhaps my poor horsemanship would slow us down, would help to prolong my arrival at the Dragon's home.

In the alley behind the hall three horses waited. I must have shown some sort of question on my face, for Elder Drewson said, "Elder Dahlish cannot make the journey up the mountain any longer. Elder Macon and I will accompany you to Greyton, where someone from Black's Keep waits to take you the rest of the way."

Greyton was a small hamlet located halfway up the mountain. On a good day it might boast two hundred souls. Its inhabitants were shepherds and their families, and as well as those who carded the wool before bringing it to market in Lirinsholme. That was their only interaction with the residents of my town, for they stayed studiously apart from us.

Well, perhaps not the only interaction. I'd heard it rumored that some of the young men of Lirinsholme would make the journey to Greyton to visit the women there, as they apparently were rather free with their favors, especially when compared to the carefully guarded daughters of the families in the larger town.

Elder Drewton helped me climb into the awkward sidesaddle, and I did my best to tuck my skirts around me in a more or less decorous manner. While I was thus occupied, the two men got on their own horses, and then maneuvered their mounts so Elder Macon was in front of me and Elder Drewson behind. I had no idea whether this was to make sure I did not bolt, or merely because they thought they'd be better able to offer me assistance this way, should I meet with some mishap during the ride.

We headed down the alleyway and then on to a narrow street fondly referred to as Pennypinch Lane. I saw then what the elders were doing—taking a course that used the quieter and less-traveled streets, and one that headed away from the town square and the crowds gathered there. After a few more twists and turns, we emerged through the northern gate, which was conspicuously untended that morning.

And then we were out on the hard-packed road that led away from Lirinsholme and up into the hills. Almost directly ahead of us was the rocky peak where Black's Keep stood, as if glowering over the valley below. The red banner caught my eye once more, and I stared up at it for a long moment, wondering whose task it was to place it there, and how the Dragon determined which would be the fateful day.

I supposed I might know those answers soon enough, although the thought did little to cheer me.

# Chapter Three

The residents of Greyton did not seem particularly curious about our arrival. A few brief glances, a whisper or two. I would have expected more, considering it had been some years since the Dragon last called for a Bride. Perhaps they had been instructed to look away.

Whatever the reason, we received no greeting, no sign that the Dragon or his retainers had even expected our coming. While unease traced its chill fingers across the back of my neck, the two elders did not seem particularly discomfited. They rode through Greyton's one shabby little street and then paused on the other side of the hamlet, where the road abruptly began a series of switchbacks up the hillside to the peak where the castle stood. From this angle, it seemed to loom over everything, as if it were about to pitch right over the cliff and down onto the houses below. Of course this was just a trick of the eyes, but still I did not look forward to making that ascent.

Up here the grass was sparser, not as green as in the fields around Lirinsholme, and the wind blew constantly. Although it was just past midsummer, and the day had been bright and cheery enough, somehow a shadow seemed to lie over this land, something that dulled it and robbed it of color. It was too warm for me to shiver, but a frisson of unease passed over me.

Movement from above us caught my eye, and I saw then that a single horse descended the perilous track.

"He comes," Elder Macon said.

"Who? The Dragon?"

The two elders exchanged an unreadable look. "Of course not, you silly girl," Elder Macon replied. "The Dragon, leaving his castle? This will be one of the Dragon's retainers, come to take you the rest of the way."

I wasn't sure whether to be relieved I would be spared the Dragon's company for that much longer, or annoyed that he would have a servant come to fetch me. Just another item for the castle, like a barrel of wine or a side of beef. It appeared he didn't rate his Brides all that highly.

Of course he doesn't, a sly voice inside me whispered. Or why would he go through them at such a rapid rate?

Having no answer to that, I merely waited in silence as the rider navigated the last of the switchbacks and then descended to where we had gathered. As he drew closer, I saw he was an older man, his iron-grey hair pulled back into a leather thong low on his neck. He rode as tall and straight as someone half his age, however, and looked at us with keen grey eyes.

"Bring her to me," he said.

"Get down," Elder Macon instructed.

"But—my horse—"

"The retainer will take you. You bring nothing with you, remember? That includes the horse. Now get down."

I untangled my feet from the stirrups and then slid down to the ground. The stranger made no move to help me or bring his horse closer, but merely waited while I crossed the few yards that separated us.

"Come now," he said, not unkindly, and reached down to pull me up into the saddle in front of him.

He must have been very strong, for I found myself hoisted into position without any apparent strain on his part. My situation was not all that different from the one I had maintained while riding sidesaddle, and yet I felt far more secure now, no doubt because I had the feeling this stranger would not do anything so foolish as to let me slip and fall. It was a little strange, to be so close to a man I had never met before. His manner, however, was so businesslike that it seemed clear enough he had nothing on his mind but my safe delivery to his master.

He uttered a brief, "Sirs," before turning the horse around and beginning the ascent to Black's Keep. I clutched the pommel of the saddle and swallowed, realizing too late that I had said no goodbyes to the elders. Well, they deserved little enough in the way of courtesy. They were only here because custom required it, and not because they cared anything for me, or for any of the Brides, for that matter.

The air felt cooler at these heights, with barely a hint of the midsummer warmth of the valley below. Or perhaps I was chilled by the enormity of what I had done...and by fears of what faced me in that dark castle on its rocky peak.

Perhaps I had gone mad. No doubt my parents would see it that way, but I must confess I didn't feel particularly mad. Apprehensive, yes. My thoughts were clear enough, although perhaps they were comprehensible only to me.

Why such a sacrifice, for someone who was none of my kin? As to that, Lilianth and I had been friends since we could barely walk, and, for good or ill, I felt closer to her than I did any of my own sisters, for all that I had a surfeit of them. My parents would mourn, and grieve, and wonder why on earth I had been possessed to do such a thing. Perhaps my mother, with a core of cool practicality that my father had never possessed, might begin to understand one day, after the hurt had begun to ebb just the smallest bit.

What waited for me in Black's Keep, I didn't know. No one had seen the Dragon, not in at least twice a hundred years, and even those were tales of greybeards spinning yarns by the fire, talking of a beast that had rained fire and wrath upon Lirinsholme for its brief moment of defiance.

I have to say that the man who expertly guided his horse up the steep mountain road did not seem particularly fearsome. If I had passed him on the streets of Lirinsholme I might not have given him a second glance, save to think he looked more like a fighting man than the craftsmen and merchants who made up the majority of the town's population. We were a peaceful folk. Possibly some of that peace had been granted by the presence of the Dragon in the mountains above our town. After all, even the boldest of barons would think twice about attacking a town that had its own draconian protector.

The rider was not the talkative sort, and that gladdened me. I could just barely retain a sort of fragile calm while silent; trying to do so while engaged in any sort of conversation would have probably ended in disaster. As it was, I tried to focus on the sparse but delicate wildflowers in shades of blue and white to either side of the path, and the welcome coolness of the wind on my cheek, and the sound of a hawk diving somewhere off to our right.

But all the while the dark bulk of Black's Keep grew closer, until finally the rider guided his horse up the last of the switchbacks—the animal blowing hard by the time we were done—and we rode onto a plateau bare of any vegetation, where the gates of the castle loomed before us. Here we stopped, and the rider helped me down off the horse before dismounting much more elegantly himself. From seemingly nowhere emerged a young man—barely more than a boy, somewhere around my sister Therella's age—to take the reins and guide the winded animal off to what I presumed were the stables, although I could see nothing at that moment but the forbidding façade of the Dragon's home.

"This way," the rider said, and led me, not through the enormous iron-barred front doors, but off to the side, to a smaller entrance that appeared infinitely more approachable.

The interior was stone, true, but rich hangings covered the grey walls, and a clerestory window high above the door let in a wash of bright afternoon light. I followed the man down the corridor and up a short flight of steps, until he paused in front of a door and knocked.

It opened, and a sturdy-looking woman some years older than my mother looked out. When her gaze fell upon me, I thought I saw the slightest softening of a pair of very firm lips, but she said only, "Goodness, what a windblown mess she is!"

"The breeze was rather brisk," the man agreed, something in his tone telling me he had had this sort of exchange with her before.

"That may well be. Off, then, for I have much to do."

He gave her the slightest sketch of a bow, allowed me a ghost of a smile, and turned and went back the way we had come. It was silly of me to feel a pang at his departure, for I did not even know his name, but he had seemed kindly enough... and a kind face is a thing to look for, when one is a stranger in the Dragon's keep.

But I had little time for wistful gazes, because the woman said, "I am Sar. I have the managing of the household, such as it is. I shall show you to your rooms, and we must get you ready."

"Ready?" I repeated stupidly.

She did not roll her eyes, but I got the impression that she rather wanted to. "For your wedding, girl. You will be wed to the Dragon tonight. What do they call you?"

"I am Rhianne Menyon." That was about all I could manage, for her words had chilled me all over. True, I had come here to be the Dragon's Bride, but somehow I hadn't thought that dubious event would take place quite so soon.

"Well enough. Now, Rhianne, follow me."

And she led me up another flight of stairs, and yet another, and then another, until I began to wonder whether I would spend whatever remained of my life climbing one interminable staircase after another. The place had always looked enormous to me, perched on its mountain peak as it was, but only as I followed Sar through its labyrinthine corridors did I begin to understand how massive the castle was, and how it could have swallowed my family's handsome town house many times over. I saw tapestries, and paintings in an archaic style that made me itch to go closer so I could inspect the artists' techniques and try to discern what types of pigments they had used. But of course Sar would allow no such dawdling, but guided me through a set of double doors and into a large chamber complete with a hearth, a sitting area with a divan and a low table, and a tall window that let in a magnificent view of the valley below.

I wanted to rush to that window, to drink in the light—it offered an ideal prospect for painting—but Sar moved straight through that room and on into the next one, which was obviously the bedchamber. The bed itself could have probably accommodated my entire family with ease, and I looked up at its enormous burgundy-hung expanse and wondered whether it was that large so it could accommodate the Dragon's bulk.

"Your wardrobe is here," Sar said, flinging open the doors of a cabinet equal in scale to the bed. From within I saw the gleam of expensive silks and damasks, and even the glint of silver and gold trim. She eyed me carefully and said, "I'll have Jaenne take up the hems. You're not as tall as the last one."

*Last one?* I swallowed at the implication and asked, "You mean...these were worn by the other Brides?"

She shrugged. "Some. We add some new and remove the older ones as necessary. Styles change...hems get worn." Another flicker of those keen dark eyes, and she added, "Good thing you're slender. We had a plump one some twenty years ago, and had to make up a whole new set. He was not happy."

One might think a Bride-devouring Dragon would be pleased with a chubby girl, but I knew better than to say such a thing aloud. I also tried not to think too much about what it would feel like to wear clothing that had belonged to a parade of other women, all now dead. Well, perhaps I could try to select only the ones in the most recent styles. At least that way they most likely would only have been worn by one predecessor.

Sar went on to show me the well-appointed little bath chamber—"hot water is on its way up"—and then proceeded, after another quick look at me, as if to reacquaint herself with my dark eyes and hair, to lay out a very fine gown of rich wine-colored damask, its square neckline and detachable sleeves trimmed in flat gold braid and what looked like tiny rough-cut garnets. With the gown went a chemise of linen so fine one could see the light through it, and then silk hose and ribbon garters to hold them up.

"You'll have to make do with your own shoes for now," she said. "I'll have more ordered, but he won't want to wait on that...let me see them."

At once I grasped my skirts and lifted them slightly so she could see my slippers. Odd how I did not entertain the notion of defying her, of saying my footwear was of no concern to her. She had about her a manner that brooked no argument.

Luckily, my shoes were fairly new, and fine enough, smooth black kid with lacings of silk ribbon. Quite the extravagance at the time, I had thought, but they had been purchased when my mother thought I had the prospect of a rich husband before me, and she had brushed aside my protests that something less costly would be more than adequate.

Well, I was about to have a rich husband, although not the one either she or I had imagined...

Sar gave an approving nod at my footwear and appeared about to speak when there was a knock at the door. At once she called out, "Bring it in!"

From the main chamber I heard the faint squeak of door hinges, followed by the shuffling of several pairs of feet. Those feet turned out to belong to two sturdy-looking manservants, each bearing a large ewer of water from which faint curls of steam emerged. Sar directed them into the bath chamber, where they poured the water into the tub. Then they hurried out, having unburdened themselves.

During this entire procedure neither one of them looked at me, even though I stood off to one side and watched the entire procedure with some sympathy. I knew just how heavy those ewers of water could be, and I only had to carry them up one flight of steps back home. I couldn't begin to imagine what it must be like to bring them all the way here, to my aerie in the Dragon's tower.

"Half an hour," Sar informed me. "Everything you need is in the bath chamber. And then I'll return to help you get ready. The ceremony is set for sundown."

Which was still many, many hours off at this time of year. I knew better than to argue, however, and only nodded. She sniffed, which might or might not have signaled her approval, and then left.

Much as I wanted to go to the window and gaze out on the amazing prospect it offered, I knew that doing so would only allow my bath to grow cold. It didn't seem quite right, after those poor servants had hauled it all the way here, and so I went on into the bath chamber.

There was no way of latching the door, which did little to soothe my nerves. I settled for taking the little table that stood under the window and placing it up under the door handle. It seemed a fragile enough barrier, but it was better than nothing.

And then I stepped out of my shoes and my stockings, and carefully removed my gown and chemise. Luckily, the gown laced up the sides instead of the back—my mother knew better than to have us wear gowns that required assistance to get in and out of them—so extricating myself from it was not difficult. I draped it over the cross-backed chair of mahogany that stood off to one side, and then lowered myself into the tub.

It did feel good, to have the warm water surround me, washing away the dust of the trail and the sticky feeling from wearing too warm a gown on too hot a day. The heat did not seem as if it would be a problem up here in Black's Keep. Indeed, I wondered what a winter here must feel like.

If I lasted until winter, of course.

I pushed that thought away and applied myself to scrubbing my limbs and back with the brush and soap provided, and washing my hair with a rinse that smelled of mint and something else, something sweet I couldn't quite place. Truly, it was quite a luxury to have a bath so soon after my last one—which had only been the night before. At home I wouldn't have had the opportunity for another two or three days.

There was no clock in the chamber, and so I had no very good idea of the passage of time, but I tried to hurry things along as best I could. There were a number of towels provided, thick and very soft, and I dried myself off and went out into the bedchamber to retrieve the chemise and other underthings from where they had been laid out on the bed.

None too soon, as it turned out, for I had just finished blotting my hair and adjusting the drawstring neckline of the chemise when Sar reappeared, carrying a tray with a number of mysterious-looking objects, along with a more prosaic hairbrush and comb.

"Sit by the window," she said. "The sun will help to dry your hair."

So I did as I was told and took a seat where she had instructed. She stood behind me and combed the snarls out of my hair, and then proceeded to brush it and brush it as it slowly dried. I wondered a little at her spending such a lengthy amount of time on this task—if she truly ran the household, wasn't she needed elsewhere for more important things?—but I remained silent as she worked.

"Well enough," she said at length. "It will finish drying while I work on your face."

"My face?" I repeated, wondering what bizarre ritual the Dragon required of his Brides before they were presented to him.

As it turned out, this "ritual" consisted of her refining my brows with a pair of bone tweezers, polishing my skin with silk, and then touching the faintest amount of some reddish powder to my lips and cheeks. I had heard that the ladies in the capital indulged in such practices, but we had little enough use of them in Lirinsholme. Each time Sar removed an errant hair from my eyebrows, I tried not to wince, and wondered why on earth the Dragon should care whether or not I looked like a court lady, when by all accounts I would be resting in his belly by the time the evening was over.

No, that was not strictly true, or fair. No one really knew what happened to the Brides. But since they were never seen again, and dragons were known to have somewhat rapacious appetites, naturally everyone expected the worst.

After she had seen to my face, Sar directed me over to the hearth, where she bade me sit as she took the last of her odd implements, a long metal tube with a wooden handle, and inserted it directly into the flames. I held my breath, wondering what tortures she planned to inflict with the device. It turned out, however, that she intended nothing more sinister than to wind my hair around it, creating a perfect series of long spiral curls. I recalled all the restless nights I'd had sleeping on rags to make my half-heartedly wavy hair curl, and decided this was a much more effective way of achieving that goal.

"There," Sar said at last, after propping the still-warm iron up against the fireplace shovel. "Now, it's on with the gown."

I turned away from the hearth and stood, realizing as I did so just how long that entire procedure must have lasted. The sun had dipped almost out of sight behind the hills to the west, although dusk itself was still some time off. I also perceived a distinct hollowness in my stomach. It had been hours and hours since the breakfast of toasted bread and cheese I had consumed at home before setting out for the town square with Therella in tow. Up until that moment I hadn't even considered such a thing, as feeding myself did not seem all that important when marriage to the Dragon loomed before me, but my body obviously had a different opinion on the matter.

"Do I get any supper?" I asked, my tone perhaps a little too plaintive, as Sar had me step into the wine-colored gown.

"You will eat...after."

That didn't sound very appetizing. Was I to dine with the Dragon? Was I to be his dinner?

Sar was busy with the lacings at the back of my dress, pulling it tight. It seemed its previous wearer had been more slender than I, or at least did not have quite as much bosom. I had no doubt that my mother would have highly disapproved of the expanse of rounded breasts exposed by the tight, low-cut bodice, but of course she was not there to comment. While Sar tied off the silk cord, I did my best to tug the chemise up a little higher.

As she came around and began to tie on the heavily embroidered and jeweled sleeves, I found myself compelled to say, "The other Brides..."

"What of them?" she asked, as she poked a ribbon through the loop attached to the shoulder seam of my bodice.

"The Dragon doesn't...he doesn't *eat* them, does he?"

At my question she paused and gave me an unbelieving stare. "Gods, no!" she replied, in tones of horror convincing enough that I thought she was most likely telling the truth. "Whatever put such an idea into your head?"

"People talk."

"That they do, and mostly of things they know nothing about. No wonder you were looking so pale, despite the paint. Thought you were going to end up in the Dragon's belly tonight?"

Feeling foolish, I nodded.

"Nothing so grim, I assure you. I'll take you to the hall when the time comes, and a priest will marry you to his lordship. Afterward, you will take supper together."

"And after that?" I might have been a maiden, but I knew what passed between men and women. But the Dragon of Black's Keep was no ordinary man.

Sar did not quite meet my gaze. "You may have noticed that I said these were your rooms. Not his. The Dragon and his Bride always keep separate chambers."

I didn't so much sigh as let out my breath slowly. My relief, however, was tempered by curiosity. So if he did not make a meal of them, and neither did he treat them as real wives, what exactly did the Dragon do with his Brides?

Asking Sar did not seem to be the best plan of action. I barely knew her, of course, but what little I had seen spoke of a no-nonsense manner that nonetheless hid its own secrets. Very likely she would either ignore my questions or tell me to mind my own business. Then again, one would think the relationship with my future husband was my business...

Years of training had taught me to hold my tongue when necessary, so I remained silent as Sar continued fussing with my sleeves. After she was apparently satisfied with every loop and puff, she went to a tall cabinet across the room, and from the top drawer she brought forth a flat box that contained what appeared, to my unschooled eyes at least, a very princess's ransom of treasures. From the gleaming jewels within she selected a necklace of gold and garnets and matching earrings. The necklace she placed around my throat, but she handed the earrings to me, obviously intending that I should put them on myself.

I did so without argument. No wonder the Dragon wished his Brides to come with no belongings of their own; he appeared quite able to provide them with whatever baubles they might require. Certainly the intricate drops of gold I slipped into my pierced ears put the simple garnet earrings I'd worn earlier to shame.

I noticed, however, that Sar gave me no rings to wear.

Instead, she returned to the cabinet, and drew forth a large hand-held mirror. "I believe he will be pleased."

That seemed to be as close to praise as she got. I peered into the silvered glass and had to consciously prevent myself from gasping aloud in shock. Now, I was not one to deny my own prettiness—why should I, when it had very little to do with me and a great deal more to do with being lucky enough to have two handsome parents?—but even so I was not prepared for the reflection that stared back at me. My hair had been tamed into sleek curls that gleamed against the wine color of my bodice, and my lips were not far off from that same shade.

Despite the tension that still lay coiled in my stomach, I couldn't help being pleased by what I saw. I guessed that quite a few people might not have even recognized me in my current guise. Then I had to laugh at myself, for of course it was a good deal easier to be beautiful when one had the luxury of spending hours to achieve such a state.

"Well enough," I told Sar, and I thought I saw her lips quirk just a little.

"Not one to sing your own praises, eh? Wise, probably." She glanced out the window, as if to determine the position of the sun, and her mouth settled into far more sober lines. "It's time to go. He will be waiting for you."

My mouth went dry then, and I wished I'd had the forethought to ask for some water or cider. Oh, well, I probably wouldn't be the first of the Dragon's Brides to utter her vows in a cracked whisper, if it came to that.

Sar went to the door and opened it, obviously expecting me to follow her.

I knew I had little choice. All I could do was follow this mad notion of mine to its conclusion...whatever that might be. So I lifted my chin and moved from the safety—however spurious it might be—of my chambers and into my unknown future.

# Chapter Four

It seemed to me a bloody descent down the castle's interminable stairs, but I knew that was only a trick of the sunset, which threw a carmine cast over everything. Still, the peculiar light only served to increase the sensation of foreboding that seeped slowly through me, like a dark flood. To make matters worse, I saw no one else during our descent, not one servant or other member of the household. I wondered then exactly how many people served the Dragon. Sar had made it sound as if there weren't that many, a contrast to the bustling households of even the wealthy residents of Lirinsholme, which certainly was not known for its grand style. The lord of Black's Keep liked his privacy, apparently.

At last we reached what I thought was the ground floor. Sar led me down the enormous vaulted corridor that seemed to divide that level of the structure, until at last we stopped before a set of double doors barred with intricate black ironwork.

"Go on," she said, after opening the one to the right.

I realized she intended me to enter on my own. Although I had only known her for a few short hours, it seemed to me then that she was the only familiar thing in my world. How could I possibly be expected to go forward to confront the Dragon alone, without a single friendly face to serve as my witness to this unnatural union?

Her expression softened as she gazed at me, at my obvious hesitation. She said, in the gentlest tones I'd yet heard from her, "It will be all right. Be brave."

That did hearten me a little. After all, I'd had the courage to step forward and offer myself in Lilianth's place. Now I must summon that same will to finish what I had started.

So I stepped past her and moved inside the chamber.

It, too, was constructed on a grand scale, the vaulted roof the height of a tall man several times over. The last traces of sunset painted the carved panels on the walls in flickering shades of russet and wine, the only light in the room, except for a pair of tall, thick candles, each sitting on its own waist-high pillar of dark marble. As my eyes adjusted to the dimness, I saw the figure of a man standing between the two pillars and started—until I realized he was quite elderly, and wearing the dark grey robes of a priest of Inyanna. Not my intended, then.

The priest extended his arms. "Come forward, child."

For one wild instant I had the notion to turn and run, to bolt through those double doors and out of the castle as quickly as my feet could carry me. Then I realized how mad it would be to try to outrun an enraged dragon on foot. Besides, I had offered myself as the Dragon's Bride. I could not back out now, even if my heart hammered in my chest and my hands felt like ice.

I stepped meekly forward until I stood a pace away from the priest. "Father."

He didn't respond, but seemed to stiffen.

We were not alone in the room.

Where he had come from, I couldn't say, but I heard the soft hiss of his long cloak as it dragged across the stone floor. The very air seemed to sigh, as if displaced by something it knew was not natural.

My heart lodged roughly midway up my throat, I turned.

At first I almost laughed in relief. This was no scaled monster of legend, no overgrown serpent-beast with eyes of fire. I looked upon the figure of a man, tall and slender, although it was difficult to make out much more than that, as he wore a cloak that covered him from shoulder to heel. The garment's cowled hood dropped low, concealing his face.

"Rhianne."

That voice—it was the sort of voice a woman might dream of, rich and yet soft, the accents rounded and full. To hear it emanate from within that hood was surprise enough; I blinked at the realization that he knew my name. But that was foolish. Sar must have told him, or sent word to him somehow.

"Yes," I replied simply, hoping my own voice didn't sound too hopelessly countrified.

"The rose, I believe," he went on. "At least, that is what your name meant in the language of old. Do you like roses?"

"I, er, well, yes," I said, and then cursed myself inwardly for my fumbling. What a fool he must think me.

"We have a rather fine garden on the north side of the castle. You must visit it when you have the chance."

Not knowing what else to say, I only answered, "Of course, my lord."

Something that might have been a chuckle escaped from beneath the hood. He turned slightly, facing the priest. "You may begin."

The old man cleared his throat and lifted his hands. I saw that he now held the traditional length of white linen used in all the wedding ceremonies I had ever witnessed. "Rhianne Menyon."

I knew what to do. Ever since I was a young child I had attended these sorts of rites, and had even dreamed from time to time of what my own nuptials might be like. Never in any of those gauze-edged fantasies had I thought I would be standing next to the Dragon himself. Like every young woman in Lirinsholme, I had always believed that sort of thing would happen to someone else.

Somehow I managed to raise my left hand, allowed him to wrap the linen around it.

"Theran Blackmoor."

The Dragon lowered his hand so that it rested on mine. A black glove enclosed his fingers, but even through the leather I could feel the heat of him, as if his flesh burned with an inward fire. I tried not to flinch, to stand my ground and not let him know how it took every ounce of willpower I possessed not to pull my hand away.

The priest wrapped the linen around the Dragon's hand as well, binding us together.

*You will not shake*, I told myself. *Or tremble, or faint, or do anything else foolish. His hand is warm, true, but at least he is not some fearsome beast, some monster. It could have been so much worse.*

I was so intent on this inner monologue that I did not hear the priest's next words. With a start I realized he had fallen silent and was waiting for me, the linen now unwrapped from our wrists and held outstretched in his hands. At once I reached out and took the linen from him and brought it to my lips in the ritual gesture, then let the Dragon take it from me so he might do the same. That is, I could only guess he had brought the fabric to his mouth, for it disappeared within the recesses of his hood and then emerged a second or two later, when he handed it back to the priest.

In silence the older man took the linen and folded it into the triangle custom required before placing it in a small brazier half-hidden behind one of the marble candle stands. With a chill I realized what was to come next.

"Close your eyes," Theran Blackmoor said.

That was not part of the ritual, but I guessed it would be unwise in the extreme to disobey. So I shut my eyes and held my breath as I felt him move closer, the heavy fabric of his hood brushing against my loose hair before his mouth touched mine.

Only for the briefest instant, and then he withdrew at once. But even in the space of that heartbeat or two I could feel something dreadfully wrong about the lips that had grazed mine, something rough and hard, as if they were not human skin at all.

Once again I fought the urge to flinch. How many of those other Brides had recoiled? Surely it must be a dreadful thing to have the woman one married shrink at one's very touch. An odd stirring of pity moved within me. For all that he had the outward shape of a man, it seemed there must be a very real reason for the hooded cloak, for the gloves.

I opened my eyes and saw him staring down at me. That is, the hood was tilted downward. I could see nothing else.

"Rhianne Blackmoor," he said, and in that voice my name was somehow a caress. "You are now the mistress of Black's Keep."

There being nothing witty or profound I could think of to say in reply, I merely curtsied. "My lord."

"Theran."

"Theran," I repeated. Perhaps one day I might have the courage to address him thus.

"And now—"

"Now?"

"Our wedding feast."

He offered me his arm. I forced myself not to hesitate, to settle my hand on top of his as if it were the most natural thing the world. Lifting my chin, I allowed him to lead me from the room.

Truth be told, it was a very odd feast. Oh, the food was abundant enough, and uniformly excellent, although my hunger might have increased its charms. However, it was a feast for two, as only the Dragon and I sat at a long table that could have easily accommodated ten times our number.

Of the chamber in which we sat, I could make out very little, since the only illumination was a single candle located next to my place setting. The lord of Black's Keep apparently had no need of such things...or perhaps it was more important to him that I have no chance of seeing what lay within the hood as he ate.

For he did eat, of roast waterfowl and wine-braised beef and a dish I had always loved, with apples and cinnamon and candied tubers, as well as salad of field greens and potatoes roasted with garlic. The bread was warm and fresh, the butter sweet and cool. With the meal came wine as well, as much, apparently, as I would like, and not the parsimonious half-glass my mother allowed me with my evening meal.

In the darkness I did not recognize the servant who brought us the food. It was not Sar, but a younger woman who somehow managed to safely negotiate the dim chamber as she brought in course after course. I for one was glad that I apparently was expected to stay in one place for some time, since I feared I might trip over the rug if I were required to move more than a few paces in the darkness.

At first we ate in silence, but then the Dragon asked, after pouring me a second goblet of wine with his own hands, "And what is it you do to amuse yourself, Rhianne?"

"To amuse myself?"

"Yes. I fear you may find it rather dull up here, if you do not have something with which to occupy yourself. Do you embroider, or sew, or—"

Perhaps it was the second glass of wine which emboldened me. "I paint."

He paused, gloved fingers only a few inches away from his own glass of wine. "You what?"

"I paint. With oils," I added recklessly. Let him know the worst. After all, what could he do? We were already married in the eyes of the goddess.

"How...extraordinary." A brief hesitation, and he added, "I would imagine that requires a number of supplies. Tomorrow you shall make up a list, so that Sar can send out for the things you need."

Was it possible? Had he just offered to get me whatever I needed? I let my fingers rest on the base of my wine goblet but did not pick it up. "They are not the sort of supplies one can procure in Lirinsholme. Lindell always had to send to Lystare for his pigments and canvas."

It must have been my imagination, but somehow it seemed as if those smooth tones sharpened somewhat. "And who is Lindell?"

"A painter who taught me what he could," I replied. "He is very good, but he made the Duke of Tralion look quite plump in his portrait, and so he has made Lirinsholme his refuge."

To my surprise, the Dragon actually laughed at that confession. "Yes, I can imagine even his Grace would not bother pursuing a hapless portrait painter all the way here. You will not mind my saying that this is a rather unusual pastime for a young woman, however."

"Do you mind?"

"Does it make you happy?"

I stared across the table at him, at the man-sized shape that was only a darker shadow in the dim room. No one had ever asked me such a thing. It was not usually a concern whether a young woman was happy or not, only that she did as her parents bade her and found some way to make peace with her lot in this life. And to have the Dragon of Black's Keep, the devourer of Brides, ask such a question made me wonder exactly how much anyone really knew about him. Very little, it seemed.

"Yes," I said firmly. "Very much so."

"Well, then."

Twenty years of being raised under my parents' roof compelled me to say, "It's all so very expensive, though. The canvas...the pigments...the linseed oil..."

"Do you think the expense concerns me?"

Oh, dear. Perhaps I had offended him. One had only to glance around the castle to know that the Dragon certainly did not lack for material wealth. I did not know him well enough—know him at all—or perhaps I would have tried to explain that my protests were not born of concern that he could not afford the supplies, but rather that one such as I did not really deserve them.

"No, my lord," I replied, in tones so meek I'm sure they would have raised my mother's eyebrows, had she been there to hear them.

"Theran," he reminded me, and I nodded.

"I suppose I shall remember that one of these days."

"We can only hope."

I thought I heard an undercurrent of amusement in his words, and I found myself smiling. My heart seemed to lighten. Who would have thought that a day which began in such dread could end with such hope? For he sounded sincere enough. Possibly, just possibly, my tenure in Black's Keep wouldn't be quite as dreadful as I had imagined it would.

After dinner he walked me to my rooms, up all those endless stairs. I did not ask where his own chambers lay. And although Sar had told me the Dragon and his consort did not share a suite, still I wondered at him taking me all this way, when it would have been so much easier to bid me goodnight in the dining chamber and allow a servant to guide me back upstairs.

Outside my door we both paused. I had no idea what to do if he asked to accompany me inside. After all, as my husband he had every right to make such a request of me. The food I had eaten, which had seemed so excellent at the table, seemed to lie heavily in my stomach.

"You will begin to find your way around, after a time," he told me. "But I thought it better to guide you here now, until you are more familiar with your new home."

"Thank you," I said, a little relieved at this statement. It seemed his motives for accompanying me here had been pure enough.

He lifted a hand. "And do not forget to give Sar that list. It will take some time to get the things you need, but I have riders who can make haste if need be."

"They do not need to do such things for me—"

"Yes, they do. You are the mistress of Black's Keep. Never forget that."

There was such urgency in his words that I could only nod. "I'll try."

"Good." He reached out then and took one of my hands in his gloved ones. I wondered if he would lift my fingers to his lips, and if I would feel that odd roughness—of scales?—once again. He did not, however, but only squeezed my hand gently before turning and going back the way he had come. A swirl of his dark cloak as he turned the corner, and then he was gone.

I stood there for a long moment, halfway wishing I had asked him to stay. His company at dinner had been pleasant, far more so than I had ever dreamed might be possible. But that was absurd. He was the Dragon, no normal man. I should be glad my first night in the castle had been so uneventful, and that I had successfully survived my first encounter with him.

With that thought to bolster me, I squared my shoulders and went inside.

My chambers were empty. I had halfway expected to see Sar waiting for me there, since she had been so attentive that afternoon. But perhaps with me now married to the Dragon, I was no longer deserving of such attention. However, it seemed someone had taken the time to prepare my bedroom. The heavy coverlet was turned back, and a vase of roses, crimson and pink and wine-tipped cream, sat on the table next to the bed. A nightgown of fine linen lay draped across the turned-back covers.

It was very quiet. In town one could always hear some sound from the streets, whether of a cart passing by or one neighbor calling to another, or even the rhythmic tap-tap-tap of the night watchman's stick as he made his rounds. Here, though, there was only silence. Even the wind had died down to nothing. If it had been colder, perhaps a fire in the hearth would have made at least a gentle hiss, but it seemed Sar had let the fire grow cold, its service in curling my hair done for the day. Truly, it had been something of an extravagance. Even at these heights, the fire had not been needed. I knew back home my mother would not dream of lighting any fire other than that in the kitchen hearth until at least mid-Sevendre.

But that thought only saddened me, as I wondered how they had fared this evening, sitting down to a table with an empty seat where I should have been. Had they wondered if I'd gone mad, or had they merely tried to see my precipitous decision as some sort of sideways retribution from the gods, a judgment brought down on their headstrong eldest child?

I truly couldn't say. I knew my parents would mourn, and Darlynne and Maeganne as well. Of Therella's reaction I was less certain. We had squabbled more often of late, possibly because she was impatient for me to be wed and out of the house so she could have her own turn as eldest, as the one who could bring honor to us through some advantageous marriage or other.

Well, I was wed now, albeit not in a manner even my sister had probably imagined. I wondered then where the Dragon had gone, whether he had returned to his own rooms, wherever they might be, or whether he roamed the castle's corridors in darkness. Did he even need to sleep?

Then I yawned, the exertions of the day finally catching up with me. Perhaps the lord of Black's Keep had no need of slumber, but his Bride did. I was safe for now at least, and I would worry about the morrow when it came. I washed my face and scrubbed my teeth, and clambered into the tall bed. It felt strange and far too large, but apparently even its strangeness was not enough to keep me from slumber. I closed my eyes, and let myself fall into the dark.

I dreamed again that night.

No nightmare visions of shadows swooping down from the heights, or even the commonplaces I might have hoped to see—my family, or Lilianth safe with her beloved Adain. In fact, I could hardly call it a dream at all, but instead just a snippet, a brief glimpse.

I had never seen the man before, or at least I did not think I had. And what I did see was little more than the outline of a fine jaw, a glint from eyes the color of the sea...or at least the sea as Lindell once described it to me, as I had never seen it with my own eyes. The stranger turned and walked away from me, dark hair blowing in an unseen wind, the ragged locks catching in the fine embroidery of his high collar.

And then he was gone.

I sat up in bed, blinking, and realized morning had come. Golden sunlight, tinted with the rosy hues of dawn, slanted in through the narrow windows on the wall opposite my bed. And with that light the image in my dream seemed to fade and disappear, just as the morning mists were burning away in the valley below.

A compulsion came on me then, a driving need to get down what I had seen before it left me completely. I pushed back the covers and climbed out of bed, rushing across the room to the small table under the windows. But its drawers were empty—no paper, no ink or pens.

I turned from the table and went into the main chamber, thinking furiously. No doubt the table out there would be as bereft of supplies as the one in my bedroom, but there were the remains of the fire from the day before. Surely there must be a lump of charcoal I could use for my purposes...

"What in the world are you doing, my lady?"

Sar's astonished tones made me draw back from my mad scrabble through the spent ashes. I stood and turned away from the hearth. Without thinking, I reached down to smooth out the skirt of my nightgown. A large black smudge appeared at once, and I let go of the fabric immediately, although the damage was done.

She was too well-trained to chide me for my heedlessness, but I saw a pucker appear between her eyebrows as she took in the results of my carelessness.

"I was looking for a piece of charcoal," I said.

"Whatever for, my lady?"

"So I could draw the—" I broke off then, for I knew if I tried to explain I wanted the charcoal to draw a picture of a man I had seen in my dreams, she would have thought me completely mad.

"His lordship said you were an artist." She didn't precisely sniff, but I could tell she was less than impressed with my avocation. "He said you had need of supplies, but I hadn't realized your need was so desperate that you'd be digging in the ashes."

"I—that is, I saw the sunrise and thought it might make a fine sketch."

Another lift of the eyebrows. "Well, I'll see that we bring you a pen and ink and some paper to start. No need for dirtying yourself, my lady."

"Of course not. I am sorry." I knew then that even the charcoal would have done me no good. The image was gone. I couldn't even remember whether the man's eyes had been blue or green. Besides, it would have been silly to waste my time on such a thing. Lindell had always told me the best paintings were those done from life, and not from the artist's mind. Too much chance of embellishing, of drawing that which was not there, if one did not have the real person or object in front of them.

"No need for apologies, my lady, but I think I had better send for another bath. I had thought this morning we could go over your wardrobe, to see which gowns would suit you best. I'll then store the rest."

I nodded, and let her sweep me away into a series of commonplaces that managed to consume most of my morning. Better that way, really. Concentrating on the fit of a gown helped to dispel some of the odd ache that had lodged somewhere in my breast, like the gnawing pain of a hunger which couldn't be satisfied. Where it had come from, I couldn't say, but it seemed to follow me throughout most of the day, akin to the persistent dull nag of a toothache. I told myself it was homesickness, or unease in my new surroundings.

Somehow, though, I knew it was much more than that.

# Chapter Five

The lord of Black's Keep was as good as his word. As soon as I had given the list of my required supplies to Sar, Theran dispatched a man named Mat and a wagon to Lystare to bring back everything I needed. In the meantime, I was provided with a quantity of paper and enough ink and pens for a small army of sketchers.

No one seemed to raise an eyebrow at my pastime, or at least they did so out of my presence. The castle was mine to roam in as I pleased, save for the north tower, where his lordship kept his suite. As he had said, there was a very fine rose garden clustered at the base of the tower, and though the tower itself was off-limits, the garden was not. True, oils or watercolors would have suited their vibrant late-summer colors better than pen and ink, but it was still something to be able to sit there for hours, exploring the differences in their branches and blooms, and finding the delicate nuances that perhaps the broader strokes of a paintbrush might not have revealed.

This was a luxury I had not looked for. When I had spoken out in the town square, I had thought only of saving my friend. I hadn't realized that offering myself as the Dragon's Bride bought me the time I had always craved for my work. No one disturbed me, save to call me in to meals. And every night I sat down with my husband.

Husband. It seems an odd word for the man who dwelt in the castle with me, for certainly we were not husband and wife in any commonly accepted sense of the phrase. I saw him only after sunset. What he did with his days, I could not say, although there were times I thought I caught movement out of the corner of my eye, as if someone or something moved in the highest chambers of the tower that overlooked the rose garden. Whenever I turned to discover the source of that movement, however, I saw nothing.

Whether he watched me in secret, I did not know, and of course I had not the courage to ask him such a thing. Instead, when we sat at dinner, he would inquire about my drawings, or the weather, or my rooms, such commonplaces as a stranger might feel safe to discuss. I wished I had the courage to make the conversation somehow more personal, but I could never find a way to do so without sounding either abrupt or downright rude, and so I rattled on as best I could, sharing shallow intimacies with someone who apparently intended to always hold me at arm's length.

The dream did not return.

Some ten days after my arrival at Black's Peak, Mat returned with my wished-for supplies. Truly, although I had been careful when composing my list, I hadn't realized what an impressive collection all those items would make when assembled in one place. I had to do some rearranging of the sitting area in my suite, and called for another table so I could properly set out all the jars of my pigments, along with the collection of fine brushes of squirrel and mink. The alcove that faced southward seemed the perfect place for my new easel, and I set it up there, intending to make the valley of Lirinsholme my first painting.

Sar seemed less than pleased with the havoc I created in my rooms, but as they were mine and not hers, she said nothing, instead settling for a few carefully timed raised eyebrows.

"And you don't mind sleeping in here with the smell?" she asked, after I had opened one of the jars of linseed oil and began mixing the first of the pigments for my study of the valley. I would need a careful combination of verdigris and umber to get the correct tint for the warm hues of the late-summer grass.

I knew that was her way of criticizing the enterprise, and smothered a smile. I had been in the castle for less than a fortnight, but I already knew she thought of Black's Keep as her place to rule, Dragon Lord or no. It wasn't that far off from the truth; I had yet to see Theran Blackmoor order anything more than another flagon of wine for our dinner table.

"It smells sweet as roses to me," I said. "Just having the pigments I need, and all that canvas! I daresay Mat brought back enough for me to make a hundred paintings."

I had thought she might raise an eyebrow again, or perhaps smile at my grandiosity, but for some reason a shadow passed over her face at my words. Then she shook her head, as if to clear it of an unpleasant vision.

"Paint as many as you like. But be sure to have Mat make the canvases for you. I can only imagine what his lordship would say if he discovered you were out in the workshops, hammering nails together for a frame."

"Well, I had to show Mat how to do it properly," I protested.

No, Sar had not been exactly pleased to find me out in the workshop, sleeves untied and tossed to the side, as I showed Mat, who seemed to be the keep's general handyman and dogsbody, how to stretch the canvas over the frame so it would be equally taut on all sides and not bunch or sag. But really, the best way to learn is by example. That was how Lindell had taught me to do it, and my first few attempts were quite pathetic. Mat did far better at it on his first try, but then, he had longer arms and was much stronger than I.

"Hmm," was Sar's response to my remark.

"Anyway," I went on, sprinkling a little more verdigris into the mixture on the thin wooden board I used for preparing my paints, "Mat is doing very well at it, so no need to trouble his lordship with tales of me sawing boards or stretching canvas."

"Thank goodness."

She left me then, stating some pressing need in the kitchens, but I really think her haste to leave stemmed more from her distaste of the scent of the linseed oil than any culinary emergency. The smell was so familiar to me that I didn't think twice about it. Besides, I had the windows open to let in the fine summer air, but I didn't mind her leaving. I had work to do.

"Sar tells me that you are quite consumed in a painting," Theran Blackmoor said to me over dinner several days later.

I wondered how often the two of them discussed me but decided, again, that there was no way for me to ask without sounding too forward. "I'm painting the valley. The hues on the hillsides are quite lovely this time of year; I want to catch them before autumn comes upon us in earnest."

"It must be quite a gift, to see things as you do."

His words made me start a little, until I realized he spoke only of my artist's eye, and not that far more troublesome one, the one which brought images to me in dreams. Since that first night, none of my dreams had been particularly vivid or memorable, and even the one that had troubled me so had faded almost completely. If it meant anything—which I doubted—most likely it had been my way of saying goodbye to any hopes of marriage to someone more suitable.

"Oh, well." Deprecating my talents came as naturally to me as breathing, and I did it without thought. Lindell had praised my work, and said it was a shame I was a girl, for I should have been plying my trade in Lystare and beyond. My family, though, tended to ignore it, save when they could use it for their own gain. No, that was not fair. I'd felt glad to be of some use, dull as the work might have been. Far better that I should have been gifted with a needle, or in the kitchens, for at least then I could have made a contribution they didn't have to hide from the world, but that was not my fate.

"Rhianne."

Although I still found myself thrilling to the sound of my name in that dark-honey voice of Theran's, I couldn't help but detect a note of reproof. To my surprise, he drew a piece of paper from somewhere within the folds of his robes and then laid it flat on the table between us, smoothing it with a gloved hand. Although the one candle sitting next to my plate did not provide much illumination, I could still see the piece of paper was one I had discarded earlier that day, a sketch of two roses clustered together. I hadn't been entirely satisfied with the shading, and so I had thrown the scrap into the waste bin in my room.

How he had come by it, I had no idea, although I guessed either Sar or Melynne, the girl tasked with keeping my rooms tidy, must have fished it out and given it to him.

"It was wasteful, I suppose. I should have used the back of the paper before I put it in the waste bin, but—"

"That is not what I was about to say." A black-clad finger traced the lines of one rose stem, then paused, still resting on the paper. "To see the truth of a thing...to be able to put that truth down on paper, or canvas...well, it is a rare gift. You should not disparage it."

"I wasn't—" I broke off, since I realized I had been doing that very thing. Well, it was never easy to shake off the habits of a lifetime. "So you don't think it odd, that a woman should want to be a painter?"

"No odder than the lord of Black's Keep being a dragon, I suppose."

It was the first time he had ever said anything about his... condition. The words sounded almost amused, if in a rueful way, and they emboldened me enough to say, "They call you that, my lord, and yet I must confess that you seem very much like a man to me."

The gloved fingers clenched on the paper, crumpling it. "Do I?"

Immediately I knew that I had misspoken, and the food I had just eaten seemed to turn over in my stomach. Why couldn't I have just held my tongue? It seemed to forever get me in trouble."My apologies—I did not mean—"

At once he pushed his chair back and stood. Wood scraped against stone, and I tried not to wince. "Count yourself fortunate that you have not seen the Dragon in his true guise...and pray that you never will."

Then he turned and strode from the room, leaving me to stare at the half-eaten food on my plate. His palpable anger had quite killed my own appetite, so after a moment I set aside my napkin and stood as well. By then I knew the way back to my rooms well enough, but still I hesitated. Perhaps some part of me thought he might return. As the minutes passed, however, it became clear that he was done with me for the evening.

Fighting a queasiness that had very little to do with the excellent meal I had just consumed, I found my way to the door and then out into the more brightly lit corridor. I saw no one, but that was to be expected. Most days I could climb from my own tower room to the ground floor and not encounter a soul. I expected that the servants, probably used to their lord's vagaries of mood, knew how to make themselves scarce when necessary.

Oh, why had I let those foolish words escape my lips? Yes, it was a thought that had been with me for some time, but I should have known better than to ask for details. And if my cursed curiosity must be sated, then I should have broached the subject with Sar, and not asked the question of the man himself.

Man. He stood on two legs like a man, had two arms and the height and breadth of a man in his prime, but I still had no idea of what lay concealed beneath his cloak. Wings and horns? I could guess, but I did not know. I only knew that he appeared a man to me, far more than a dragon.

I reached my rooms and let myself in, closing the door softly behind me. It was far too dark for painting, but I found I had little taste for that. I could only hope Theran wasn't so angry with me that he would not sit down to dinner with me the next day, that perhaps his ire would burn itself out in the dark hours of the night.

Even though I had no intention of picking up my paintbrush, I sat down in the chair in my little alcove. The windows were still open to the night air, and I welcomed the feel of the small breeze that whispered its way past the mullioned glass and played with the loose hair about my shoulders. If I closed my eyes and concentrated on the scents of dry grass and the faint lingering traces of linseed oil, perhaps I could forget that ugly little scene in the dining room, forget the anger in Theran's voice.

From somewhere above me came a high, piercing cry, one that seemed to chill the very blood in my veins, even though the night air was quite mild. I had heard that cry before, once, in my nightmares.

Although some part of me wanted to fling the windows shut, to run back to my bed and draw the bed hangings around me, I made myself stand and go to the casement. Fingers gripping the cool, rough stone, I leaned out just enough to get a clearer view of what had made that sound.

Black circled against black, blotting out the stars. There were no moons, and so I could not see anything clearly, but I thought I could make out the shape of enormous wings as something—someone—moved through the air above Black's Keep. And perhaps it was just a fancy, but I thought I saw the glitter of eyes, green as emeralds. Those eyes seemed to pierce the darkness and find me where I stood.

For one long moment I remained frozen in place, my own gaze meeting that of the monster. A shudder went through me, and I gasped. I had heard hunters describe the way rabbits might go still in such a manner, when caught by a predator's stare, and indeed, it seemed to me that I was unable to move, that I could not force myself away from the open window. The shadow moved closer, and the breath strangled in my throat. It would dive now, drop through the black night and tear the life from me, just another Bride to bleed out her last in one of the castle's high towers.

But then the shape moved off, and that hard green gaze turned elsewhere. I gasped and pushed myself backward, then grasped the windows and flung them shut, heedless of the glass.

They held, and I rushed to fasten the latches. A silly precaution; that enormous shape could have broken the mullioned windows with hardly a second thought. Better to have something there than nothing, though, and I stumbled out of the alcove and on into my bedchamber, where I closed the windows as well, and shut the door, though it had no latch.

Then I sat on the bed, arms clutched about myself, as if that would do anything to stop the trembling which had overtaken my body. At last the tremors subsided somewhat, and I forced myself to look at the nearest window, now safely hidden behind a fall of crimson damask.

It seemed clear to me now that the Dragon of Black's Keep was more than simply a title.

Sleep ran from me that night, ran like a quarry chased by a persistent hunter. Sometime in the dark hours of the morning I finally fell into an exhausted slumber, and the dream came upon me once again.

This time I saw him only in profile, catching a glimpse of a fine, long nose and that same sculpted jaw. Once again, though, he turned away, seemingly swallowed in a blaze of blinding white light. Even in my dream I blinked. And then he was gone.

I sat up in bed, and realized that wash of bright light was only the sun, now pouring in through the window. But hadn't I pulled the curtains the night before?

At the moment I couldn't quite recall what I had done in the depths of my terror. And even now, my thoughts seemed less consumed by my discovery that the lord of the castle was, in fact, a dragon than the vision even now fading from my mind's eye.

I pushed the covers aside and fairly leapt from the bed, intent on the pens and pencils scattered across the worktable in the alcove. A pencil came to hand first, and so I grasped it and found a clean piece of paper, then began to sketch. A few quick strokes to get down those clean features, although even as the pencil moved across the paper I wondered whether I was getting it right, whether his nose was not quite that aquiline, and whether the longish hair touched the top of his collar or brushed past it. And as I sat there the image was gone again, and I was left only with those hasty pencil marks to prove I hadn't conjured him completely from my imagination.

From the other room I heard the sound of footsteps. Melynne with my breakfast tray, most likely.

At once I was overcome by the impulse to hide what I had been doing. I shoved the half-finished sketch between a few sheets of blank paper and turned to face the doorway. My greeting to Melynne died on my lips, for it was not she who faced me, but Sar, looking grimmer than I had ever seen her.

She carried a breakfast tray, but all it held was a bowl of hot wheat cereal, and not even some of the raspberries that grew wild along the mountain roads. This time she did not bother to disguise her sniff as she took in my posture at the worktable, the pencil still clutched in my right hand.

"At it already, my lady?" she inquired in acid tones.

It did not take a good deal of perception to realize she was angry with me, and I knew the probable reason why. It must be an unsettling thing to have one's lord and master take to the skies in the form of a dragon, even if that sort of thing had happened before.

"Just some scribbling."

Another sniff, and she set down the tray in the single empty space on my table. Even so, one edge of the tray nudged a paintbrush, which fell onto the floor and rolled off into a corner. She did not bother to retrieve it.

Perhaps it would have been better to bear her anger in silence, thank her, and have her leave, but I felt a little flare of irritation myself. After all, how was I to know that a few unguarded words would be enough to raise such an ire in Theran Blackmoor that he would apparently be forced into his dragon form?

Beyond the annoyance, though, was worry over what I had said to him, and his reaction to it. With the return of the bright morning light, the terrors of the night before seemed to pale somewhat. He had not attacked me, although it certainly had been within his means to do so.

"Was he—was he very angry?"

This time her dark eyes narrowed, but then she seemed to pause and truly look at me. I thought I saw her mouth soften just the slightest bit, although she said nothing.

"I didn't mean to upset him," I went on, my words rushed, spilling over themselves. "Truly I didn't. It's only—well, too many times the words come out before I have time to think of them. I should learn to guard my tongue. The gods know my mother has told me that often enough."

Somehow the image of my mother chiding me for some long-forgotten transgression, and the memory of the disappointment in her voice, brought a choking sensation to my throat. Hot tears caught at my eyes, and I blinked. I did not want to break down now, not here in front of Sar, but thinking of my mother only brought to mind the understanding that I would never see her again, never hear one of her exasperated sighs or her warm, rueful laughs. And with that realization came a flood of sorrow I didn't even realize had been pent up inside me until I let it go.

I bent my head and wept, bringing my hands to my face in a childish attempt to conceal my misery. But then I felt Sar's arms go around me, and one hand stroke my loose, tangled hair.

"There, there, child," she said. "I won't say not to weep, because I know it's hard, to be torn from everything you've known and brought to a strange place."

"I didn't—didn't mean to hurt him." I brought up a hand to wipe away the tears, and from somewhere within her voluminous sleeves Sar extracted a handkerchief and pushed it into my damp palm. After I had wiped my eyes and blotted my nose, she said,

"I don't suppose you did." Arms crossed, she surveyed me for a moment, and again her expression softened, as if she truly saw me for the first time. "He thinks very highly of you."

"He—he does?"

"Indeed. And I don't say that lightly, for it is not his way to praise others."

The hurt I had caused him must have been all the worse for that. Oh, why did I not stop my foolish tongue before it uttered things I would only wish later unsaid? The fears of the previous night seemed very far away. At the moment I could only think of how he must have felt when I had so lightly broken the fragile regard that had begun to grow between us.

"I want to apologize," I said. "Will he see me, do you think?"

She hesitated. "I will have to see. He is always weary...the morning after. Perhaps later today."

"Of course." What must it take from him, to have his body rent asunder and turned into something so alien? Weary? I would think he'd wish to sleep for a hundred years after such a cataclysm.

"Eat," Sar told me, and her tone was already more brisk, as if she had decided on a plan of action. "I'll send up Melynne shortly to assist with your bath. It does no good for you to berate yourself further. Paint, and wait, and I'll see what I can do."

Her words reassured me a little, and I nodded. She took her leave of me then, but I did not immediately pick up the spoon and eat my breakfast. Instead, I drew out the little sketch I had made and stared down at the half-finished features of the strange man.

*Who are you?* I wondered. *And why do you haunt my dreams?*

The Dragon Lord agreed to see me at sunset, in the rose garden.

Ever since my painting supplies arrived, I hadn't paid much attention to my appearance, save to take great care that none of my gowns became spattered with paint or stained with linseed oil. Of course Sar made sure my hair was tidy before I went down to dinner each night, but even she hadn't seemed overly concerned with how I looked, as long as I was more or less presentable.

That afternoon, though, I put aside my paints early and took great care to brush my hair and choose a becoming gown of a smoky dark teal color, and to put on some jewels of gold and enormous black pearls. If I had been asked, I'm not sure I could have given a very coherent explanation as to why I felt my appearance was so important on this one occasion, when in the past I had not given it much thought. Perhaps it was something as childish and simple as thinking the Dragon would be less likely to devour a pretty-seeming young woman. Or perhaps I wanted to show him that I did care what he thought of me, that my previous carelessness had been no reflection on him.

Almost imperceptibly the days had begun to shorten, and the sun was slipping toward the horizon, the light growing warmer and somehow slanted. "The golden hour" was what Lindell called it, that magical time when the world seems to be limned in warm hues, and everything appears somehow both more real and yet insubstantial at the same time.

The roses seemed to be touched by that same magical paintbrush, and for a second I wished I had my own paints with me, that I might capture the beauty of the hour before it was gone. But no. I had more important things to occupy my time.

A shadow at the edge of my vision, and then he was there, standing only a few feet away. It was the first time I had ever seen him outside the castle walls...unless, of course, one counted my brief glimpse of that dark shape circling overhead.

He said nothing, no word of greeting, and although I had told myself to watch my tongue, I felt as if I should say something. So I moved toward one of the rosebushes and laid a hand against one of the blooms, fully open and a deep crimson. The gold at its heart seemed to echo the ochre-washed skies above us.

"They are so beautiful," I commented, my tone deliberately casual. "Do you ever walk here, my lord? I confess I haven't yet seen you in the gardens."

"I can see them from my window."

The words sounded almost too neutral. I turned and looked up at him then, but of course I could see nothing within the hood. The black-gloved hands hung at his sides.

"But can you smell them?" And I bent to breathe deeply of the rose blossom.

"Well enough."

I could not be angry with him for being curt. Probably I should be glad that he agreed to see me at all. "I would like it if you would walk with me here sometimes."

That seemed to take him aback; for the span of a few heartbeats he was silent, and it seemed as if the hood tilted slightly so he could regard me from a different angle. "You would wish that—to spend more time with me?"

"Yes," I said simply, knowing as I gave him the answer that it was no more than the truth. I wanted to know more of him, this odd husband of mine. Our dinners together had taken on something of the air of a ritual, but surely there should be more contact than that.

"You are not frightened of me?"

"I was last night. I am not frightened now."

"Because you face me in the daylight, and I appear to you as a man."

"No."

"No?"

It seemed the best gift I could give him was the truth. "Because last night you were not a man, and yet you did not hurt me. I angered you—unwittingly, that is true, but still I want to tell you how sorry I am for that. I should not have asked questions to which you did not want to give answers."

It seemed he sucked in his breath then, and he turned away slightly, as if regarding the blue mountain peaks to the north of us. A breeze came from somewhere to tug at the edges of his cloak, but I noticed the heavy fabric around his face did not move at all. Perhaps it was weighted in some way to keep it from shifting.

At last he spoke. "You are a very unusual young woman, Rhianne Menyon."

"Am I? I suppose one might think so, what with the painting—"

"That is not what I meant. You have every reason to fear me, and yet you stand there and do not shy away, even though you know I am not as other men."

I laughed then. "Well, you just implied that I am not as other young women, so I think that means we are actually rather suited to one another."

There seemed to be a ripple of laughter in his own voice as he replied, "Is that so?"

It seemed the most natural thing in the world for me to move closer to him, to reach out and take those gloved fingers in my own. Again, they seemed very warm to the touch, and I couldn't help wondering what lay beneath them. But I wouldn't think of that now. I had to let him know all was well between us.

At first his hand felt stiff, as if he was not sure I wouldn't pull back as soon as I realized what I was doing. But then his fingers seemed to relax, and wrapped themselves around mine.

"Much better," I said. "Shall we go in and see what Sar has planned for dinner?"

"Yes," he replied. "Let us go in."

# Chapter Six

That meal had far more of the feel of a celebration about it than the feast which had greeted us after our nuptials. The fare was plain enough—roast pig, and wild rice, and some of the last of the summer's squash—and yet we lingered over it as if a dozen courses had been laid before us.

I told him of my painting, and he spoke of the art which adorned the walls of the castle. "Some of it I chose myself, years ago, before I could not leave the castle."

"So you...traveled?" It was on the tip of my tongue to ask, *So you were not always as you are now?* But I did not have the courage to give voice to the words.

Somehow he seemed to know what I was thinking. He poured another measure of wine into my goblet and then into his own before replying, "Once I was no different from other men."

I didn't quite know what to say to that, so I only drank a bit more of my wine and waited.

Again there seemed to be an undercurrent of amusement in his voice. "Does that surprise you? What is the current tale in Lirinsholme? That I was born in this inhuman form as a punishment to my parents for their harsh treatment of the townsfolk?"

"One of the tales," I said frankly. "But the most prevalent one is that you were cursed by a sorcerer. It seems rather silly to me, as the last mage in this part of the world disappeared more than five hundred years ago."

"Five hundred years." His tone was musing. "Has it really been that long?"

I set down my goblet and stared at him, aghast. To be sure, that was the tale I had heard for most of my life, but I'd always thought it must be an exaggeration. Yes, the Dragon had reigned over Lirinsholme and its environs for time out of mind, but people's recollections grew hazier as the years stretched on, and I really hadn't thought it could have been that long in reality. Trapped in this castle, in an alien body, for half a millennium?

"You seem surprised," he remarked. "So you did not think the legends had any truth to them?"

"Legends generally don't."

He chuckled. "So the dreamy artist actually has her feet planted firmly on the ground?"

"I'm the eldest of four daughters. I didn't have much choice."

Another laugh, and he lifted his goblet and drank. "I can see the truth in that."

Emboldened by the lightness in his voice, I asked, "So what really did happen? I must say that it seems rather excessive, as curses go."

At first he was silent, and I held my breath, worried that once again I had asked the wrong question, had broken the delicate rapport between us. When he spoke, however, he sounded more sad than angry. "I cannot speak of that."

*Cannot...or will not?*

Still, my common sense hadn't completely deserted me, and so I only nodded instead of asking yet more questions. I speared the last bit of roast pig with my fork and lifted it to my mouth, wondering what on earth I should say next. After I had swallowed the morsel, I ventured, "It must be a very great thing to be able to fly."

"One might think so. I found that the novelty palled somewhat after the first century or two."

I supposed it might. I tried to think of what he did to fill all those endless days and came up with nothing. If I had been trapped in the form of a monster for centuries, I thought I could have painted—the shape of his hands appeared human enough to hold a paintbrush—but I saw little evidence of such hobbies on the Dragon's part. Then again, I had never seen his rooms. I didn't know what might be hidden there.

He waved a hand. "But never mind that. Tell me more of this painting of yours."

It was a diversion, I knew, but one I was willing to follow. And so I went into a detailed, and, I fear, rather dull description of all the pigments I was using in the painting, and how I had to work quickly, because autumn was swiftly approaching and the colors of the prospect would begin to shift and change any time now. But the Dragon seemed interested, and I was happy to leave more troubling topics behind us. I did not want a repeat of that dreadful night where he flew through the darkness, crying out his pain and wretchedness, as if only in the dragon's form did he have the power to give voice to his sorrow.

By speaking of lighter things, I found it easier to pretend that all was well in his world.

Although it was true enough that I needed to complete the large painting soon, the next day I instead took my small easel and my palette to the rose garden, where I undertook to paint the roses I had noticed the day before. The canvas likewise was of modest proportions, not even a foot square, but within that small space I hoped to capture some of the beauty and the warmth of the flowers in their late-summer bloom. It would be my gift to him, some small part of me he could take back with him to his solitary rooms.

Again I thought I saw that watching shadow in the corner of my vision, but every time I glanced upward, the windows were empty of all onlookers. Very well. I had hoped for the painting to be a surprise, but if my lord wished to watch me as I worked, there was little enough I could do about it. I took care not to lay on the paint too thickly, for I wanted to give it to him that week, and even a piece of such a modest scale would take a few days to dry.

It was a good day's work; I found myself satisfied enough with the shading of the flowers, the velvety texture of each petal. Perhaps I could see if Mat might build me a suitable frame for it, something simple but elegant. I thought I had seen some carved molding tucked away in a corner of the workshop, left over perhaps from an earlier refurbishment in the castle. It might suit, as it had only a simple carved beaded border, nothing too heavy.

Mind humming, I packed up my things and returned to my tower room. Little enough time remained before dinner, only enough for me to take off the smock I'd had Sar make for me, and to pull away the ribbon that held back my hair and arrange my wavy locks in a more or less becoming pattern over my shoulders.

I paused then in my primping, one hand still resting on my hair, the paint stains on my fingers somehow incongruous against the blue silk of my gown as it gleamed beneath the dark strands. My reflection stared back at me, one eyebrow lifted slightly.

*All this, to meet a man who is not even a man? What should you care what he thinks of your appearance?*

I turned away from the mirror and flung my hair back over my shoulders. Common courtesy, I told myself. No, my family was not fine enough to dress for dinner, but woe betide any of the Menyon daughters if she should arrive at the table without her hair brushed and her face and hands clean. Gods only knew what my mother would have said about the paint stains on my fingers. I had been careless lately, and the oil paints were far messier than the glazes I used for my father's pottery.

Yes, it was common courtesy. Simple enough.

I wouldn't let myself think it was anything else.

A few days after that, my rose painting was ready, the frame kindly put together by Mat, as my rough carpentry skills, while barely up to the task of building a canvas, certainly did not lend themselves to putting together a picture frame that was serviceable, let alone handsome.

Theran took it from me at dinner and turned it over in his hands. By this time, he had allowed somewhat more adequate lighting in the dining hall, and so at least I was assured that he could actually see some of the details of the painting. Then again, the lit sconces on the wall and the large candelabra in the center of the table might had been put there solely for my benefit. Perhaps his enchanted dragon eyes could see perfectly well in the dark.

"It's beautiful," he said, one gloved finger touching the glowing petal of a flower briefly. "I shall treasure it always."

"It's just a trifle, but I thought it might help you to remember the rose garden when the snows of winter come."

"It is far more than a trifle, but yes, it will help to keep a bit of summer alive. I fear you will find the castle…rather gloomy in the wintertime."

"I always rather liked winter," I said. "Especially after a first snowfall. Everything always looks so white and clean."

He did not reply at once, but instead stared down at the painting for a long moment, as if trying to commit the colors and shapes contained therein to memory. Then he said, his tone rough along the edges, as if touched by some previous pain, "You may find that winter here is not quite as much to your liking."

What on earth was I to say to that? I fumbled for a reply that would be both noncommittal and yet breezy, to show that his words had not troubled me. But that would be a lie, because of course they had. What lay ahead for me, here in Black's Keep? So far everyone had been most accommodating, and I'd found my tenure in the castle much more comfortable than I had any right to expect. What was to be the fly in this honey pot? I didn't dare ask.

"Oh, I daresay it might be confining when the heavy snows come, but as long as I have my paints and my easel, I assure you that I shall be able to keep myself amused."

He nodded then, and turned the conversation to other things. And although he sounded pleasant enough, I knew he was troubled. I also knew I dared not inquire as to the cause.

There were so many things I could not ask...

The dream came to me once more that night. This time I was better suited to meet it.

As soon as my eyes opened the next morning, I pushed myself out of bed and went to my easel, stumbling a little in the dim light before dawn. Setting aside my half-finished painting of the valley of Lirinsholme, I grasped another canvas of roughly the same size and set it in place. A pencil, then, to work out the rough lines of his features, the high brow, the mouth with lips thin but also beautifully shaped. I worked feverishly, desperate to get down every detail before they fled my traitor mind as they had done twice before.

The sun had just begun to peek over the hills to the east when I stopped, knowing that I would get no more from this sitting. Still, I had accomplished far more than I had previously, as the face of a man stared back at me from the canvas. Rough, of course, with far more detail that still needed to be filled in…if my chancy dreams would allow it. But now I had something to work with.

Driven by the same need for secrecy that had made me hide the first sketch I had made of him, I pulled the canvas from the easel and set it back behind several blank ones that had not yet been pressed into service. The valley of Lirinsholme returned to its previous position of honor, although I must admit my appetite for painting it had waned considerably.

Although his face was now hidden from view, this time his features seemed to haunt me, as if my putting their entirety in physical form had given them some sort of anchor in my mind. And even though I was nowhere near the stage where I would begin to apply paint to canvas, I found myself contemplating the mixture of azure and viridian I would need to compound to match their elusive sea-colored depths.

Melynne came then with my breakfast tray. I was glad enough of the distraction, and gladder still that it was the maid who had come, and not Sar. Melynne, though a sweet enough girl, was not blessed with much in the way of discernment, while I worried that the much sharper Sar might have seen my distraction, and wondered at it.

I knew I could never begin to explain myself. How could I possibly tell that no-nonsense person I seemed to be obsessed with a man I had seen only in my dreams, a man who was most definitely not my husband? That, I feared, would not go over very well. By the time I descended the stairs to take my morning walk in the gardens, I should have had a respectable space in which to compose myself. Sar need never know something was amiss.

As for the rest, well, I could only hope the madness was temporary.

The days seemed to fly by. I awoke one morning some six weeks after my arrival in Black's Keep and realized it was my birthday. I was twenty now, and if all had gone according to plan, I would have been safe from the Dragon, free to pursue my destiny. That is, free to pursue the destiny of being married to whatever man, young or not-so-young, whom my parents deemed suitable.

If I had been home, I would have been greeted in bed with my favorite seedcakes. There would have been presents—a finely carved hair comb from my mother, perhaps a new set of paintbrushes from my father, a clumsily stitched handkerchief from Maeganne, a little brass bauble for my neck chain from Therella.

I had been more or less successful at keeping the homesickness at bay, but the thought of my family, of those homely comforts that were now gone forever, brought stinging tears to my eyes. I told myself not to be foolish, that my life here was better than I could ever have hoped for, but such sensible advice did not seem to do me much good. For the first time in several weeks, I had no motivation to go to my hidden canvas, to continue my halting progress on the strange man's portrait.

The painting of Lirinsholme, now almost complete, seemed to mock me from its position on the easel. What had I been thinking, to paint the one thing I could never have again? Oh, once upon a time I had scorned my provincial upbringing, wished I could go make my fortune in Lystare, or even brave the great journey to see the capital of Sirlende, the great city of Iselfex, reputed to be one of the wonders of the world. Now, though, I thought I would give a great deal to see Lirinsholme's narrow streets again, and to hear my mother's voice or the laughter of my sisters.

But as there was little I could do to change my current situation, and because my mother had drummed into me the notion that sitting around and moping did no one any good and could actually do a great deal of harm, I made myself get out of bed. I dried my eyes on a handkerchief I retrieved from the top shelf of the wardrobe, and opened the windows and drew in deep breaths of the bracing morning air.

On an impulse, I pulled out the canvas of my unknown man and stared for a long moment into his eyes. They had been one of the first things I colored, and their elusive aquamarine depths seemed to look past me rather than at me. As much as I might have wanted to find answers there, I saw nothing but more questions. So I sighed and replaced the painting in its not-so-secret hiding place amongst my blank canvases...but not before I pressed two fingers to my lips and then laid them against the painted mouth of the stranger. Nothing in return, of course...no response save me shaking my head at my folly.

I had not bothered to tell Sar or Lord Blackmoor that it was my birthday. It appeared to me a foolish indulgence in a place where every dinner seemed to be a birthday feast, and where my every wish was granted.

Save, of course, my wish for freedom.

So it was a quiet day, and one in which I did not expect anything out of the ordinary to occur. I settled myself in my alcove and vowed that I would finish that damned painting of Lirinsholme. Autumn was fast approaching, the oaks and elms on the higher hillsides already beginning to be touched with bright color. I realized with a pang that somewhere down in the valley below, Lilianth would be wed to her betrothed very soon.

*May she have more joy in her marriage than I have*, I thought then, and then chided myself for being so self-pitying. Perhaps Theran Blackmoor was not the sort of husband a young woman might dream of, but he had treated me very well, with kindness and respect, which was probably more than I would have had at the hands of Liat Marenson. That realization made me thank the Dragon Lord for his patience and his regard. Things could have been so much worse. And since I had been careful to guard my tongue and to be as amiable as possible when in his presence, we had had no repeats of that terrifying night when he circled the ramparts of Black's Keep in his dragon form.

A sudden commotion from the courtyard below made me stop and set down my paintbrush. The castle and the grounds surrounding it were not a place of hustle and bustle; it was clear Lord Blackmoor maintained only enough staff to keep the household running and not more than that. We had no strangers here. Whatever shipments of goods were necessary to the maintenance of the kitchens and the castle itself were brought here by its servants. Wandering traders and the like knew better than to approach the Dragon Lord's doorstep, preferring the much more hospitable audience they might find in Lirinsholme.

Curiosity awakened, I lifted the easel out of the way so I could better peer down into the courtyard to see who—or what—disturbed the peace of Black's Keep. The window was open to the cool afternoon air, and so I had only to place my hands on the lintel and lean over to identify the cause of the commotion.

"I will see her!"

The voice was familiar. My gaze rested on him, just as I realized who it was.

My father.

He sat, somewhat clumsily, on the back of a large, ungainly brown horse—Traes Mackinrod's Thunderer, if memory served. What my father had said to persuade the blacksmith to part with his prized horse, I did not know, but at the moment I thought the "how" was far less important than the "why."

I watched as Sar came bustling out into the courtyard, followed by Mat and two guardsmen whose names I did not know. She said something, in tones low enough that I could not hear her, but my father only shook his head and retorted,

"I am her father, and it is her birthday! I will see her!"

Strange enough that my normally mild father would have taken it into his head to come here, when such a thing was forbidden. Stranger still that he should roar and cause a clamor, as if he had borrowed some of Traes Mackinrod the blacksmith's bluster along with his horse.

I knew it was entirely possible for Mat and his two companions to remove my father bodily if need be, but I did not want things to come to such a pass. An impatient pause as I drew off my smock, and then I was running for the door, hurrying down all those interminable staircases as fast as my slipper-clad feet could take me.

Although at that time of day Melynne and the other housemaids should have been preparing the dining chamber for dinner, I found them clustered around the great double doors which opened on the courtyard, peering out and whispering to each other as if they watched one of the puppet shows in Lirinsholme's marketplace.

Worry for my father made my tone far more curt than usual. "I daresay his lordship will be less than pleased when he learns you were spying on other people's business rather than attending to your duties."

At my words all three of the maids snapped upright, eyes going wide. Melynne in particular looked startled; I daresay she had never heard me speak in such a fashion before.

"I - I'm so sorry, my lady. Only we heard the noise and—"

" —And went to eavesdrop on something that is no concern of yours. Go on—you know you should not be here."

They went, scurrying away with nervous squeaks and chattering, sounding more like a trio of house mice than young women of my own age. Satisfied that I had reduced the audience somewhat, I stepped out into the courtyard.

"Master Menyon," Sar was saying, "you must come away. You know it is forbidden for you to come here."

"And why is that?" he replied. "A man forbidden to see his own daughter? Preposterous!"

"Father," I said quietly, having paused just beyond the bottom of the steps that led up into the castle.

He stopped then and looked over Sar's head. Our eyes met. Something of the wild expression that had overtaken his normally mild features ebbed away. Ignoring Sar, he dismounted clumsily and came toward me, hands outstretched.

"Rhianne. Oh, Rhianne." And he bowed his head, as if he did not want me to see the tears in his eyes.

I almost wept, too, seeing his face and hearing his voice, when I had thought I would never do either of those things again. But I knew I must maintain my composure; although Sar had stepped back, as if in deference to the lady of the castle, her dark eyes were keen as she watched me. My response would tell her much of how I viewed my place here.

"Father," I said, quietly and firmly, "do not think I am not happy to see you, but you know you should not have come here."

"Or what?" he replied. "Will the Dragon come to strike me dead? I have set foot in this accursed place, and yet I still breathe."

"Yes...on his sufferance, no doubt. Do you not think he knows of your presence here?"

"I care little for that."

I wondered whence came this false bravado. Was it that brush with death he'd had earlier in the summer, when his heart betrayed him so suddenly? I couldn't begin to guess, but

I supposed it did not matter one way or the other. What mattered was getting him safely on the way home again.

"Well, then," I said, in a voice I feared was a trifle too hearty. "You see me now. Do I not look healthy and well?"

He surveyed me then, taking in my rich gown, the sapphire drops at my ears. His eyes narrowed as he noticed the paint stains on my fingers. "You are painting, then?"

"Every day. His lordship has been most generous in providing me with supplies."

I had not meant the words to sting, but I saw my father flinch slightly. He said, "That is something we could not give you. Instead you painted pottery at your father's whim, and took the brunt of the blame when the subterfuge was discovered."

At once I understood. The gods only knew what thoughts of guilt had assailed him in the weeks since my marriage to the Dragon. My poor father thought it all his fault, that I had given myself to the Dragon as the only way of saving my family. And perhaps at the time that had been part of my reasoning, but not all. I knew I couldn't begin to explain to him how this place, odd as it might seem, had become home to me.

"Dear Father," I said, and took his hands in mine. "You mustn't blame yourself. I took the risk willingly...as willingly as I came here to be the Dragon's Bride. It was my decision to make. And I am happy here. Truly."

At those words he looked down at me in wonder, as if by studying my face he might find the answer to such an unfathomable riddle. "Happy?" he repeated at last.

"Yes. Happy. It sounds strange, I know, and a month ago I would not have believed it myself. But, as I said, I have as much time as I would like, and the Dragon has been kind to me. Very kind..." I added, trailing off as I considered the odd lord of this castle, the man haunted by an evil curse, someone who should have had every reason to view the world with hatred and suspicion, and yet who somehow, inexplicably, had made me feel welcome here.

My father was silent for a long moment, watching me. Perhaps he saw the truth in my features, or perhaps he'd only come to his senses enough to realize that, strange as it might seem, my existence was not the horror he had imagined. He cleared his throat. "I brought your presents."

"You needn't have—"

He cut me off. "I wished it. Your mother wished it." And he turned from me and busied himself with one of the saddlebags, as Sar looked on with raised eyebrows and I prayed to whichever gods might be listening that the lord of the castle was occupied elsewhere.

The gifts were very close to what I had imagined, although my mother's gift was a fine ebony-backed hairbrush instead of a comb, and the bauble Therella had sent was a needle case for my chatelaine. Never mind that I avoided needlework like the plague. But my father had brought me some fine-tipped squirrel brushes, and Maeganne had made me a handkerchief with my initial clumsily embroidered in the corner, while Darlynne's gift was a little bottle of water smelling of lavender.

"They are lovely," I said, as I fought against the choking sensation in my throat. "Tell Mother and Therella and Maeganne and Darlynne that they are just what I wished for."

My father nodded. "We think of you every day, Rhianne. Do not think you are forgotten."

"I hadn't." Then, after a quick glance at Sar, whose mouth tightened slightly, even as she nodded, "And how is Lilianth? Her wedding is three days hence, is it not?"

"Yes. Some thought it ill-mannered of her, to go ahead with the wedding after she had been chosen and not gone—"

"—Because I stepped in for her! What foolishness it would have been for her to have not gotten married after all that!"

He said nothing at first. Then he nodded slowly. "You gave much for your friend."

I did not bother to say that she would have done the same for me, for in truth I did not think she would have, had our positions been reversed. I did not love her any less for that, but she and I were very different people. "And I have received much as well. Tell Lilianth that—and Mother, too."

Perhaps he caught the warning glance Sar shot him then, because he only replied, "I will," before pulling me into a rough embrace, during which he wouldn't quite meet my eyes. Still with his gaze averted, he climbed back up into the saddle with the over-caution of someone not accustomed to the task.

"You will take care," he said.

I almost said I had no real need to, but then I recalled the dark shape of Theran's dragon form, circling above the castle that was his prison. All had been calm enough since then, though I knew better than to trust things would go on in such a fashion. "I promise...if you promise as well. I hope you have not tried to haul your own clay lately!"

"As for that," he said frankly, "what with business the way it's been..." He caught himself, but the damage was done.

So the good people of Lirinsholme had not relented, even though the wayward daughter had sacrificed herself on the altar of Black's Keep. Ah, well. Prejudices died hard, newly formed ones possibly even harder than old beliefs that had had a lifetime to mature. At least the Dragon's bride price would ensure they did not want, although it was a difficult thing to have one's life work discarded all because of a single ill-considered decision.

"The ground will be too hard soon anyway," I pointed out, and he even smiled a little. "But look, Father—the sun is beginning to set. You must be down the mountain before dark arrives."

He looked unhappy at those words, although he did not try to argue. There would have been no point—we both knew his skills on horseback were negligible at best.

"Farewell, Rhianne," he said simply.

"Farewell, Father." It must have been the newfound maturity of my twenty years that allowed me to keep my voice so calm, so level.

He turned the horse around. I noticed he did not look back as he crossed the courtyard and went on through the castle gates. And then he was gone.

Sar approached, and I held my breath, wondering what words of recrimination she would have for me. But she only gazed at me for a moment and said,

"Come inside, my lady. It is almost time for dinner."

# Chapter Seven

"You should have told me it was your birthday," Theran Blackmoor said.

With my fork I pushed aside a fatty-looking piece of venison and instead tackled the compote of spiced apples that had accompanied it. "I didn't think it mattered. You've already done so much for me—"

He raised a hand. "All I've done is try to make you comfortable here. But a birthday...a birthday is special."

"Sar has prepared a wonderful meal."

A rueful shake of the hood, and he reached for his wine glass. At least, it seemed that small movement of his head was rather aggravated. I fancied that over the days and weeks I'd come to know his moods and gestures a little better, even if I could not see his face.

"I am told that modesty is becoming in young women, but you might try a little less of it from time to time. It does not suit you all that well."

"What is modest about not drawing attention to one's self?"

He laughed outright then. "I would say avoiding attention is one of the basic characteristics of modesty. Come now—you are a woman of the world now, having left your girlhood behind. I would like to hear you say one praiseful thing about yourself."

At first I hesitated, thinking perhaps he meant to jest with me, but as he remained sitting there, watching me with his head cocked and the wine glass still in one hand, I realized he was in earnest. Good gods, what on earth was I to say?

Stumbling over the words, I managed, "Well, I am—that is, I have been told that I am a rather good painter."

"You have been told you are a good painter. Do you need the words of others to convince you of this?"

Of course I didn't, not really. I knew I was good. Better than good, really, but it was difficult to shake off years of my mother admonishing me to never boast, to only nod meekly if someone commented on a sketch or the texture of a pudding or the sweetness of my smile.

I lifted my head and looked directly into his unseen features. "I am an excellent painter."

"Much better. What else?"

"What else?"

"There is more to you than your paintbrushes, Rhianne. What would you say if I told you your beauty rivals that of any of the court ladies I have ever seen?"

"I would say that it has been a long time since you were at court, my lord," I replied tartly.

Another laugh. "And I would say you are correct in that point, but my memory has not faded with the passage of years. I know whereof I speak."

I knew I should have come up with some rejoinder, some words that would have asserted my own ordinariness while not sounding contradictory. At least, that is what my mother would have wished of me. But she was not there, and, odd as it might sound, I found myself enjoying Lord Blackmoor's approval. So I said, in meek tones I was sure did not fool him for a second, "As you say, my lord."

If I'd been able to see his eyes, it was very likely that they'd have had a wicked glint. But there was no mistaking the amusement in his voice when he spoke. "I do say, Rhianne. But since I have obviously discommoded you, let us move on to safer subjects. You say that your painting of Lirinsholme is almost complete. What next, then?"

Relieved he'd abandoned the discussion of my charms, I went on to explain how the ivy on the castle walls had just begun to turn with the first frosts, and how I wanted to do several paintings—a triptych, I hoped—in which I could catch those elusive colors before they were gone. It did not take me much encouragement to hold forth at length about painting, and so I was able to fill up the rest of the meal's discussion with commentary on my future projects.

Upon reflection, I realized there was one good thing about that hood. At least with it concealing my husband's face, I could not as easily tell if he were bored by me or not.

That night Theran accompanied me to my rooms. I did not know precisely why; perhaps he thought it a gentlemanly gesture, as it was my birthday. At the door, I hesitated, wondering if I should ask him to come inside. Surely it would be a friendly gesture to ask him in to sit by the fire for a few minutes. I didn't see the harm in that, as Sar or one of the maids always kept the door between the sitting room and my bedchamber closed—most likely to hide the clutter of my paints and easel.

"Sar left the fire going, since the evening promised to be chilly," I said, one hand resting on the doorknob.

Theran seemed to pause as well, as if not entirely sure how best to respond. Then the hood dipped slightly. "You wish me to come inside?"

"Just—just for a few minutes," I faltered, wondering if he had interpreted my invitation as something else entirely.

Again a brief silence. "I would enjoy that."

Not entirely sure whether I should be relieved or alarmed, I turned the knob and went inside, my husband following like a silent shadow. A fire did, indeed, crackle welcomingly in the hearth, and I saw on the low table in front of the divan a crystal decanter of some amber-colored liquid and a few small glasses. Well, Sar had mentioned that she would leave me some of the local honey liqueur, proclaiming it to be just the thing to ward off the chill of autumn nights in the castle.

"A drink?" I inquired, moving toward the table. At least the act of pouring us a few glasses would do something to fill up the silence.

"I see that Sar has sent up some *methlyn*. A little, perhaps. It is very strong."

"So she warned me." I lifted the decanter, which was heavier than it looked, and tipped a little of the liquid into each of the glasses.

Theran approached and took one of the glasses. "Happy birthday."

I grasped the one remaining and raised it as well. "Thank you."

We both drank—that is, Theran managed a practiced sip of the liquid, which was much thicker than wine or cider, and far more searing. I swallowed a mouthful, gasped, then coughed quite inelegantly.

"Sar didn't warn you?"

"She might have mentioned that it took some getting used to, but..." I blinked my watering eyes. "I see now what she meant about it keeping me warm—I feel as if someone just poured Keshiaari fire down my throat!"

"Some water, perhaps?" A ceramic pitcher sat on one of the side tables, and he went to it and poured a measure into one of the pitcher's matching goblets. I took it gratefully and drank, thus cooling my abused throat somewhat.

"Thank you."

I couldn't see his smile, but I guessed there might be one hidden under that hood. He retrieved his own glass and took another sip. "Practice, my dear Rhianne."

The last thing I wanted was to swallow any more of that searing stuff, but I also didn't want him to think me a coward. So I went and picked up the glass I had abandoned on the table, and forced myself to take the merest of sips, barely more than an exhalation of fumes over my palate. That seemed a little more manageable; this time the liquid going down my throat had the warmth of a welcome fire, and not the searing heat of a dragon's breath.

"Better?"

"Much."

A silence descended, but this time it somehow felt companionable rather than awkward. Theran stepped away from me, going to stand only a few feet from the hearth. His robes looked very black in contrast with the golds and reds and ochres of the flames. He drank from his glass again, draining it. I wondered at him being able to stand that much, although perhaps his body was more suited to such heat than mine.

He spoke then. "Your father loves you very much."

His words took me aback. There had been a questioning note to the remark, as if he were not entirely sure of the answer.

"Well...of course. I am sorry he came here, though. I know that it isn't done."

Theran turned toward me, empty glass dangling from between his black-clad fingers. "It isn't done, Rhianne, because no one has done it in the past five hundred years. Until now."

His tone was so neutral I could not tell whether he was angry or not. "He only wanted to make sure I was well..."

"There is no need to make excuses for him." The Dragon Lord paused, as if checking himself. "That is, it is understandable why he came. You should not worry on his account."

"You won't—you won't retaliate?"

"Of course not!"

There was no mistaking the vehemence of those words. Again I had misjudged him, this odd husband of mine. "But there must be some reason why family members are forbidden to visit the Brides..."

"'And go forth, taking that which is his, and leaving behind the things of your childhood,'" Theran said. "Do you know what that is from?"

It sounded familiar, but although I had been taught to read and write, books were a luxury in my household. I could not place the phrase.

He seemed to take my silence as tacit admission that I did not, in fact, recognize the passage. "It is from the *Book of Inyanna*, where it discusses how a young woman must leave her family and make a new one with her husband. A tenet which is perhaps adhered to more strictly here than elsewhere, I am sure. And it is not always wise to come here, because the family may find—" And then he paused, possibly recalling at the last instant that some things were better left unsaid.

*May find what?* I wanted to ask. But if he had stopped himself, I guessed he would not confide in me.

"So it has become something of a tradition," I ventured, and he nodded, as if relieved that I had not pressed the issue.

"Precisely." He moved back to the table and poured himself another glass of the *methlyn*.

I might have sucked in my breath slightly at the thought of two such glasses drunk so closely in succession. Whatever the cause, Theran turned back toward me.

"No fears, Rhianne. It does not affect me in quite the same way it does you."

Unfortunate that I had been so transparent. I managed a smile and replied, "I imagine not, or you would be doubled over coughing right now."

A chuckle. "Quite right...although it seems you've acclimated yourself to it somewhat."

"Perhaps." To be sure, I had essayed one or two more careful swallows, but I thought it was safe to say that the *methlyn* would never replace wine as my drink of choice.

His air seemed to change then; somehow he appeared taller, as if he had straightened within the enveloping robes, and the hood was tilted down toward me. "And it never occurred to you to leave?"

"Leave?" I repeated, unsure of what he was asking me.

"With your father. I was not there—it is possible you would not have been stopped."

"I would never—" I burst out. Then, in somewhat calmer tones, "That is, such a thing would never have occurred to me."

"And why not?"

"It would not be the honorable thing to do," I replied calmly. That sounded very noble, but I knew there was far more to it than that. "I mean...that is to say..."

He said nothing, as if content to watch my verbal floundering.

Damn it. Perhaps it would have been better to say nothing, but I did not want him to think that he had bested me. "Why should I leave?" I asked. "I have everything I need here."

At that he went very still. The dark robes could have been carved from basalt, so unmoving were they. Finally, "You do?"

My cheeks flushed with sudden heat, although whether my blush was from the methlyn or something else entirely, I could not say. I thought I was being careful with the heady liquor, but perhaps it had loosened my tongue more than I had guessed, although more than three-quarters of what I had first poured still remained in the glass I held.

"Well, I can paint as much as I want, and Sar has been very kind, and—"

"And?"

Oh, it was too much. I had not been raised to know what it was like to carry on this sort of a conversation with a man. If one could even call Theran Blackmoor a man. Be that as it may, while I'd had long discussions on painting techniques with Lindell, and of course interacted with my father on a daily basis, I had no real experience of what it was like to speak of anything save the weather or the most mundane inanities with someone of the opposite sex. So far I had skirted my inexperience by speaking of my paintings and other such commonplaces with Theran, but I realized we had crossed some sort of threshold here. Once again, it would have been far wiser to keep my mouth shut.

Then again, he was my husband. Why should I hide things from him? Well...besides my painting of the strange man, safely hidden behind stacks of canvases and the closed door to my bedchamber.

Since I had already begun, I thought I might as well go ahead and truly stick my foot in it. "And I like being with you... speaking with you."

He said nothing for a long moment. I found myself holding my breath, wondering if I had made some drastic blunder, said the words no woman in my situation should have uttered.

Although he stood only a few feet away, it seemed as if a very great distance separated us. He appeared to stare down into his half-full glass, but then set it on the table before walking toward me. I did not move. I don't think I could have, even if I had wanted to.

He stopped then, although he stood very close to me, closer than he had been since the night of our wedding. Once again I felt the heat of his body, only this time, instead of being troubled by it, I yearned for it. I wanted to know then what it would be like if he reached out for me, drew me into his arms. What it would feel like if his lips met mine in earnest, and not in the cool kiss of ceremony.

One hand reached out as if to touch my loose hair, but he stopped, gloved fingers a scant inch from my head. I saw then that they were trembling.

"No," he said clearly. "I will not do this. Not to you."

And he turned and fled the chamber, leaving me to watch as he slammed the door, and to wonder what I had done wrong. For the longest time I could do nothing but stand there, staring at that closed door. Then, almost as if it belonged to someone other than myself, my right hand lifted, and I bolted down the remainder of the contents of my glass, blinking at the sudden tearing in my eyes and telling myself that it was only the *methlyn*. Only a reaction to the bite of the liquor, and nothing else.

I was glad of the dream this time, glad I could focus my attention on something other than Theran Blackmoor, if only for a little while. This time it seemed as if the stranger turned toward me and smiled. His was a beautiful smile, illuminating his whole face, accenting the laugh lines around his eyes. I wished I could somehow paint that smile into the portrait, but the set of his mouth was quite done already.

That didn't stop me from getting out of bed and grasping a pencil, and picking up my sketchbook. Just a quick study, something to get down the lift of his mouth and the crinkles at the corners of his eyes. Perhaps when I was done with the first portrait I could do another one, this one with him smiling.

I set down the pencil and shook my head at myself. Madness, really, as the first painting was far from finished. Besides, who had ever heard of a portrait wherein someone smiled? Portraits were serious matters, after all, a way of immortalizing oneself, and, I thought, giving one's ancestors some idea as to what their forebears looked like. At least, that was how Lindell explained it to me, and since he had painted a great many members of the peerage, I supposed he knew better than most.

The stranger smiled up at me from the paper, and I scowled. "I suppose you find this all very amusing," I said aloud. "But you have done enough mischief for one day."

And I closed the sketchbook, turning instead to the painting of Lirinsholme's valley. Truly, the piece was done, to all intents and purposes. I had thought perhaps to deepen some of the shadows cast by the stands of oak and elm which bordered the town to the south and west, but on further inspection I deemed that not to be necessary. No, all it needed was further time to dry, and then it could be framed and hung. Where, I had no idea; I thought Lord Blackmoor would decide where best it would reside. It was something I could discuss with him at dinner...if he could even bring himself to speak to me.

I didn't quite sigh, but I felt little of the accomplishment I had thought I would experience once this, my first grand painting, was finished. Perhaps with time I might become more seasoned to his lordship's vagaries of mood and not allow such things to temper my own spirits. At the moment, though, I could only wish I had stopped myself before revealing truths he apparently didn't wish to hear.

Despite it being sandwiched between several other canvases, I felt the pull of my unfinished painting, the draw of the stranger's eyes. Almost without thinking I stood and went to retrieve it, to hold it up in the clear morning light that streamed through the windows. Although the man's expression was serious enough, I had painted in the smallest lift at the left side of his mouth, as if he were secretly amused by something.

*As well you should be*, I thought, staring down at his features, which were slowly becoming as familiar to me as my own. *What with haunting my dreams over and over, and making me waste valuable paint and canvas on something I dare not show to anyone else...*

Almost as if I had summoned her with my thoughts, I heard the door in the outer room open and Melynne enter, calling, "Breakfast, my lady!"

At once I grasped the painting and dropped it down between the two blank canvases which had hidden it previously. My panic seemed foolish to me—after all, if Melynne did chance to spy the painting, I could always tell her it was of someone I had known in Lirinsholme, a cousin or something similarly harmless. But for whatever reason it felt vitally important to me that she not see it, and I did sigh in relief as I turned away from it just as she came in through the door.

She seemed not to notice anything amiss, but only set the tray down on the table next to the bed. By this time she knew better than to clear any space on my worktable for such things. "There's more of that pear sauce you like, my lady, and wheat griddle cakes. I noticed you hadn't been wanting your tea the past few mornings, but seeing as it's turning brisk—"

Tea sounded like an excellent idea after the *methlyn* I had drunk the previous night. "That sounds wonderful, Melynne. I was thinking the dark green gown today."

"Of course, my lady." She bobbed a curtsey and went over to the wardrobe, then began to lay out my clothes for the day.

It didn't matter to me all that much what I wore, as long as it was more or less suited for the day's weather. However, by setting her to the task immediately, I gave myself a chance to eat my breakfast and drink my tea in silence, uninterrupted by any chatter. I liked Melynne, although it felt odd to be giving orders to someone only one or two years younger than myself, but that morning I found myself disinclined to conversation. My thoughts kept replaying that odd exchange with Theran the night before. I could have sworn he wanted to be closer to me, and yet he had run from me as if I were the dragon in human form, not he.

Although I hadn't much luck with Sar in the past, she seemed the most likely candidate for questioning. Of course

I couldn't speak to my husband of such things, not when he had made it so clear that there were to be no real confidences between us. So I ate my food and treated my aching head with several cups of bracing tea, and vowed to go in search of Sar as soon as I was able.

I found her in the kitchen gardens, supervising the harvest of the last of the herbs against the onset of our first hard frosts. We had had a few light ones, ice crystals clinging to leaves and glittering like diamonds, only to melt almost as soon as the sun touched them, but the nights already grew colder, and the elms and oaks had begun to put on their autumn cloaks of red and gold and brown.

By some good luck the two kitchen maids assisting her had just finished plucking the last of the rosemary and thyme, and had gone scampering back indoors with their baskets of herbs to prepare them for drying. Sar watched them go and then turned, her eyebrows lifting slightly in surprise as she saw me standing there.

"My lady," she said formally.

"Sar. I thought I might speak with you."

"Of course, my lady," was her automatic reply, but something in her manner turned guarded, as if she guessed I might guide the conversation in directions she did not particularly want to go.

"How long have you been here at Black's Keep?"

She blinked at the question, although she replied readily enough. "Going on twenty-eight years now. I was younger than you when I first came."

"And did you—that is, were you summoned here?" Somehow I had the impression that service to the Dragon Lord was not exactly voluntary.

"Good gods, no. I volunteered. That is, the steward at the time, Steen Larens, his name was, came to Greyton looking for a few likely lads and lasses. Even then I knew I didn't much want to spend my life the way my mother had, bearing children until she—well, it didn't much appeal to me."

I'd heard certain less-than-savory things about Greyton, how the young women there were rather free with their virtues. Of course no one would say such things in front of me, but Lilianth had heard from her cousin who had it from her older brother that some of the young men of Lirinsholme would travel up the mountainside to amuse themselves, and how such things were brushed aside in the tiny hamlet.

"Otherwise, it would all be cousins marrying cousins, and the children would be born with crooked limbs...and worse," she added, dropping her voice to truly sepulchral levels, as if to hint at defects best left to the imagination.

I saw no sign of any such a thing in Sar, but there could be any number of explanations for that. Looking into her level brown eyes, I knew better than to ask whether she and her siblings shared the same father, or whether she had decided it was better to serve the Dragon than to be thought a plaything for the young men of Lirinsholme.

"So you came to Black's Keep..." I prompted.

"So I came here and worked in the kitchens, and Master Larens was pleased enough with me that when he felt he could no longer continue his duties, he put me in charge."

"And he went back to Greyton?"

"Of course not. The Dragon takes care of his own. Master Larens had his rooms still, and when he passed he was laid to rest out there." She gestured vaguely toward the northeast, to a stretch of forested land I had not yet explored.

*The Dragon takes care of his own.* Save, it seemed, his Brides, who had to be replenished every five years or so. "You know him well, then?"

Her gaze sharpened. "The Dragon keeps his own counsel."

"But after twenty-eight years..."

"It seems a great span to you, I know. And yet it is a short time for his lordship. He does not view such things the way you and I do. And he is not one to share confidences."

Apparently not. I had thought from her earlier reactions to some of my transgressions that he must have spoken to her of me, but now I guessed her disapproval had stemmed merely from her responses to his outward actions. Well, it seemed I had run up against a dead end.

Stubbornly, though, I refused to admit defeat. "He must speak to you of some things, though. How else do you get on?"

"As I always have, my lady. He gives his commands, and I do my best to follow them."

"And does that make him happy?"

"Happy?" she repeated, as if she had never thought to associate such a word with the Dragon Lord. "It is not for the likes of me to comment on his lordship's happiness."

"And what about the likes of me? I must confess, I have lived here for six weeks, and yet I fear I know little more of him than the day I came to this place. Does he hold all his Brides at such lengths?"

"I would not presume to comment on such a thing."

"Who better than you?" I cried, my tone becoming wild. "For you have been here all these years, and seen these young women come and go. Did they, too, break themselves upon him like a ship foundering upon the rocks?"

"My lady, do not distress yourself—"

"There is no need for that. I find that his lordship does it for me."

And because I could feel my eyes begin to fill with tears once more, I turned from her and fled the gardens. No doubt she thought me a foolish girl, always either weeping or asking questions that had no simple answers. My rooms offered a spurious comfort at best, but they were the only place I could think of to go. Once there, I flung myself on my bed, thinking I could cry it out and have done, but somehow my tears seemed to dry themselves once I was alone.

All I could do was sit there and think of the way his voice sounded, like silk and honey, and the brief, bitter heat of his touch. I was his wife, and yet he would not let me be that in truth, little as I knew of such things. I only knew that some part of me yearned for him in a way I couldn't explain, ached for something I knew I could never have.

Had they all died of a broken heart, these Brides of his? Once I might have laughed at such a notion, no matter what the songs and stories might say of lovers wasting away and dying, all because of a heart betrayed. Now, though, it seemed not so far-fetched. I had reached out to him, and he had even reached out to me...only to turn from me at the last moment.

*You know what he is,* I tried to tell myself. *Most likely he only seeks to protect you. How can one such as he have anything close to a normal life?*

That sounded logical to me. Unfortunately, I didn't want logic. I wanted him.

Somehow I knew he was the one thing I could never have.

# Chapter Eight

He did not speak of what had passed between us that one evening, and so, perforce, neither did I. From time to time I caught Sar watching me with troubled eyes, and from that I guessed she was not quite as indifferent to the situation as she pretended to be, but what could she do? The management of the household lay in her capable hands, but his lordship's heart was his alone to govern.

Oh, we rubbed along tolerably. Mine was not a temperament much suited to brooding, and I had not grown up in a household with three sisters without learning a good deal about getting along even when personalities clashed. Not that Theran Blackmoor and I did much clashing—we spoke of the weather, of my painting, of the food Sar set before us, and not much more than that. The little bit of ground I had thought I gained the night of my birthday was long gone.

Not that he did not show me courtesy. My painting of the valley of Lirinsholme was framed and given a place of honor in the main hall, so that anyone entering would see it almost before anything else. This might have been more of a gesture if anyone except the same score of people had an opportunity to see it; my quiet home back in town seemed a veritable whirl of social gaiety compared to the stillness of Black's Keep. There were no visitors, and perhaps the maids chattered in the kitchens as they prepared the meals or sang as they swept the stairs, but if they did, I never heard them.

Once I had thought all I needed was unlimited time to paint, but I began to realize even that was not quite the blessing I once deemed it. My parents had not possessed the resources to have us taught the harp or lute, and I had no voice for singing, so I could not use music to fill up some of the empty hours. Sar brought me embroidery silks, an elegant carved standing frame, and some fabric. I used that to while away a few afternoons, even though I still disliked embroidery...and even though I couldn't help wondering whence came that frame, and whether it had belonged to one of Theran's erstwhile Brides.

The dreams of the stranger came to me at least once a week, and I continued on his portrait, although to what end I couldn't begin to imagine. The work went slowly, however, as each dream seemed to reveal a detail hitherto unnoticed, and I found myself continually painting over sections I had thought already completed. Once or twice I tried telling myself that I was being ridiculous, that I should abandon the thing and move on to something else. After a day or so of neglecting it, though, the dreams would return with even greater force, as if compelling me to return to the painting, as if trying to tell me I could not leave it undone, and so I always went back to it despite my internal objections.

His was not the only painting that occupied my time, of course. I dutifully painted the triptych of autumn ivy leaves I'd already planned, working quickly before the subjects of the paintings fell quite away from their vines. I tried to amuse myself with doing watercolor sketches of various members of the household; Melynne quite blushed when I gave her the one I had done of her, while Sar only shook her head and attempted not to look pleased.

"And have you nothing better to do with your time than this?" she asked, although I thought she was rather tickled by the small portrait I had done of her.

At the time I had only shrugged, but truly, I really did have nothing better to do with my time...

And then autumn was truly upon us, the dark hours colder and colder. A fire burned in my chamber night and day, and the gowns Melynne or Sar laid out for me were no longer silk and linen but wool and velvet. Frost shimmered in the dead grass, and I saw storm clouds gathering on the mountaintops to the north. Winter was not here yet, but it threatened. That was the way of things in our part of the world, the summers glorious but too brief, autumn a burst of color remembered before the long dark nights came upon us and the snows wrapped everything in their solitude.

A fire was lit in the great dining chamber where Theran and I took our evening meals, although it did not seem to help all that much, being situated at the far end of the room from the dining table. I wished I had the courage to wear a cloak to dinner, but the one time I had mentioned it, Sar gave me such a scandalized look that I promptly abandoned the notion.

Still, I couldn't help rubbing my hands against the chill as I sat there one night at the end of Octevre, and hoping that the first course would be a bowl of warm soup so I could wrap my fingers around it.

"You are cold?" Theran asked.

At once I put my traitor hands in my lap. "Not at all, my lord."

"Rhianne."

I knew that note in his voice. Lifting my shoulders, I said, "This chamber is rather chilly, yes. I'll admit that it is beautiful, but consider me duly impressed. Do you not have someplace a little cozier where we may eat?"

A pause. "There is...a smallish room in my own suite where I have sometimes supped alone. It does have quite a pleasant hearth. Would that suit you better?"

"Oh, yes," I replied at once. Whether my alacrity was spurred merely by the thought of eating my dinner in more comfortable surroundings, or whether it was inspired by my curiosity to see his chambers, hardly mattered. Of far greater importance was the fact that he seemed concerned for my comfort...and was not adverse to having me join him in a part of the castle that had been hitherto off-limits to me.

"Can you hold on for one more night? For I think Sar might be rather discommoded if we asked her to serve elsewhere this evening with no notice."

"Of course, Theran," I said, and let him go on to discuss the first touches of snow that had begun to decorate the mountaintops to the north. Inwardly, though, I found myself only wishing for an end to the evening and to the day that followed, so I might finally see his chambers for myself.

What I had expected of those rooms, I hardly knew, but what greeted me there was certainly not any of the rather confused visions that had crowded my mind's eye. True, his suite was large, much larger than my own, with a great room twice the size of my sitting chamber, and a small eating area, a study, and a library offering tantalizing glimpses through each of their respective doorways. The door to the far left was shut; I imagined it must be what led into his sleeping quarters.

The furnishings were heavy and ornate, the upholstery rich wool velvet, but what surprised me more was that every tabletop was covered with small but intricate contraptions whose purpose I couldn't begin to identify. Like me, he had a large worktable, this one located in an expansive alcove with windows that looked to the north and west. On the table were all sorts of tools, small hammers and picks and other instruments I didn't recognize.

Theran stood to one side, watching me as I entered. He said no word as I moved through the room and went almost without thinking to the worktable so I could inspect the half-finished device there more closely.

"You made all these?" I asked. I knew better than to reach out and touch the delicate object, but I cocked my head to one side so I could see underneath just a little, get a closer look at the tiny gears and wheels and what looked like small glittering jewels.

"Yes," he said, crossing the room himself so he could be by my side. Not too close, of course; no risk of those robes brushing against me this time. But still, I found myself very aware of his presence.

Again I had to tell myself not to touch, not to disturb the tiny components. "What are they for?"

"Oh, various things. I must confess that half of them do nothing at all, save to move and make a pretty distraction for the eyes. See here." And he stepped away from me, going to a handsome sideboard carved with the shapes of running deer, and touched one tall, slender device. At once it whirred into motion, its tiny golden vanes shimmering in the light, moving in a complicated yet delicate dance.

I clapped my hands together. "It's beautiful!"

"Thank you." He extended his gloved finger again, and the movement stopped. "It is something to while away the hours. Sar chides me sometimes for using up so many candles, but—"

"You—you do not sleep?"

At first he did not reply, but only stood there, staring down at the device as if he had never seen it before. Then, "I fear that is a solace deprived me."

I could not even begin to comprehend what that must be like, not only to be cursed with apparent immortality in his inhuman form, but also to be denied even a few hours of blissful emptiness where he could forget what he was. Even with dreams of a stranger tormenting me, I would not have given up those hours of sleep for anything in the world. And what on earth could I say in reply to such a statement?

Luckily, I was saved from having to think of an answer, for Sar appeared then, two of the maids in tow. They all carried covered dishes in various shapes and sizes, and bustled over to the eating area I had spied earlier. The table had already been set, so it was a simple matter for the three of them to put the serving dishes in their designated places.

After they were done, the two maids scurried back out again, but Sar turned to Theran and inquired, "Will there be anything else, my lord?"

"No, Sar, that will be all."

She bobbed a curtsey and went out, but not before shooting a curious glance in my direction. Perhaps I was the first Bride to ever request warmer eating conditions. I found that difficult to believe, and resolved to ask her the next time I saw her.

In the meantime, though, the Dragon Lord had extended his hand toward me, indicating that I should come and take my place at the table. I did so, happily noting that it was much warmer up here. A fire roared in the hearth, and heavy curtains at the windows did an excellent job of barring any errant drafts. In this smaller room, the stone walls were covered with tapestries, and I supposed they helped as well.

"Better?" he asked, after I had seated myself.

"Much better. I could almost imagine it's midsummer again."

This was, of course, an exaggeration—I would not be wearing such a thick wool gown in Julende, and blazing fires were not of much use in Augeste—but he seemed to agree with my assessment, or at least not argue with it, for he nodded. "An excellent idea, Rhianne. My apologies for not thinking of it sooner."

"No matter," I replied airily. "We are here now, are we not?"

"That we are. Soup?"

"Yes, thank you."

And so we ate, and talked of commonplaces once more, even as my mind churned with the revelation he had made just before Sar arrived, that he did not sleep, and apparently sat up nights working on those lovely little instruments, all to keep himself occupied. I wondered if he removed the gloves as he worked, and what his hands looked like without the dark leather covering them. His lips had felt rough, as if they were covered in scales. Were his hands the same way? Did he have claws?

I must have shivered a little at that thought, for he said, "Are you cold after all? Perhaps the fire is beginning to die down—"

"No, no, not at all," I told him. "It's lovely in here, and the food is lovely as well. I must thank Sar for being so accommodating as to bring our dinner up all those additional flights of stairs."

"It is her duty to accommodate me."

It was on my lips to tell him that was quite a high-handed thing to say. Then again, he had been lord of this castle for centuries. I supposed he knew nothing other than having people jump at his every command, no matter how whimsical it might be. My tone was somewhat gentler than I had first intended as I said, "Perhaps it is, but I find it no great chore to thank her for doing her duty well. It cannot be an easy thing, to manage a castle."

The hood tilted to one side as he apparently considered my remark. "No, perhaps it is not. I hadn't given it much thought, as she always seems to do what needs to be done."

"So you see, then. Not that my home could compare to Black's Keep, but there are always so many things to be taken care of—planning and preparing meals, laying the fires, cleaning, washing the linens, washing the dishes, drawing water for baths—"

"And you did all this yourself?" Of course I could not see his face, but his voice sounded distinctly amused.

"A good deal of it, yes, my lord. We had one maidservant to assist us, but my mother always said mischief finds a use for idle hands, and so we were not idle all that often, as you might imagine."

"It sounds as if your mother might be a good deal like our Sar."

In truth, she rather was, in her brisk, no-nonsense approach to most matters, and her estimable ability to follow up on all the household details, no matter how minute they might be. In appearance they were not much alike, save perhaps in coloring; my mother still retained some of her youthful beauty, while I guessed Sar had never possessed much even as a young girl. Despite that, though, they had a similar set to their chin whenever they thought I was being difficult. Perhaps that similarity was part of the reason I had adjusted to life in the castle far more quickly than I had any real reason to.

And perhaps, somehow, it was why I now thought of it as home. Easier to think that than to contemplate that it had anything to do with the enigmatic figure seated across from me.

"In some ways," I said hastily, hoping that he had not noticed my hesitation.

He made no reply to my comment, but only returned his attention to the excellent meat pies that formed the bulk of our dinner that evening. I did so as well, although I found myself glancing past him from time to time so I could catch a glimpse of those lovely little devices in the other room. What else about himself had he kept hidden from me?

After dinner he seemed disinclined to send me back to my own rooms, but instead showed me into his library, which appeared equally astonishing in its own way. Some ten years before I was born, an enterprising young man in Sirlende had devised a way to print books with some sort of mechanical type, thereby putting a good many scribes out of work, but also making books far more readily available than they had been heretofore. Still, they were expensive, and most people I knew owned only one or two, if even that many.

But here were...hundreds? It was hard for me to say for sure, as all four walls of the chamber had bookshelves from floor to ceiling, and all of those shelves were full. Theran had so many books that they were also piled up on a table in the center of the room, and even stacked on the floor beneath that table.

"Do you read?" he asked.

"I was taught, that and to write and to figure. But we didn't have much opportunity for reading. The only books in the house were the primer my mother used to teach us, and a cookery book she received as a wedding present, and a history of Farendon." I didn't bother to add that the history must have been written for the sole purpose of sending its unfortunate readers to sleep, as it was dry as dust.

"Ah, none of that sounds very interesting." He went to one of the bookcases and selected a thick volume bound in dark green leather, with gold lettering stamped on the spine. I couldn't make out the title from where I stood, however. "I had thought perhaps if you wanted to give your fingers a rest from painting, you might try reading something...if you could read, of course. Not all of—that is, not all girls your age can."

No, they couldn't. Lilianth could barely manage to write her own name; her parents had not set the same store in learning that my own did. I knew the Dragon probably meant that not all of his Brides had been able to read, which did not surprise me. After all, those girls had come from both wealthy families and poor. At least that much could be said for the selection process, horrible as it might be for those involved. There was never any hint that the more powerful families in Lirinsholme influenced the process in any way so their own daughters might be spared. In fact, a Bride had been selected the same year my mother married my father, and the unfortunate girl in that instance had been the daughter of one of the elders.

I pushed the thought of that long-dead young woman aside and said, "That sounds like a lovely idea. It has been wonderful to paint so much, but I must confess even that can become tedious after a while. One cannot curl up next to a fire with a painting—not unless you're willing to risk an explosion. Linseed oil is quite combustible."

He laughed and said, "Yes, far less risk of that with a book. I thought you might like to try this one." And he held it outstretched in one hand, so that I had to approach and take it from him.

My fingers brushed against his as I retrieved the book. Whether he had meant for me to do so or not, I couldn't say. Another one of those little shivers traced its way down my spine, and I swallowed. I should not allow myself to react to him so. After all, with every revelation he seemed to show himself as less human, as something that had not been a man for many, many years. And yet...

And yet I wished it could be otherwise. Hold me at arm's length he might, but I found myself wanting more of his company, wishing to hear his voice, yearning for ways I might think of to bring us together more, rather than these formal dinners and nothing else.

Foolish, I knew. We could be nothing more than temporary companions, before...before what? My time here would not last forever. I did not know what lay in store for me, but it could not be pleasant, or the Dragon would not have need of a new Bride every five to seven years. It wasn't as if he kept multiple wives around the castle, the way I'd heard was the custom in far-off Keshiaar.

For the greater part of two months I'd been able to keep the fear at bay. It rose now, clawing at me, seeming to tighten my throat, and I forced myself to swallow.

"It is not to your liking?" Theran asked.

I blinked, and looked down at the book I held. "*Tales of the Age of Magic*," I read aloud, and glanced up at him. "I thought such things were not to be written or spoken of."

"In some places, perhaps. We are moving into a more enlightened time. Men are beginning to understand the value of knowledge, of history. It is better to learn from our mistakes so that we do not repeat them."

Something in his voice, some sharp edge to the normally smooth accents, made me wonder if he spoke of his own mistakes rather than those of the long-ago mages whose hubris had brought about the near-collapse of our civilization. I could not ask, however. Somehow I knew he would not reply.

"I hadn't thought of it that way before," I said.

"Many haven't. That does not make it untrue."

I clutched the book, flipped it open. The print was clear and very black; it was of the highest quality, and I found myself wondering where he'd gotten it. Then again, supplies came to us from the capital when necessary, and I supposed it would be no great task for Theran to send his agents to several booksellers to procure a batch of new titles at the same time they were gathering together cloth and tools and casks of wine and whatever else might be needed at Black's Keep.

"I will be very careful with it," I told him, shutting the book once again. I did not think it would be polite to read it any more closely until I had returned to my chambers.

"I trust you will." It seemed as if he paused, staring down at me. Once again I felt that urge to reach out to him, to lay my hand on his arm and move closer, but something seemed to prevent me. And then the moment was gone. He turned away, saying, "It grows late. No doubt you wish to retire for the evening."

My mouth opened to make some protest, but I quickly shut it. Anything I might have said would have sounded unutterably foolish. *I could stay and watch while you work...I could curl up on that divan before the fire...I could stay here through the long, dark night.*

There seemed little for me to do but nod, and clutch the book more tightly to myself.

"And can you find your way down to your rooms, or would you like me to show you the path?"

Perhaps if I asked him to guide me, I could spend a little more time in his company...but for what? So I could face another awkward farewell before the doors to my own suite?

"Thank you, Theran, but I marked the path as you brought me here, and I think I know the way. Thank you for dinner, and for the book."

"You are most welcome," he replied, although something in his tone sounded almost doubtful, as if he were now wishing he had not given me the option to decline his company.

Since I had well and truly put my foot in it, as Sar might say, I could only nod and force myself to move toward the door, to open it and walk slowly out into the corridor. Even as I did so I halfway hoped he would ignore what I had said and follow after me.

Of course he did not.

Although it was, as Theran had said, quite late, I found myself restless when I returned to my rooms, not ready to retire meekly to my bed. The fire looked as if it had been stirred up recently; no doubt Sar had sent Melynne to check on things before she went to bed. Even though I was the lady of the castle, I did not receive nearly as much fussing-over as I had heard was the custom for high-ranking women. I was expected to undress myself and braid my hair for the night, and return my clothing to the wardrobe.

I did all these things, and washed my face and scrubbed my teeth as well, but instead of climbing into bed, I gathered up my warm woolen dressing gown and returned to the sitting area with the book Theran had given me. The firelight was just bright enough to read by, and sitting close also helped to keep me warm.

The book felt heavy and unfamiliar in my lap. Yes, I could read, but I had never done so for mere pleasure, as a way to pass the time. Well, I had plenty of time to pass now.

Crisp paper crackled under my fingertips as I flipped past the first few leaves, which were blank. Then there was some sort of page acknowledging the printer—in Lystare, as I had suspected—and an illustration I suspected had originally been a woodcut, with its thick emphatic black lines. It depicted a high tower with lightning bolts shooting from the top, no doubt the artist's idea of what a mage's fortress must have looked like. Facing the illustration was a title page, which read, "Tales of the Age of Magic. Being a True Account of the Birth of Magic, and of the Manner in Which Mages Came to Power. With Knowledge Never Before Set Down by Men."

I almost laughed then. Nothing like a brazen declaration of one's merits to get things started. I supposed the author or authors had to do something to make their book stand out from the rest and convince a browser in a bookshop to part with his hard-earned coin. No mention from whence this information had come, or whether its verity could be established. Best to approach its contents as mere tales for amusement, and not an actual history.

The first section or story was titled "The Coming of the Althuri." Who or what the Althuri were, I had no idea. Certainly I had never heard of them, although I would be the first to admit I was no scholar. No time for that in a place like Lirinsholme, where commerce was the order of the day. Not that I'd ever heard of a woman being a scholar, although I knew some women were admitted to the Order of the Golden

Palm, where they were trained to be doctors. But even a doctor had a practical purpose, whereas a scholar seemed to have little.

Frowning somewhat, I forced myself to focus on the page before me. "For generations the origin of magic has been the subject of debate. Whence came this scourge that laid men low? Was it an ill humor that arose from the ground and infected the minds of those susceptible, so they gained unholy powers? Was it an affliction with them from birth? No, none of these things, but instead a taint passed on by the Althuri, a race of great power who came to this world to spread their evil seed, to give us the means by which we might destroy one another..."

I yawned then, and blinked my watering eyes. If the entire tome was to be this tedious, I thought it would take me a very long while to get through it. Oh, I knew the mage wars had been terrible, cataclysmic events that almost destroyed the world...but that was so very long ago. No need to tell me how evil magic was; I'd heard such things since I was in the cradle. And if I needed any additional proof, then Theran Blackmoor's pitiable condition was more than enough.

A thought struck me, and I flipped past the foreword, looking to see if my husband's strange curse was mentioned in the book. It did not appear to be, but I did see a chapter titled "The Tale of Alende the Cursed and the Fair Allaire."

That sounded a bit more to my liking. After all, Theran was most definitely cursed, and he thought me fair. Perhaps I could glean some bits of wisdom from the old tale. I settled the book more comfortably in my lap and began to read.

It seemed that Alende inherited a barony in the eastern reaches of Farendon. He was good and kind, and much loved by all he met. In those days even a baron would have a mage in his employ, but Alende did not follow the tradition, saying he had everything he needed in this world, and that a mage could do little to improve his lot. As one might have guessed, such pronouncements did not sit well with one Melarde, a mage of some renown in that part of the world, and who had thought to take service with the baron, as Melarde's own lord had just passed away.

The mage went to visit the baron, and sought to impress the young man with his powers. But Alende only laughed and said that while it was clear that Melarde had great skill, still the baron had no need of a mage, and bade Melarde find patronage in Lystare. This response angered the mage, who had thought to settle down in his old age in a comfortable position, rather than try to curry favor with the more demanding courtiers in the capital city. He approached the young man a last time, again with a great show of his powers, but Alende was unmoved, saying, "No one doubts your skill, good sir, but I am content, and think I can do well enough without the aid of magic or mages."

This upset the old man, who scowled fiercely and replied, "You are content now, in your youth and beauty, but will that contentment last when all who look upon you cry out in fear?" And he spoke words of great, horrible power, and a grave disfigurement struck the handsome young man, twisting his features so that he appeared more as someone horribly burned, all traces of beauty gone.

The young baron fell to his knees and wept, and his people cried out in horror. Then Melarde was gone, vanished in the manner that mages had, leaving poor Alende to his pain and his grief. And so he spent many years alone, his face and form covered in a heavy hooded cloak, so that none could see his disfigurement.

I paused then, for the tale sounded eerily familiar, although the young man in the story did not seem to have been turned into a dragon. But his isolation certainly was an echo of Theran's. Was that why my husband had given me the book, so I might see this tale and understand his own pain a little better?

A log fell with a soft thump in the hearth, and I jumped, then shook my head at myself. I had no idea how late it was, but I had a feeling I would regret this late night the next morning. The reasonable thing would have been for me to shut the book and return to it when I awoke. That idea seemed quite unappealing, however, so I flipped my braid back over my shoulder and bent toward the closely printed page once again.

The years passed, and Alende came to uneasy terms with his condition. He tried to be a good and just lord, but he felt his loneliness, felt time slipping away. He was the only son, and his estates had no heir. But he knew he could not expect any woman to marry him, to bear his child, when he was so unutterably ugly.

On Midwinter Eve a traveler came to the gates of his castle, seeking shelter from the bitter cold. The traveler was a young woman. Her train had been attacked by brigands, and she had fled in the night, and had seen the lights of the castle through the darkness.

Alende welcomed her, and found himself moved by her beauty, but he knew better than to expect anything of her save a few moments of companionship before she went on her way again the next day. The snows were deep, though, and she could not be expected to travel again before the weather cleared. And so she stayed on, fearing the hooded lord at first, then coming to see his gentleness and his quiet good humor. They spoke for long hours, and a rapport grew between them, even though Alende dared not hope that she would see him as anything but a friendly companion at best.

But although Alende was wise in the ways of many things, the heart of a woman could not be counted among them. He did not see how Allaire sought out his company, or lingered for days in his castle when she could have safely returned to the road. The curse had placed a barrier between him and the world, and his vision was trapped within it.

Then came a day when the snow was all melted away, and the birds sang in the trees, and the first buds began to show on the flowers that lined the walkways of the castle grounds. Alende went to Allaire and said, "The thaw is truly upon us. It is safe now for you to return to your family and friends."

She turned wide eyes upon him and said, "Do you weary of my company, my lord?"

He replied, "Of course I do not. But I had thought you must have tired of mine."

Her laughter was sweeter than the birdsong outside the window. "All this time spent together, and yet you know so little of me?"

And she went to him, and pushed back the hood, and smiled, seemingly untroubled by the ruin of his face. Then she kissed him, and kissed him again. Alende was so startled he made no protest at first, but at length he took her hands and pushed her away, saying she must be mad to do such a thing.

In reply she only laughed, and told him it was the madness of love, that she had grown to love him without knowing what his face looked like, so what difference could it possibly make now? He stared down at her in wonder, and realized she spoke only the truth, and cared little for his disfigurement. Joy filled his heart, and he drew her to him and kissed her back, before asking if she would stay with him forever, and be his wife.

They lived a long and happy life together after that, and although her love did not cure what the curse had done to his face, it did heal the blight in his soul, for he had found someone who could look past his scars to see him as he truly was. And their love became a beacon for all around them...

I closed the book. Was this what Theran was trying to tell me? Did he want me to see the story of Alende and Allaire so I might learn from her courage?

It seemed odd to me, though, that I had already tried to reach out to him, and had been rebuffed. Theran's did not seem to be the actions of a man inviting a woman to love him.

A puzzle, and one for which I appeared to have no answers. My common sense told me I should go to bed and think on it anew the next morning. The world's troubles could not be solved in a day, as my mother used to say. So I got to my feet and set the book down on the low table next to the divan, then put myself to bed.

Even as I did so, I thought of Theran, alone in his rooms, tinkering with those lovely little instruments he had devised as a way of filling the empty hours. What would he do if I arose from my bed and went to him now, asked to stay? Would he laugh, or would he let me in?

I feared I wasn't quite brave enough for that yet. I closed my eyes, and willed myself to an uneasy sleep.

# Chapter Nine

Perhaps it was simply because I had kept myself up so late, and was so much wearier than usual, that my sleep that night was black and dreamless. When I awoke, however, I felt curiously unrefreshed, as if I had not really slept at all.

The pot of bracing tea Melynne brought up for me in the morning helped a little, although my mood was not improved by the view I caught of the lowering day outside my windows. I'd had some notion that perhaps a walk in the garden might help to clear my head, but the storm clouds I saw told a different story. I was barely into my second cup of tea before the rain had begun to stream down the glass.

Melynne seemed quieter than normal that morning; perhaps she had caught something of my ill humor. At any rate, she laid out my clothes in silence, and was equally quiet as she gathered up my breakfast dishes and prepared to leave.

"Do you like it here?" I asked abruptly, and she paused on the threshold, brown eyes wide. She seemed alert and wary, rather like a young doe perched to flee.

"Like it, milady?"

"Does it suit you, being in service here? Or would you rather have stayed in Greyton?"

Once I had put the question in those terms, she seemed to relax a little. "Oh, it's much better here than in Greyton, milady."

"How so? Isn't your family in the hamlet? Your friends?"

"My ma died when I was born, milady, and my da a few years after. I lived with my aunt until I was old enough to come here. I think they were glad of having one less mouth to feed."

She spoke simply, with no apparent design of eliciting my sympathy, and yet my heart went out to her. How hard to be left alone, and with relatives who saw you only as a burden. I thought then how lucky I had been in my own family, despite their little faults and foibles.

"I see. But your friends?"

"I have all the friends I need here, milady. Besides, Mat and I—" And she broke off, blushing a little. No doubt the servants were not supposed to admit their liaisons to their masters.

"That's good to hear," I said, smiling so she would know I did not disapprove of her relationship with Mat, whatever it might be. "Having someone special makes the day go by more quickly, I would expect."

She answered only with another blush, and some downcast eyes. I began to understand why Sar sometimes complained about Melynne not being quite as quick to answer the bell as she should…no doubt she was stealing a few moments with her young man.

Since it seemed clear that she did not wish to reveal any more than that, I thanked Melynne and let her make her escape before I could embarrass her any further. After she had gone, my smile faded. Yes, there might be a bit of romance hiding in Black's Keep…but not for me, apparently.

My mother would have told me that self-pity was a most unattractive quality in a young lady, but she was not there to scold me. And although I had begun to develop some sort of rapport with Sar, I guessed she would be properly horrified if I tried to discuss anything of my nascent feelings for Theran Blackmoor with her.

I knew I should shake off my dark mood and go back to my easel, but the paints and brushes oddly held no allure for me that day. And although I did go to my painting alcove, I ignored the tame landscape that was my "public" work in progress. Instead, I pulled out my half-finished portrait of the strange young man, then sat there, staring at it for a long while.

The sea-colored eyes seemed to gaze back at me, holding their own secrets. I had neglected the painting for several days, although at that moment it scarcely seemed to matter. It was only a diversion, a foolish fancy. A waste of good canvas, really, for a portrait of someone who lived only in my own fevered dreams. Didn't I have enough to worry about without allowing myself to be consumed by visions of a man who didn't even exist?

A strange humor possessed me, and I set the painting down on my worktable and seized my largest brush, then mixed up a quantity of paint, pale as new cream. A fitting tint to cover his enigmatic features, to blot out the knowing eyes and the mouth with its quirk in the corner, to make the canvas blank again so it could hold a more worthy subject.

I held the brush over the canvas for a long moment. My hand began to tremble.

*No.*

The voice was as clear in my mind as if the speaker were in the room with me, although I was quite alone. I even glanced over my shoulder, thinking perhaps Theran had entered the suite while I was preoccupied, but of course I saw no one. He had never come to my rooms during the daylight hours.

Shaking, I set down the brush on the easel. A drop of paint had fallen before I did so, and it gleamed like a tear on the young man's cheek. Without thinking, I lifted a piece of gauze from among the oddments on the table and blotted the errant drip away before it could do any further harm. It still left behind the palest of smudges, but I knew I could fix that.

And I realized then I could never destroy the portrait. What it meant, I did not know, but I had already poured too much of my soul into it. Perhaps it would never be finished—perhaps it would stand as mute testimony to my obsession when I was gone from this place. But stand it would.

With a sigh I turned and plucked my apron off its hook, then pushed up my sleeves. No point in dripping paint on my fine gown of green wool. I had not thought I would have any set occupation that morning, but obviously the portrait had other ideas.

I hadn't dreamed of him, and yet my brush moved with an alacrity I'd only seen before on those mornings when his face was still fresh in my mind. His hair filled in under its quick flashing strokes, painting in what had only been a sketch before, bringing to life the heavy dark waves as they flowed back from his high brow. Not black, but the deep, rich hue of earth new-turned in the spring, unlike my own hair, which gleamed with shades of mahogany in the sunlight. From there I moved on to his dark, straight brows, the lines of lashes that framed the gleaming blue-green eyes.

Another brush, another tint, and this time I traced the light shadows under the high cheekbones, along the jaw line and the slightly pointed chin. I dipped my brush back into the paint, frowning as I studied my handiwork and tried to determine whether I had made those shadows too pronounced, whether I should go back and lighten them ever so slightly—

"My lady?" came Sar's voice from the outer room.

I started and nearly dropped my paintbrush, but luckily none of the paint spattered. "I'm working," I called out, even as I laid aside my brush and gathered up the portrait so she could not catch a glimpse of what I was doing. The canvas was far too wet for me to slide it between two other paintings, and so I had to settle for slipping it under the table. I could only hope Sar would not look too closely; she tended to avoid the alcove, as she still could not seem to abide the smell of the linseed oil.

Perhaps that was why she did not come in immediately, but remained in the sitting chamber as she replied, "It's past noon, my lady. I've brought you a tray."

"Oh," I said vaguely, my gaze straying to the windows. The rain still beat down, so there was no sun to give an indication as to the passage of time. Had I really been consumed in my work for almost four hours?

It came upon me like that sometimes, only not usually for quite so long. I wondered what had possessed me then. Perhaps I had only needed that moment of indecision, that brief space where I thought I would destroy the portrait, to rouse my passion and invest myself fully. Odd, because I had tossed aside sketches with impunity in the past. Perhaps it was only the value of the canvas that troubled me, although Lindell had told me he often painted over works he wasn't pleased with, not exactly being overburdened with wealth himself.

I didn't have time to puzzle over the conundrum any longer, however, for I knew if I lingered much longer, Sar would be sure to come into my sleeping chamber, linseed smell or no. Better not to risk her sharp eyes seeing the portrait in its not-so-secret hiding place under my worktable. So I wiped my hands on the rag I kept for that purpose, then untied my apron before setting it aside and going out to meet her in the outer room.

Sure enough, a tray with a large bowl of soup and a small loaf of bread waited for me there, accompanied by a flagon of cider. Usually it was Melynne who brought my luncheon, but perhaps she was occupied elsewhere.

"Thank you, Sar."

Her dark eyes looked sharper than usual this morning, but perhaps that was just my guilty conscience. Why precisely I should feel so guilty, I couldn't quite say. For some reason, the portrait felt so secret...so *illicit*, somehow...that I knew I would stumble over my words like an adulterer admitting a transgression if I ever had to explain its presence.

"You can paint well enough, in this sort of light?" she inquired, with a lift of her shoulder toward the charcoal-colored skies outside.

"Oh, yes," I replied, grateful that she had broached a more or less neutral subject. The finer points of technique were always something I liked to discuss—and if she were inquiring about that, less likely that she would ask to see what precisely I had been working on. "Sometimes it's almost better, you know...no glare to contend with, no harsh shadows."

"Hmph."

By this time I knew her well enough that I understood her non-reply as her way of saying she wouldn't presume to contradict me, but that she also didn't quite believe my statement. Well enough; I wasn't going to bother explaining myself to her. I thought she liked me but also thought I might be a trifle touched in the head, at least when it came to my painting. I guessed none of my predecessors had quite the same all-consuming passion for any of their avocations...at least, mine were the only Bride-painted works hanging about the castle, unless Theran took them down whenever a new wife arrived.

Deciding a new tack was probably wise, I asked, "Is that beef and barley soup? It smells wonderful."

No doubt she noticed the deflection, but she only nodded. "Cook made up a new batch this morning. Thought it might be a warming antidote to a gloomy day."

"It is."

Another nod, but this time I caught her giving me a searching look, as if she found something amiss in my expression or my manner. I tensed a little, even though I told myself I was being foolish. After all, I was the lady of the castle. It was not her place to question me. Never mind that her no-nonsense manner reminded me a little too much of my own mother. Even after several months in the castle, I had to school myself not to snap to Sar's commands the way I would have if I still lived at home and they had been delivered by my mother instead of someone who was in fact one of my servants.

A hesitation, and then she said, "Well, enjoy your luncheon, my lady. His lordship says you will be taking your dinner in his rooms again this evening?"

"This evening, and for the rest of the winter, I don't doubt, unless we have an unexpected warm snap."

"Very good, my lady."

And then she took her leave of me and went. I stood there, staring at the shut door for a long moment, wondering at the diffidence I had seen in her aspect. Truly it couldn't have been that much of an imposition for Theran and me to dine in his chambers, as he must have his other meals brought there anyway. Perhaps it was just that Sar did not like to have her routines disturbed. Yes, that must be it.

Satisfied that I had explained away any oddness I might have noticed in her manner, I sat down to my meal and ate hungrily enough. Painting can be hard work, even if that which one paints is seen only through the mind's eye, and has no true substance in this world.

I spent much of the rest of the afternoon in the same manner, working quickly and without stopping. This time I created nothing that I thought I might have to paint over later, and when I finally stopped a little after sunset—or at least what I guessed must be sunset, as I could see nothing of it through the sullen rainstorm that seemed to have descended on the castle—I was much farther along in the portrait than I had ever dreamed I would be. True, I was not done, and still some weeks off from being done, but for the first time I thought I might reasonably finish the portrait sometime this winter.

What I would do with it then, I couldn't imagine. Hide it under my bed, most likely. I couldn't see Theran being terribly pleased with my hanging a picture of some unknown man in my rooms, even if I had conjured him from my own imagination and a combination of features I thought pleasing. Those sea-colored eyes I had seen the previous summer in a young man who'd come to Lirinsholme in the train of a traveling merchant from Purth, and the heavy fall of dark hair was quite similar to that of Kellin Strathelme, who was apprentice to Master Mackinrod, the blacksmith. Not so odd, I supposed, to invent someone who combined qualities I found attractive, when I lived day to day with someone who refused to show me his face.

With that thought I realized I should tidy myself up for dinner. Once again I set aside my apron, and washed my hands vigorously before brushing my hair. I had worn no jewelry while I was working, but I slid a pair of earrings with dark green stones I didn't recognize into my ears, and fastened a matching necklace around my throat. I stood for a moment, regarding my own reflection, wondering if I might see something there that Sar had noticed.

But I looked much the same as I always had, although perhaps there was just the slightest hint of darkness below my eyes—from my restless night, no doubt. I had heard that the ladies of the court used powder and paint to hide such things, but Sar had only used such subterfuges on my wedding day. They were not a permanent addition to my toiletries. Just as well; I shuddered to think what my mother might say if she ever discovered that her daughter had stooped to dabbing powder on her face or stain on her cheeks.

As I left my chambers and headed for Theran's quarters, I thought of the tale I had read the night before, of Alende and Allaire. She had been brave enough to love him despite his scars, and they had lived a happy life, even if he was never restored to his former self. Was this what the Dragon Lord wished to teach me? Would I have the courage of Allaire, who had looked into the baron's face and seen only the man she loved, and not his deformity?

The memory of those rough lips against mine returned to me, and I drew in a breath. Truly they had not felt human, and yet Theran seemed so much a man to me, from the measured woodwind tones of his voice to the spare elegance of his movements.

And what would you know of a man? some part of me seemed to scoff. You, who have never even stolen a kiss in the alley behind your parents' house, or caught the fancy of a single young man?

To be fair, my experience was not large. In truth, it was nonexistent. Some might have thought this odd, since I had been deemed more than pretty by the standards of my town, and certainly my family was good enough. Perhaps it was simply my obsession with drawing and painting, which, though my parents tried to suppress talk of it as best they could, still made me the subject of some bemused speculation. Nor did it help that I had spent a good deal of my spare time learning what I could of the craft from Lindell. The gossips must have known that he had a longstanding understanding with Melisse, the keeper of the Dragon's Head, but I suppose those same busybodies did not find that relationship salacious enough, instead preferring to manufacture some sordid explanation for his interest in me. That could do much to shred a girl's reputation, even if there were no truth in it.

If there had been talk, I never heard it, although that meant little. My parents did what they could to shelter me, and Lilianth did rather more. She would never hear one ill word spoken of me, and recalling that about her made me doubly glad I had stepped in to take her place here at Black's Keep.

I wondered then what on earth she would have made of Theran Blackmoor...or he of her.

No doubt they could have gotten along well enough, once she got past the bitter disappointment over losing Adain. But I had a feeling they would have had very little to say to one another. Hers was a sunny disposition, but she was not one to think deeply on things, and I thought Theran might have become impatient with such a quality after a while. And whatever would she have done to keep herself occupied? True, she was very clever with a needle, but one can only do so much of that before it begins to pall. I had a sudden vision of Theran's rooms with their delicate little pieces of machinery all covered in doilies made of the tatted lace Lilianth excelled at, and had to suppress a grin.

Then I was at the door to his suite, and I hesitated before lifting my hand to knock. Should I mention the story, or only thank him for the loan of the book and perhaps attempt a white little lie...*I was so tired last night that I only read the introduction...it was so big a book I didn't know where to start...*?

I felt uncomfortable about lying to him, though, and the excuses sounded feeble even to me. If he had given me the book to provoke some sort of discussion, then I would discuss what I had found within its pages.

That settled, I lifted my hand and rapped smartly on the door.

Inside the fire blazed, and although the rain beat as heavily on the windows here as it did down in my rooms, somehow it seemed cozier, more welcoming. Perhaps it was only that the air held a toothsome smell, the source of which I discovered to be a small pot Theran had sitting over a brazier.

"They do this in Purth," he explained, directing me toward the table in front of the divan, where some cut-up bread and sausages awaited us. "It seemed like a good idea for a stormy night."

"What is it?"

"Only melted cheese. Come—try some."

So I followed his lead and picked up one of the long bone-handled forks from the table, speared a chunk of bread with it, and dipped it in the pot. The cheese began to drip, and Theran laughed and quickly fetched a plate from the table, then held it beneath the chunk of bread. Steam wisped up and away from it, bringing with it a delectable aroma that reminded me it had been quite some time since the soup I'd consumed at noon.

The taste of it was better than I had even imagined, sharp with the tang of pale wine and some other seasonings I couldn't quite identify. "May we have this every rainy night?" I asked, this time choosing a piece of sausage to dip into the mixture.

"I fear Sar might have something to say about that. She did not think it a proper meal, but I argued that it would amuse you, and so she relented. But I would not press my luck."

"One might think she is the true ruler of this house and not you, my lord."

"Ah, you have discovered our secret. I may hold the title, but it is she who sees how things are ordered around here...far more than I."

I smiled at him and watched as he expertly skewered a piece of the fine white bread with its chewy crust and dipped it into the pot. He was able to maneuver the morsel into his mouth without dripping a bit of cheese on the hearthstones, his cloak, or the rug, which seemed quite a good feat to me.

We ate in companionable silence then for a while, bites of cheese and bread and sausage punctuated by sips of crisp white wine that might have been part of the original recipe for the dish. At length, though, I began to feel somewhat full from all the rich food and finally set down the long-handled fork.

"I simply cannot eat any more," I declared, and took a breath. I could have sworn my gown didn't feel quite that tight when Melynne laced me into it that morning.

"Not even the spiced peach compote Sar brought up?"

"Oh, dear. Perhaps in a quarter-hour?"

He nodded and poured me a little more wine. I had gotten used to it during my time here, and so several glasses didn't make my head swim quite as much as they once had. Even so, I realized I had been a little intemperate in washing down all those delectable morsels of bread and sausage, and therefore took only the smallest of sips from the newly refilled glass.

It was probably the wine, however, that prompted me to say, "Theran, why did you give me *Tales of the Age of Magic* to read?"

The hooded head turned toward me. "I thought it might amuse you."

"And that is all?"

"Why else?"

His tone sounded casual enough, but I thought I caught a slight edge to his voice, as if he had not been expecting my question and was caught off-guard by it.

I probably should have let it go. But I was weary and, perhaps, just the slightest bit tipsy, both factors which did nothing for my sense of discretion. So I said, "I read 'The Tale of Alende and Allaire.'"

"Indeed? I am surprised you got that far in a single evening."

"I skipped ahead."

In brittle accents he replied, "Do you always do that with the books you read?"

"I hardly know, as this is the first real book I've had a chance to read. But the foreword was so dusty dry that I felt I had to find something a bit more interesting to keep me awake."

"Ah."

That was all, just a single syllable which could have meant anything. Undeterred, I plowed ahead. "I found it very fascinating, my lord. In fact, I was up quite late finishing it."

He said nothing, instead staring at the fire as if something in its flickering depths intrigued him.

"I found it compelling that Allaire could ignore what the mage had done to Alende, could instead admire him and care for him because of who he was and not what he looked like."

Still the silence stretched on, the hood facing forward and away from me, as if he could not bear to see my face. He shifted, and I saw the gloved hands tighten on the fine wool that covered his knee. Finally he said abruptly, "It is only a story."

"Indeed? For the title page of the book declares that it is 'A True Account of the Birth of Magic.'"

"Perhaps that much is true, but I doubt the entirety of it is 'a true account.' As with many other works of that nature, the author most likely gathered up what tales he could and published them all under that title, whether they were relevant or not."

"If that is your opinion, then I wonder at you giving it to me in the first place."

He did turn and regard me then; at least, the hood shifted in my direction. "I thought it might make for better reading than many of the volumes in my library, given your...limited opportunity for study."

"Oh, I see," I replied, not bothering to hide the edge to my voice. "So you thought to give me silly fairy tales to read, as I am only a poor uneducated girl who couldn't possibly comprehend anything more scholarly!"

"That is not what I said."

"Perhaps, but I have a very good idea that it is what you meant." The bread and sausage and cheese, which had tasted so wonderful only a short time ago, began to churn in my stomach. Indeed, I wondered if I might be sick. Perhaps it was the wine. Yes, that had to be it.

"Rhianne, don't be foolish—"

"So now you think I am a fool," I countered, and got to my feet, albeit rather unsteadily. "Well, don't let me inflict my foolishness on you any longer!"

He stood as well, a rather ominous upheaval of dark robes. One edge of his cloak caught my wine glass, and it spilled to the rug, although he appeared to pay it no heed. "Rhianne, please—" He reached out toward me but then pulled up abruptly.

So he couldn't bear to even lay his hand on my arm. So be it. An odd little ache rose inside me, a hard knot of tears just waiting to be shed. I would not give him the satisfaction of seeing me dissolve before him, and so I turned and fled, running for the door, which I slammed with a satisfying bang behind me.

I ran then, feet slapping on the cold stone of the steps, the air frigid against my burning cheeks. The sickness seemed to fill my throat and I gulped, willing it to stay down until I reached the safety of my own chambers.

Once there, I ran for the chamber pot, thinking the rich food would surely come back up again. But instead I only choked and coughed, and realized the spasm of nausea had passed. That did little to reassure me, however. I stood and poured myself some water, then drank half of it without stopping. I almost expected the queasiness to return, but it did not. The knot inside me seemed to release, and I wept then, burying my face in my hands and giving in to the misery.

I could not even say why I was so forlorn, save that Theran and I had quarreled, and my hopes for how the evening might have gone were irretrievably dashed. It had seemed so simple to me before—we would discuss Alende and Allaire, and I would hint that I understood Allaire's feelings completely, and then...

And then what?

If he had taken me in his arms, had pressed his lips to mine as a true lover should, and not with that light brush of mouth against mouth he had given me on our wedding day, would I have surrendered to him? Could I have looked past whatever destruction that long-ago mage had done to his face and person, and embraced him only as Theran?

I did not know, and now it seemed as if I never would. Oh, quarrels had their way of mending themselves, I supposed. That is, I had heard my parents raise their voices to one another on more than one occasion, but those rifts were never that deep, and seemed to pass as if they had never been. Whether it would be that way between Theran and myself, I could not say. I only knew I felt so weary as I readied myself for bed that I wondered if I would sleep the next day through.

# Chapter Ten

He came to me in my dreams that night. The stranger, that is, not Theran.

I stood in a great wooden hall, surrounded by gaily dressed, chattering folk, and realized I was at Lilianth's wedding party. The chamber appeared to be the large reception room of Lirinsholme's Brecken Hall.

Truly it seemed as if almost everyone in the town was there, wearing their best and drinking ale and cider and mead—curious how my dream should be so detailed, as I knew neither Lilianth's parents nor Adain could afford to serve wine at such an event. This seemed to matter little enough, for everyone appeared to be in fine spirits. The hall itself was bright with autumn leaves and garlands of berries, and the bride was resplendent in her gown of the silk and linen fabric we had picked out on that day which now seemed so long ago.

I looked down and realized I was wearing the finest gown from the wardrobe Theran had given me, the wine-colored damask with the gold braid on the neck and sleeves, the trim gleaming with the dark blood color of uncut garnets. More of the sanguine gems gleamed at my throat and on my fingers, although waking I wore no rings.

Music filled the hall, and I found myself going time after time to the dance floor, this time with Lindell as my partner, the next with Adain's younger brother Mikhel, even once, improbably, with the Elder Drewson, who proved to be quite light on his feet, and who bestowed upon me an admiring glance that I thought odd, even though we danced only in a dream.

But then I saw him.

He made his way through the crowds, dark head held high. And though everyone wore their best to honor Lilianth on her bridal day, he outshone them all. His doublet was of dark green velvet, and a heavy necklace of gold and onyx hung from his shoulders and and dropped across his chest.

This was the first time I could recall seeing all of him, seeing his entire form instead of only his face. Somehow I hadn't thought how tall he would be, how elegantly he would wear his garments.

We might have been alone in the hall. He moved through the revelers as if they were shadows, and came straight for me. Closer, closer, and then he was so near I could have reached out and touched him...if I'd only had the courage to be so forward.

He bowed, a gesture worthy of the king's hall. "May I have the honor?"

So courtly, and so out of place in his velvet and gold. The forest shade of the doublet seemed to reflect in his sea-colored eyes, turning them almost green.

Somehow I found my voice to reply. "Of course."

He took my hand and led me to join the other dancers, where we all faced one another in a long line. A pang went through me as he released my fingers so we might perform our honors to one another before the dance began. I had never thought that I would touch him, never thought I would feel the warmth of his hand against mine, and I only wanted him to hold my fingers tightly in his for as long as possible. True, we would touch one another throughout the dance, but it was not the same thing.

The music began, however, and I had no time for regrets. This dance, called "Grey Mare," was one I usually enjoyed. But in my dream I could only curse its lively nature, which meant there would be only limited contact between my dream man and myself. How I longed for musicians to play a Sirlendian verdralle, so he might take me in his arms. But the dance was still deemed quite scandalous, especially out here in the hinterlands. Quite possibly it was danced every day in the king's court in Lystare...but we were very far from there.

The stranger did not speak, not even to offer his name. We only traced our steps around one another, down the set and back up again, until at last the song ended and everyone applauded.

Then he did say, "Something to drink?" to which I nodded and followed him to the refreshment table. He poured a cup of cider for me but did not immediately hand it over, instead leading me away from the crowd and up a narrow flight of steps until we emerged onto a small balcony which, I realized, was the same spot where the elders had drawn the name of the Bride from a polished urn.

I saw no urn this night, and the air was fine and mild, just as it would have been on that day in early Sevendre when Lilianth's wedding took place. The stars glittered overhead, so close it seemed I could reach out and touch them. Neither of the moons had risen yet, but I knew Taleron would be full, and Charis waxing past three-quarters. An auspicious day for Lilianth, or so the lore of such things went. I wasn't sure I believed the moons and the stars really had that much bearing on our lives here on solid ground.

The stranger handed me the cup and I drank, letting the cool sweetness of the cider slip over my tongue and down my dry throat. He stood quite close, and once again I was struck by his height. In my dream I thought I could even feel the heat coming from his body after the exertions of our dance, although I saw no sheen of sweat on his brow.

"Thank you for the dance," he said, a commonplace, but still I thrilled to hear him speak. Something about his voice sounded oddly familiar, as if I had heard him once in passing in Lirinsholme, although certainly I did not know his face.

"You are most welcome," I replied, feeling—strange as it might seem in a dream—oddly shy now that we stood alone and face to face, with no one else to note our exchange. He only nodded, and I hesitated, unsure as to what I should say next. Casting about for something safe and polite, I ventured, "Lilianth looks very lovely, does she not?"

"Yes, she does." His tone was almost too warm for my liking, but then he added, "She is very lovely indeed, but she does not hold a candle to you, Rhianne."

I opened my mouth to protest, for I had always thought Lilianth much prettier than I, with her pink cheeks and dimples and forget-me-not eyes. Whatever words I might have been about to say were smothered, however, as the stranger pulled me toward him and pressed his lips to mine.

A dream kiss should not count, I suppose, and yet nothing in my life had ever felt as real as that. His mouth was warm, and he tasted of sweet cider. Sweet, too, was the scent that seemed to cling to his dark hair, something fresh and herbal I couldn't identify. I'd never realized how solid a man would feel, pressed up against me like that, how my whole world could shrink down to just the taste and smell and feel of him.

The cup of cider fell from my hand and clattered against the wooden balcony. The stranger jerked backward at the sound. "Oh, no..."

"What?" I asked, for I clearly heard the distress in his voice. "What is wrong?"

"Goodbye, Rhianne," he said, and he began to grow hazy and indistinct, as if he were made of mist and was blowing away with the morning breeze.

"No!" I cried, and reached for him, but it was too late. He was gone.

I sat up then, my breath coming in great heaving gasps, and I realized I was in my own bed, with the hangings drawn about me and three heavy blankets below the silken coverlet to provide extra warmth. No one else here to keep away the chill of the early winter night; I was all alone.

A wave of despair hit me then, blacker than the night in which I had found myself. I pulled in a dragging breath, trying to keep the tears at bay, but it was no good. He was gone, had never been there at all. The first sob out of my throat seemed to pierce the very air itself, and then I was weeping, the tears on my cheeks the only warmth in the chamber.

How real he had seemed, but I knew now he was only fancy, something I had conjured to provide some comfort, here in this place where I was so very alone. Never mind Sar's little kindnesses or Melynne's chatter—I was not here for them, but for the Dragon Lord, and whatever he had expected of me, it was clear I had fallen far, far short.

Although I knew it was foolish to get out of bed, I somehow couldn't remain there. A candlestick and a little wooden box of matches sat on the table next to my bed, and I seized a match and lit the candle. It gave enough light for me to reach under my worktable and pull out the portrait.

Ah, yes, so very, very close. The laugh lines around his eyes were more pronounced in person, and his mouth just a tiny bit wider, but nevertheless the likeness was remarkable. One would have thought I'd had him sit for me.

Then I shook my head, realizing how mad that all sounded. How could I refer to seeing him in a dream as "seeing him in person"? One was no more real than the other. Perhaps the dream felt more real, simply because he moved about and spoke...and kissed me...but he still lived only in my mind. He was a specter, a ghost, a combination of qualities my mind had assembled as its ideal man. And in my mind was the only place where he would ever exist.

My hands shook as I poured myself a cup of water. If my mother were here, no doubt she would blame all of this on a surfeit of cheese. At that thought I almost smiled. What I wouldn't have done to have her with me, to have her soothe and scold and tell me I was being silly and that it would all be better in the morning.

But she was down in Lirinsholme, snug in her own bed with my father snoring softly beside her, and I had no one to come and push away the darkness. The tears returned, even though they had begun to lessen, and this time I had no more will to fight them. I only returned to my bed and buried my face in the pillows, so that my sobs might be known to no one but me.

"Rhianne."

I made some sort of incoherent sound and pulled the covers more closely over my head.

"My lady."

Since it was Sar, I knew she would not go away, but that didn't mean I had to give her any encouragement. "I don't feel well."

"Ah," she said, and I could have sworn I heard satisfaction in her voice, even muffled as it was by the heavy coverlet and blankets. "I told his lordship no good would come of eating all that cheese. I don't care what they might do in Purth, but—"

"That's it," I said from behind the blanket. "Definitely the cheese. I think I would like to go back to sleep."

"Of course, my lady." The sound of her footsteps on the wooden floor was clear enough, even buried in linen and wool as I was.

Then I froze, still burrowed into the bedclothes. Had I, in my abandonment of despair last night, left the portrait of the stranger sitting out in plain sight? I honestly could not recall, and of course I could not get up to check, not with Sar standing right there.

Hardly daring to breathe, I lay in my bed, listening as she set down what sounded like a fresh pitcher of water next to the bed, followed by the hollow clank of a pewter plate being placed next to it.

"I've left you a roll and butter, in case you feel like eating later," she told me.

"Mm-hmm," was all I could manage, but apparently that was enough for her. Her footsteps moved away, and the door closed behind her with a solid thunk.

I forced myself to lie in bed for a minute or two more, just in case she had forgotten something and decided to come back into my bedroom. However, I heard nothing except the anxious beating of my own heart, and so I judged it safe enough to emerge.

After pushing back the bedclothes, I climbed out of bed and surveyed the chamber with some trepidation. The portrait was nowhere in sight. What had I done with the blasted thing? I hoped I wasn't so far gone the night before that I had shoved the still-damp canvas between other paintings, where I might damage its surface. But no, it wasn't in the stack of canvases in the alcove, and neither was it stashed beneath my worktable.

Somewhat flummoxed, I stood and planted my hands on my hips and gave the room another careful inspection. Had my dream presented some truth I hadn't wanted to recognize? Had the impossible happened, and the stranger in the portrait somehow taken on life and walked away?

Put so baldly, even in the privacy of my own thoughts, the notion seemed ludicrous. Then again, I supposed a person might think a man being turned into a dragon was a ludicrous notion, and yet here I was, living in that very dragon's castle.

"Damn," I said aloud.

I racked my brains, but I could recall nothing very clearly of the moments before I went to bed, save that I was feeling nauseated, yet not enough so to be physically ill. Had I even touched the portrait? I couldn't remember.

In desperation, I dropped to my hands and knees to search under the bed. A pair of blue-green eyes gazed back at me, and I gave a little gasp before realizing it was only the stranger's painted eyes meeting mine, due to the angle at which the canvas lay.

"You have been a very naughty boy," I remarked, and grasped the painting by the edges so I could extricate it without touching the painted section and thereby risk damaging it.

In response he only watched me, still with that hint of a secret smile in the corner of his mouth.

"Laugh if you must," I said sternly, and got carefully to my feet. "I suppose you think me a very great fool, and perhaps I am. Still, you are going safely back here for now, until I decide what on earth I should do with you."

His features were so lifelike, so close to my recollection of the dream from the night before, that I halfway expected him to respond, for the painted mouth to open and tell me what a silly young woman I was. But of course nothing of the sort happened, and so I only tucked him away in his special hiding place, in a corner behind the canvases that angled in such a fashion so it could fit neatly without touching any of my other half-finished paintings.

I supposed I should work on one of those, but the thought did not appeal at all. Or perhaps I should simply crawl back into bed and languish there the rest of the day. That appealed to me even less. What I really wanted, I realized, was some fresh air. The storm of the night before had quite blown itself out, and now the sky outside my windows was a deep, calm blue, overlaid with clouds so thick and fluffy they looked as if they had been sheared right off one of Master Marenson's sheep.

How I would explain venturing outside, when I had just claimed I wasn't feeling well, I had no idea. But the freshly washed world outside beckoned, and besides, I knew it would not be long before the first snows came and I would be trapped in this castle all winter, lucky if I could make a circuit or two of the rose gardens before the next storm swept in.

That seemed to decide things. I braided my hair back into a thick plait, and donned one of my simplest gowns, the dark blue wool one with the wheat-colored embroidery about the neckline. The rest of it was quite unadorned, however, so it seemed the best choice for tromping around outside. That reminded me there would most likely be mud, and so I put on a pair of calf-high boots instead of my usual slippers, and drew out the wine-colored cloak of heavy wool that I had worn only once so far, when I had walked with Theran in the gardens not three days ago. The wind had blown from the north that afternoon, promising storms. Well, they had come...both inside and outside the castle, unfortunately.

One advantage of the small staff Theran kept at Black's Keep was that no one seemed to pay much mind to my comings and goings. Not that I came and went all that often, as I spent most of my days painting away in my own rooms. Still, it was a relief to know I could slip outside my chambers once I was dressed, and drift down the stairs to the northern exit with no one apparently the wiser.

Even if someone were to see me, it was the same route I would have taken to go to the rose gardens, and no one would have made much note of my presence there. Sar, perhaps, would have made a comment about the mud and how it was not a good day to go outside, but I did not see her or anyone else, and so made my escape easily enough.

The gardens, however, were not my destination. Beyond the now-bare rosebushes and the colored gravel walks, the forest rose, dark and secret. I knew that sometimes Mat and other men of the household would ride there, to hunt deer and squirrels and even the occasional boar, but I did not much fear encountering any of the men today. They had brought in two fine bucks several days ago, and did not plan to go out again for a day or so more. At least, that was what Melynne had told me, glowing with pride that Mat should be such a fine hunter in addition to being the keep's general craftsman and jack of all trades.

Why I sought the forest now, I could not exactly say. Perhaps it was only that I had looked off into its expanses from my bedroom window for so long that it seemed a natural thing to explore it before the winter weather closed it off to me until spring. Something about those dark firs and pines, the naked branches of oak and elm, seemed to draw me to them, and I went willingly enough.

The air chilled my face and hands almost at once, for in my rush to leave the castle I had forgotten to put on my gloves. I buried my cold fingers in a fold of my cloak and pushed on, moving past the rose garden and through a yellowed and patchy expanse of grass. Beyond that was a tall hedge with a gate built into it; luckily, the gate was not locked, and I lifted the latch and moved on through. For the first time since I had come to be the Dragon's Bride, I was outside the grounds of Black's Keep.

It was very quiet. From somewhere far off I thought I heard the chattering of a brook as it rushed over a stony bed, but otherwise there was no sound, not even of birds or small forest creatures. Or larger ones, I thought, reminding myself that boars sometimes frequented these woods. Well, I would have to hope I'd hear a boar coming; it couldn't be that difficult, considering the heavy carpet of dead, rustling leaves underfoot.

I had no very clear idea of where I was going but kept moving vaguely northeast. The grey towers of the castle were still visible over my right shoulder, and that comforted me. The stories of my youth were full of tales of children and young women who had gotten lost in the woods and had met unfortunate ends, and I had no desire to number myself one of them.

The air smelled of damp earth and the vague musty scent of decaying leaves. Above that, though, was the tang of pine needles, sharp and aromatic. I breathed deeply, glad of the crisp morning breeze. Odd how I had felt so cold indoors, and yet now enjoyed a chill that must surely be greater here. Perhaps I had grown weary of the castle without even realizing it, tired of the smell of linseed oil and woodsmoke and human sweat.

Whatever the reason, I felt my spirits lift as I walked along, free—if only for a little while—of the tension between Theran and myself, the undercurrents that swirled through the keep. I did not pretend to understand them. To be sure, I hardly understood my role there. I was not a wife in anything but name, and Sar might call me the lady of the castle, but she ruled that place, not I. What purpose a Bride served, I couldn't begin to guess.

I pushed those thoughts away and continued doggedly forward. Whatever had happened between Theran and me could wait. For the moment I only wanted to enjoy this brief taste of freedom, even if I knew it couldn't last.

Had any of the other Brides come this way? Surely they, too, must have longed for their freedom, wished to flee. I wondered then at my easy escape. Did Theran not worry that one of his unwilling Brides might try to run away, run from the confinement of the keep and its cursed lord?

The forest fell away from me, and I emerged into a clearing, pale with the last remnants of summer's straggling grass. Then I blinked and looked more closely at my surroundings, and realized it was not a true clearing…or at least not a natural one.

It was a graveyard.

Rows of grey headstones marched away from where I stood. They all appeared to be more or less uniform in size, coming up to around my knees. Some force seemed to compel me to approach the closest stone, although the dread rising in my throat had already begun to tell me what I would find.

*Liselle, Beloved Bride.*

"No," I said aloud, although some part of me knew my denial was foolish. What else could have happened to all those young women, so that Theran would need a new wife every five or seven years or so?

Footsteps dragging, I moved to the next one. The name was different—*Delianne*—but this stone, too, said, "Beloved Bride."

How could he have loved any of them? There were so many…so many, I realized. I tried to count, found the landscape blurred as my eyes filled with tears. At least sixty, probably more, but I could not tell for sure. And how much longer until I lay there as well, beneath a stone that read, *Rhianne, Beloved Bride*?

"My lady!"

The voice was male, but not Theran's. Besides, he had never addressed me thus. I turned and saw Mat stumbling from the edge of the forest, his broad, handsome face tight with worry.

"Sar sent me to find you," he said, pausing a few feet away from me. I noticed he studiously avoided looking at any of the headstones.

"Why does that not surprise me?" I responded. "How on earth did she even know where to look?"

"Dellah saw you go out through the door in the hedge, and she told Sar."

So there had been eyes watching me, even though I hadn't noticed them. No real surprise; Dellah's domain was the kitchens, and I should have guessed that she might be able to note my comings and goings from one of that chamber's several windows.

Not that it really mattered, considering what I'd found. What did any of it matter?

"Come, my lady," he continued. "This is not place for you."

"Not yet, anyway."

His eyes widened a bit, and I saw him cross his fingers behind his back, making the sign against the evil eye. He did not, however, contradict me, but said only, "'Tis cold, my lady, and the clouds are coming back in. Best to get you back home."

*Home?* I thought. *Is that what Black's Keep is supposed to be for me? It seems only a temporary way station, a stopping point before...before...* And my mind hesitated and stuttered to a stop there, for I could not bear to give the horrible notion any further shape and form.

"All right," I said wearily, for I had no doubt he would throw me over his shoulder like a sack of meal and carry me back that way if necessary. I might have been the Bride of Black's Keep, but I was not the one who issued the orders.

The look of relief that passed over his features might have been comical under different circumstances. He nodded, said,

"Very good, my lady," and did not move until I had turned away from the forlorn little graveyard and begun moving toward the southwest, down the narrow trail that had brought me here.

It seemed in this, as in all else, I could only do as I was told.

# Chapter Eleven

"So he did kill them," I said baldly, as Sar set my muddy boots by the fire so she could brush the dirt away once they had dried.

She straightened and shot me an indignant look. "He did not lay a hand on any of those poor girls."

"Do you really expect me to believe that they all died of an ague, or a fall down the stairs, or from eating the wrong type of mushroom? I know there are many ways to die in this world, Sar, but it does rather stagger comprehension to think they all died under perfectly innocent circumstances!"

Her hands tightened in her apron. "Believe what you like, but his lordship had nothing to do with any of their deaths."

"Hmph," I replied, and drank of the spiced wine she had brought me.

There had been no words of recrimination, no scolding. I'd had to remind myself that Sar was, in fact, a servant, and that it was not her place to question my actions, for I'd been certain I was about to receive the sort of dressing-down I hadn't gotten since the time I was eleven and thought it a good idea to use my father's glazes to paint my fingernails red. I'd overheard one of my mother's acquaintances describing such a procedure taking hold in the court, after a visit by a Keshiaari princess who tinted her fingernails, and had thought it sounded like a jolly fun idea. My mother hadn't thought it jolly at all, of course.

Sar hadn't been jolly, either, her jaw tense and her mouth more than a little strained. She said nothing as Mat handed me over to her. I wasn't exactly marched upstairs, but her manner told me that I had better not suggest anything else besides going straight to my rooms.

Of Theran, I saw no sign.

"It is...unfortunate...that you saw what you did. You should never have gone there, my lady, nor left the castle grounds on your own. It's dangerous in the woods, what with the boars and the bears—"

"Do not forget the dragon," I put in.

Her mouth tightened further. "The dragon would never trouble you, my lady, and I think you know that very well."

"Do I?"

She turned from me then, the set of her shoulders communicating what courtesy would not allow her to. How she probably wished she could give me the talking-to she so clearly thought I deserved.

"You are not well," she said, after a pause. "You should not have gotten out of bed in the first place. I do think you should allow yourself to rest. This will all look much better to you tomorrow."

I didn't quite see how even an extended period of rest would help me to extinguish the grim vision of those rows of gravestones, of the realization that all of my predecessors lay buried not more than a mile from where I now sat. Even ten years of sleep, like that which had captured the enchanted princess from the tale my mother used to tell me when I was a little girl, would not be enough to erase that sight...or the questions it aroused.

Besides, if I slept...if I closed my eyes...who was to say they would ever open again?

Something of my dismay must have shown itself in my face, for Sar's tone was gentler when she spoke again. "You have nothing to fear," she said, and somehow I heard the truth in her words, although I guessed it was not the whole truth. "And he knows nothing of any of this, so we can keep it as our secret."

Her words did seem to lift a burden I hadn't noticed I was carrying until it was gone. Truly, Theran was probably still angry with me after our exchange the previous night. I didn't want to think what his response might be if he learned I had left the castle unaccompanied. Not only that, but that I had discovered something no doubt he wished to remain hidden.

"Thank you, Sar. I think I shall sleep now. Don't worry about bringing me any supper—I'll make up for it at breakfast."

She nodded, a little of the worry seeming to lift from her brow, and she appeared even more relieved when I set down my goblet of spiced wine and made my way to my bedchamber. Since I had already removed my mud-spattered woolen gown, it was a simple enough thing for me to shrug off the heavy quilted robe I'd put on over my chemise and then slide into bed.

I closed my eyes, more for Sar's benefit than because I thought I would actually sleep. She seemed to putter about in the outer room for a minute or two more before I heard the door close.

The wind wailed past the tower, rattling the windows in their casements. Mat had been right; another storm was coming in. Nothing to be surprised about, of course. This was the season for it. I supposed I should have been glad that the snow had held off so far. We were only a few days into Novedre, but snowstorms had been known to come earlier than that.

Perhaps it was the keening of the gale outside that stirred up my restlessness. Not that it really mattered. I knew sleep would not come to me this early, so many hours before the time I usually laid down my head. And besides, that dream of mine had taught me the portrait was not yet right, that there were still many things about it I needed to correct, close as it was to its subject.

Sar had built up the fire, and some of its heat penetrated into my bedchamber. Cold drifted past the cracks in the windows, though, and I gathered up my heavy dressing gown and put it on before going to the alcove and fishing out the portrait from its hiding place.

Out came my palette and brushes as well, and I set to, working to get those crinkles around his eyes just so. Altering the shape of his mouth would take more time, and so I set that task aside for later. If I could get at least this part right, I would feel as if I had accomplished something today.

I worked away, as the stormy gray half-light outside my windows faded into dusk and then black night. At some point I set down my brush long enough to light some candles, but that was the only respite I allowed myself. Too much to do, too much to do, I told myself as I dipped my brush in the paint, using tiny strokes to define the troublesome areas around his eyes.

Finally I set down the brush, mainly because my hand had begun to cramp. I had no way of knowing how many hours I had spent in my frenzied work, but the castle around me was quiet and still, save for the ever-present keening of the wind. Apparently Sar had taken my words at face value and stayed away.

Meaning that Theran had taken his dinner alone. I doubted it was the first time, and I tried to ignore the pang of guilt that went through me as I pictured him sitting by himself at the round table in his chambers, his ingenious little devices whirring and shimmering away in the next room. Why should I feel guilty? It was he who had insulted me, not the other way around. And I was not the one with a graveyard full of dead wives barely a mile away.

That thought brought home the events of the day. I had done a good job of shutting them out while I was working. Perhaps I had thrown myself back into the painting in such a frenzy precisely because I wanted to forget what I had seen.

Not so easy, though. I could see it clearly as if it still lay before me, that forlorn little clearing with its ranks of neat grey headstones. Someone obviously took care to keep it in that condition, for the area had been clear of weeds, and I thought

I had even spotted the remnants of wildflowers lying on several of the graves. Whose grim duty was that? Mat's? Sar's?

What would Theran say, I wondered, if I went to him and asked outright what had happened to all those young women?

*What happened to them...and what will happen to me?*

He would give me no answer. What was it he had said? *I cannot speak of it.* But that had been in reference to the curse, and not to his Brides...unless they were one and the same.

Secrets lay heavy upon the castle, and I knew I would get no answers to them. Reason enough for me to keep to myself, to stay away from Theran Blackmoor. If he could not do me the courtesy of explaining even something of my reasons for being here, then I saw no point in extending him any particular favor.

That sounded very fine and proud. Whether I would be able to do such a thing for any period of time remained to be seen.

Weariness came over me then, and I knew I might finally be able to sleep. I cleaned my brushes and put everything back in its proper place, including the portrait. Before I settled it in its corner, I held it out at arms' length, studying the man's face. In my dream those lips had touched mine; it seemed I could feel them still. But that had been no true dream, only a wistful fancy. If it had been true, he would be here with me now, in the flesh, and not in this flat frame, with arms that could not hold me, and a mouth that could not kiss me.

It seemed then as if I could not bear to gaze at him any longer. I hurried to put him back in his hiding place, so I would not have to torture myself with that which could never be.

"It's clear as day," Lilianth was saying to me as we paused at Alina's stall to ponder the various potatoes and turnips and leeks. "You obviously care for him. So why not tell him?"

The sky above us was a clear, bright blue, but we both wore cloaks and scarves, and I could see my breath hanging on the morning air. Not summer, then, but perhaps a fine early winter day on a rare respite between storms. Beneath her cloak I thought I saw Lilianth's belly rounded in pregnancy.

Foolish, of course. Not that dreams had to make any particular sense, but I knew even if she had been with child when she wed Adain, she would not be showing so much barely three months later.

"I can't just come out and tell him," I protested, picking up a string bag of golden potatoes and inspecting it carefully to see if it hid any half-rotted specimens. "That would ruin everything."

Her blue eyes were wide and guileless, a mirror of the sky. "Why?"

"Because—because—because he's the Dragon! It's not as if he's the goldsmith's apprentice!"

"All the more reason."

I pulled a pair of copper coins from the purse at my belt and handed them to Alina, who had not appeared to pay much attention to Lilianth's words. Just as well; even in a dream I really didn't want someone overhearing such a frank conversation.

"You don't know what you're talking about," I said, gathering up my potatoes and moving on to the next stall, where skeins of brightly dyed wool hung from the wooden crosspieces.

"Don't I? At least I know what it is to be in love...and I see all the signs in you."

"Indeed?"

"Indeed. You moon over him constantly, worry about what he thinks of you, wish to be in his presence even though you do nothing to make such wishes a reality. It's either love or an attack of some extremely ill humors."

"The physicians of the Golden Palm don't believe in humors," I pointed out.

"They wouldn't. Anyway, we were not talking about them, but about you. What's the worst that could happen, if you told him the truth?"

"He might—he might laugh at me."

"Do you really think that is what would happen?"

No, I didn't. I knew he had enough courtesy in him for that. But I also knew he was very good at keeping his own counsel and maintaining a certain distance between us. There were times I thought he actually enjoyed being in my company, true. Yet he never confided in me, and never did anything to make me think he wanted anything close between us.

"He doesn't want to care for me," I told Lilianth. "Not when I'm going to die like all the rest of them."

"How do you know that you're going to die?"

"Because they all died."

"That doesn't mean you have to."

I knew there had to be some way to point out the flaw in her logic, but somehow it escaped me at the moment. Frowning, I said, "Perhaps it's my fate."

"I've never heard you talk about fate before."

"I never lived in a cursed castle before."

She lifted her shoulders and gave a little chuckle, as if conceding my point. "All right, then. Look at it this way. Perhaps you are going to die. Would you not rather he knew the truth before you were gone? We always regret the things we have not done, not the ones we actually had the courage to try."

"I don't know about that," I said slowly. "I'm still regretting those boiled sprouts your mother made last spring."

"That is not what I meant, and you know it."

Somehow I didn't recall Lilianth being quite this wise in real life. But that was how dreams went, I supposed. We saw things in them as we wanted them to be, not as they really were. Why else would I have dreamt of kissing the stranger in the portrait?

Perhaps that was not completely accurate. Once upon a time, I did have dreams that were true, that showed things as they happened, or were about to happen. It seemed I had not had one, though, since I arrived in the castle. Was it because I had nothing left to see of any importance, or because something in the castle was blocking the visions from appearing to me?

Abruptly I asked, "Who was that man at your wedding?"

"Which man? There were many in attendance."

"I don't see how you could have overlooked him. He was tall, and wore a green velvet doublet with a heavy gold chain across his shoulders."

Her fine brows drew together in a frown. "I saw no one like that."

"He and I danced 'Grey Mare' together, and then...we stepped outside."

"Did you?" Her eyes glinted. "And what precisely did you do outside?"

I said nothing, but instead pretended to be interested in a collection of pewter plates at the stall where we had paused.

She laughed then. "Ah, I see. So you went outside to kiss this stranger, and now you don't know how you feel about the Dragon Lord of Black's Keep."

That seemed to sum it up neatly. Never mind that the stranger was no more real than the conversation I was presently having with Lilianth. But perhaps she had the right of it. Perhaps this inner obsession with someone I had never actually met or seen with my own eyes was somehow preventing me from admitting that I had come to care for Theran, more than I wanted to say.

Had any of the rest of them loved him, those women who lay sleeping in that secret clearing? And had he loved any of them back?

"Perhaps they all died of a broken heart," I said, echoing my musings of some days earlier.

In my dream I had made no mention of the place where all of the Dragon's Brides took their final rest, but Lilianth only nodded as if she knew exactly what I was talking about. Then she tilted her head and gave me a searching look. "People don't really die of a broken heart," she said. "That sort of thing is just for stories. Something else killed them, Rhianne, and you need to find out what it was."

"Before or after I tell my husband I'm in love with him?" I asked, in semi-teasing tones, but she appeared to take me seriously, considering my question before replying,

"Afterward. You are both so busy building walls right now. If you don't stop soon, you'll never be able to tear them down."

I was about to comment on her sudden sagacity, but she seemed to grow insubstantial before my eyes, to waver and then blow away like mist on the morning breeze. All around her, the familiar streets of Lirinsholme likewise began to disappear, the buildings and people and smells and sounds dissolving into nothing. A bright light touched my eyes, and I awoke.

The sun streamed through curtains I had forgotten to close the night before. Unlike the previous storm, this one seemed to have been short-lived.

I blinked, and just as they had done in my dream, the words from my conversation with Lilianth blew away, leaving my mind as if they had never been there. Such was the way with dreams, but this time I had the impression I was forgetting something vitally important, if I could only recall what it was.

However, the harder I tried to hold on to those wisps of memory, the more they slipped away. My head ached, and I found myself feeling disinclined to get out of bed. Well, Sar had told me to get my rest. What did it matter whether I slept the day away or not? Even the thought of getting up so I might paint more was not appealing, and so I rolled over in bed, pulled the covers more tightly around me, and drifted off back to sleep.

No dreams greeted me that time, nothing but oblivion unbroken until I heard Sar's voice from somewhere above me.

"My lady!"

I rolled over, noting vaguely that the bright sunlight had quite gone. Sar held a tray in both hands; behind her broad silhouette I could see the dim traces of a sullen sunset through one of the windows. Had I really slept the day through?

It seemed so.

"I thought you might like some supper," she said, her tone uncharacteristically hesitant. "Or do you still feel ill?"

I paused to consider. The ache had gone from my head, though I still felt oddly listless. But my stomach apparently decided that it had had enough of lethargy, and growled.

Something that might have been the beginnings of a smile touched Sar's mouth. "Not so ill you couldn't eat, I wager."

"I could try something," I admitted.

Suddenly brisk, she set a clever little four-legged tray down on my lap. It was the sort of meal an invalid would be likely to enjoy—potato soup thick with cheese, a fresh wheaten roll, a mug of cider. I set to with more energy than I'd thought I would be able to muster, demolishing the roll and most of the soup before I'd even stopped to decide whether I was all that hungry.

"You seem to be on the mend," was all she said, but a certain gleam in her eye told me she was almost amused by my wolfish appetite.

"It would appear so."

I didn't wish to waste time on speaking then, not while I still had some of that delicious soup to eat. Perhaps I could be excused; it had been a very long time since my dinner the previous night. And although I had not forgotten the shocks of the day before, they'd already begun to take on a hazy, dreamlike quality, as if they had happened to someone else.

Sar bustled about, putting away the clothing I had dropped across a chair, placing my boots on the floor of the wardrobe, even condescending to straighten the brushes and little jars of pigment I'd left sitting on my worktable. I thanked the goddess I'd retained enough presence of mind to hide the portrait of the stranger where it could not be easily spotted. I did not wish to have that conversation this evening...or ever, if possible.

Luckily, enough of the scent of linseed oil hung about my workspace that Sar had no wish to linger there, or perhaps it was just that I had finished all of my supper, giving her an excuse to return to me. Whatever the case, she stepped back toward the bed and retrieved the empty tray.

"Very good, my lady. It is probably best if you sleep some more, to regain your strength."

"I've already slept the day through," I protested.

"True enough, but rest is the best thing when you're not feeling well."

I supposed so; I hadn't been ill enough in my short life to know for sure. We Menyon girls had always been a robust lot, soldiering on when most of our acquaintances sniffled and coughed their way through the long winter season. At any rate, this hadn't been that sort of illness.

Assuming it had been an illness at all. If I were the sort to find drama in everyday occurrences, I would have said it was simply the sting of Theran's cold words, followed by that gruesome discovery. Such things might be enough to send some girls to their beds. I'd never been the sort to suffer the megrims…and besides, my mother wouldn't have allowed such a thing for even two minutes.

Curiously, though, I found I was weary after eating, and probably could sleep again. So I said, knowing it would make Sar happy, "I do think I will shut my eyes for a while."

"Very good."

I did close my eyes, but not all the way, watching her through my lashes as she set the tray down on my bedside table for a moment so she could move the bowl and cup closer to the center where they'd be less likely to fall. Her expression was more troubled than I would have expected, given that I had done as she wished, and promised to sleep some more. She shot me a troubled little frown, her forehead puckering, before she shook her head and picked up the tray, then went out.

She hadn't shut the door to my bedchamber, most likely so the heat from the hearth in the other room could penetrate to where I slept. I found myself wanting to dream, but as sleep overtook me this time, it was deep and black, depthless as the ocean, taking me with it.

And so it went. I slept that night, and the day after, and the next night, rousing myself only to take a little food and attend to such necessities of hygiene as were required. Sar did manage to coax me into a hot bath the morning of the third day, and braided my hair herself as I tried not to let my face crack from yawning. It seemed I could not get enough sleep, no matter what I did. The line of worry between Sar's brows only appeared to deepen as time passed, and I wished I had the strength to tell her I was fine. Somehow I lacked even that motivation, however.

That evening came a diffident knock at the door to my bedchamber. I rolled over in bed, blinking. How long had I been asleep this time? It seemed only a few hours had gone by since Sar last checked in on me.

"Yes?" I managed, pushing myself up against the pillows.

"Rhianne."

*His* voice, but hesitant, as if I were the master here, not he.

Oh, good gods. I knew I must look a mess, my disarray something that could not be cured by a hurried primping. Still, I reached up to run my fingers through my hair and arrange it more or less neatly over my shoulders. The covers I pulled up more tightly about myself, although truly the heavy linen of my sleep chemise revealed very little.

"Come in," I said. My own voice sounded rusty and dry. I should have poured myself some water before asking him to enter.

Too late, though, as immediately the door to my bedchamber opened and he stepped through. So many days had passed since I'd last seen him that his height and the sweep of his dark robes startled me a little. My breath caught, and I looked down at my hands where they were knotted in my lap.

"Sar said you have been sleeping a great deal," he said. Although the words were calm enough, I thought I caught an edge of tension to his tone. "Perhaps it is time I called in a physician to see you."

"Oh, no," I replied at once. "Surely that isn't necessary."

"You are not ill after all?"

"No—I, well, that is, I was. Or I think I was." How on earth could I describe the lassitude that had overtaken me, the utter weariness which had no connection to any actual exertion? "But I think I am getting better."

"I am glad to hear that."

Surprising myself, I asked, "Are you?"

The hood turned toward me. "Of course I am. Do you think it pleases me that you have been ill?"

"No, of course not." I found myself ashamed of the implication in my previous words. Then it came out in a rush, perhaps driven by the days I had spent not knowing if he were angry with me, "Only that I thought you were displeased with me, and perhaps if I had angered you, then you would not be as bothered by my being ill."

"Oh, no." He moved toward me and reached out with one gloved hand, as if to touch my arm where it lay on top of the coverlet. As always, though, something stopped him, and he paused, irresolute. "I have been very worried about you."

I hadn't known until then how much it mattered to me what he thought, how he felt. Relief coursed through me, with the return of an energy I had not felt for several days. His hand was only a few inches from mine, and I grasped his fingers, feeling the soft, warm leather like a caress against my skin.

Barely a whisper as he asked, "You do not fear me?"

I didn't even have to stop to think. "Of course not," I replied. "You have given me no reason to fear you."

He made no reply, but only tightened his fingers around mine. I felt again the heat of his flesh through the thin leather, the force of his being. How I wished it could be more than this, but at least it was a start.

"Stay with me," I said.

"Of course. Would you like me to read to you?"

"Very much." Anything to hear more of that mellow, mahogany voice.

With apparent reluctance he released my hand and went into the other room, where I had left Tales of the Age of Magic sitting on the table in front of the divan. I couldn't help but wonder whether he would read me "The Tale of Alende and Allaire," but of course he was far too circumspect for that. No, he drew a chair up to my bedside and opened the book to its proper beginning, "Of the Coming of the Althuri."

I must confess that I was rather more interested now I had Theran reading the story to me, rather than trying to slog through it myself. Truly, it seemed fantastic beyond belief, that beings from a world other than ours would come here and fall in love with our women, thus bringing the gift—or curse—of magic to their offspring. But that is how it was put forth in the book, and I was so caught up in Theran's reading of the tale that I did not want to stop him and ask questions.

At length he came to the end of that particular tale, with the last of the Althuri driven into hiding and those who carried the strain of magic going out into the world and selling their services to whatever kings and lords had the means to pay their prices. Theran closed the book and said, "It grows quite late, Rhianne. I think it is time for you to sleep."

"Sleep? When that is all I have done for the past three days?"

"Yes. It's true that you have spent much time abed, but you should sleep now, and try to rise in the morning at your usual time, so you are back in the same rhythm as the rest of the household."

These words were so sensible, and so like something Sar or my mother would have said, that I could hardly gainsay them. So I merely nodded and said, "Yes, Theran."

"That is very meek, and quite unlike you. You do promise not to get up in the middle of the night and paint a portrait of Sar, or some such?"

I laughed then, as much from relief at the teasing note in his voice as from the image of me being driven enough to paint Sar in the wee hours of the morning. Of course, there was no way I could confess to him that I'd had more than one of those nighttime painting sessions, not when the subject was someone he might conceivably see as a rival, ridiculous as that might sound.

"I promise. I shall sleep the night through and then eat all my porridge in the morning."

"Sar actually brings that to you? I shall have to speak to her."

"No—no. I was only teasing. Sar brings me proper breakfasts of bacon and bread and eggs. No gruel, I assure you."

"Ah, that is a relief." He stood, and this time I saw no hesitation as he reached over and touched my hand. "Sleep well, Rhianne."

"I will."

The dark hood bent perilously close to the candle flames as he blew out the tapers in the candelabra one by one, but he rose without having suffered any harm. "Perhaps a walk in the rose garden tomorrow, if the weather allows?"

"I would like that very much."

He nodded and went out, leaving me alone in the dark. I didn't mind it as much this time, though. A soft wash of dim light still came in through the doorway from the last of the fire in the hearth, and it heartened me somehow. His footsteps sounded across the stone floor, and then I heard him shut the outer door.

A deep breath, then another. I should sleep, so I could walk in the gardens with my husband the next day.

And darkness claimed me.

# Chapter Twelve

"Oh, well," Sar said, as I looked in despair at the snow falling outside. "It's come this early before, and I daresay it will again."

"But Ther—but his lordship and I had planned to walk in the gardens today!"

"No reason why you still shouldn't, if you're feeling well enough and bundle up. It's a dry, light snow, by the looks of it. You should have no trouble walking, as long as it doesn't get any worse."

These sturdy, no-nonsense words did something to hearten me, but still I found myself angry, frustrated that the snow couldn't have held off for just another day. Foolish, of course. The weather did what it willed, and all of my cursing would do very little to change it.

"You will—you will tell his lordship that I fully intend to still walk with him after I have eaten and dressed?"

"Of course, my lady. Don't fret about that. Now, finish the rest of your breakfast, and see how you feel then."

There being little else I could do, I ate the last of the cold chicken and biscuits on my plate, my eyes fixed on the grey skies outside. Was the snow letting up a little? It seemed to be coming in brief flurries, rather than in the steady veils of white I had spied when I first woke up.

"And you are doing better today?" she asked as I pushed the plate away and set it back on the tray.

She should have been comforted on that point, since I had taken my meal sitting in a chair and with the tray on the table beside me rather than while still in bed should have told her that much. But just in case she needed extra reassurance, I nodded and replied, "Very much so. Whatever it was, it seems to have gone now."

"Good," she replied, but I noticed that she still frowned a little, absently, as if she didn't quite realize what she was doing.

I honestly couldn't think what had her so troubled. To be sure, after the plague that had devastated Purth and Seldd, and some of the regions of my own country that bordered those two lands, I could understand being concerned over every cough and fever. However, as that had been almost five years ago, and Lirinsholme had never been touched by the disease at all, the chances of my being ill with anything so dire as the plague were very low. Besides, I hadn't coughed, and I had no fever. My only symptoms had been that odd lassitude and the unnatural amounts of time I had spent asleep.

Perhaps some of the other Brides had been sickly, and that was what concerned her now. After all, I had no idea what caused their deaths.

*Something else killed them, Rhianne, and you need to find out what it was.*

The words sounded so clearly in my mind it was as if I had spoken them myself, but that internal voice was not mine, and I did not recognize it. Somehow I thought I should, for something about the words seemed familiar, but I could not remember why or how.

I knew I should attempt to determine what had happened to all of Theran's erstwhile wives. The only way I could possibly prevent the same thing from happening to me was to discover the cause of their premature deaths.

Exactly how I was supposed to accomplish such a thing, when prying the smallest bit of information from either Theran or Sar had already proved to be more difficult than prising a pearl from a particularly stubborn oyster, I did not know. Sar had already told me Theran had nothing to do with their deaths. That should have reassured me. In some ways I suppose it had—after all, one does not want to believe that the man one loves is a killer. However, with the most likely suspect eliminated, that left me with very little to go on.

It must have something to do with the curse. But since Theran could not or would not tell me anything of its particulars, and Sar professed ignorance in such matters, I had no idea where I could find such vital information. Even if the details of the curse had been written down somewhere, the most likely place would be in Theran's library somewhere. I somehow doubted he would give me free rein to go through his things so I might find the vital piece of information I needed.

"I thought your blue wool gown, my lady, and of course your boots, what with all that snow."

"What?" I had to pause and make myself consider Sar's words. Then I nodded. "Certainly. It is my warmest gown."

With that decided, I stood and allowed Sar to take my breakfast tray away so I could get dressed in privacy. And even though the gown was of stout, sturdy wool, and my boots likewise thick and warm, I still gave the leaden skies outside a dubious look. Not that winters in Lirinsholme couldn't be severe. But at least in town we were somewhat sheltered by the fiercest blasts of the winds, and the snow did not drift quite so deep. Here on the heights, exposed to every gust, we had no shelter from winter's worst.

That didn't stop me from fastening my cloak tightly around my throat and slipping on a pair of fur-lined gloves. The gods only knew the corridors of Black's Keep were cold enough on their own, far away from the hearths that struggled to keep the individual rooms warm. I was not premature in making sure I had bundled myself carefully against the chill.

I hurried down the steps, as much because of a desire to keep warm as because of my eagerness to see Theran again. Since Sar had disappeared as soon as I was done eating, I had to presume she'd gone to tell his lordship that I would be out and about soon.

It seemed my speculations were true this time, for almost as soon as I stepped outside I saw his dark form outlined against the snowy white that covered all the rosebushes and trees, and lay piled thickly on the ground. He turned almost at once; the wind caught at the hem of his cloak, but as always the edges of the hood moved not at all.

"Rhianne. You are quite sure you're well enough to be out in this?"

"Of course," I replied stoutly. It wasn't that bad, actually. Although an icy wind blew, my own cloak protected me well enough, and the snow had stopped falling, save for a wayward flake here and there. "The fresh air tastes wonderful."

"I wasn't aware that air could have a taste."

"Of course it can. Today it is crisp and cold, like mint."

"Ah." He turned so he faced into the wind, and I wondered how much he felt within the muffling hood, whether the crisp air I had just described even made it in that far so he could feel or taste it. "There is a bit more shelter from the wind down at the end of this alley, where the oak tree grows. Let us walk that way."

"Lead on," I told him and then stepped close, so I could slip my gloved hand in his. I felt a tremor go through him as our fingers twined around one another, but he did not try to pull away. Instead, his grip tightened on mine before he began to guide me to the spot he'd indicated.

The wind did seem to howl a little less here, the oak tree's spreading branches offering some shelter even though they were bare of leaves. Above us the grey bulk of the castle loomed, a darker shade against the sullen sky. Although the snow had let up for a time, I guessed it would not hold off for much longer, and I was thankful I had decided to meet Theran now instead of waiting to see if the day improved any.

He stood quietly beside me, hand still in mine as he gazed over the now-barren garden. I wondered what he was thinking.

"So is it all true?" I asked.

"Is what true?"

"The story you read to me last night, about the Althuri. Did those who practiced magic truly have a strain of blood in them that wasn't quite human?"

"So it is claimed." He let go of my hand and made rather a show of pulling his cloak more closely to him. "Certainly I would like to believe that the perpetrator of my particular curse was something less than human."

So many questions I wanted to ask. Since I had had very little luck along those lines, I held my tongue, thinking on the best way to approach this. "Did mages do a lot of that? Cursing people, I mean."

"If it suited them, or if they were paid well enough to do it. Some claimed to take the high road and not indulge in such dark matters. However, it seemed in the end most of them would cast those sorts of black spells, if it suited them or enough money changed hands."

"And—and this mage," I ventured, trying to ignore the chill seeping up through my boots. "Did he cast the curse of his own volition, or was he paid to do it?"

"Oh, entirely of his own volition." The words sounded brittle enough to break off and shatter in the icy wintry air.

"He must have been very angry with you."

"I suppose he was."

"Why?"

"I cannot tell you that."

I was actually surprised he'd told me as much as he had. Getting him to divulge the reason for the casting of the curse was expecting a bit much. Still, I now knew one thing. Whatever had happened, whatever had gone wrong, it sounded personal somehow.

"We should go in," he said abruptly. "It's beginning to snow again. See?" And he lifted one black-clad hand to catch some of the falling flakes, which melted as soon as they touched the leather covering his palm.

"It's not that bad yet. I like the snow."

"It can be lovely...if one is safely watching from indoors. And you are only just risen from your sickbed."

"It wasn't that kind of sickness," I pointed out. "I never had a fever. The cold should not matter so much. Besides, surely you don't really feel the cold. Your hands are always so warm."

"Oh, I can feel it. It may not affect me the same way it affects you, but that is not to say that I am entirely comfortable in it."

I gazed up at him, at the tall figure wrapped in its heavy robes. The wind had begun to pick up, and despite my protestations otherwise, I knew I could not stay out here much longer. Not unless I had another layer of clothing to shelter me from the bitter cold.

"Two may be warmer than one," I said, and before I could lose my nerve I went to him, burrowing into his robes so they spread around me. The wool of his doublet was warm and slightly scratchy against my cheek as I laid my head against his chest and wrapped my arms around his waist.

His breath went in and he went still, so still I wouldn't have known he still breathed, save for the beating of the heart within his breast. And then his arms were around me, holding me close, as I let the heat from his body warm me through, making it seem as if I stood outside on a hot summer day, and not a raw snowy morning in mid-Novedre.

"Rhianne..."

I didn't know if he'd said my name aloud or whether I'd just imagined it, so soft were those syllables as they were whispered into the icy air. Perhaps I should have said something as well, but for the moment I only wanted to stay within the protective circle of his arms, only let his warmth keep me safe from the storm. But then I realized how soaking wet my feet were, how the combined weight of both our cloaks still wasn't enough to keep out every piercing draft.

Very gently, he released his hold on me and stepped back. "We must go in. You should not be out in this."

Away from the heat of his body, I could feel every searching gust of wind, every sharp prickle as the snowflakes blew past the hood of my cloak and bit my exposed skin. "Y-you may be right," I stammered.

I thought I heard him mutter something under his breath, but I could not make out the words. He reached for me again. This time, though, he did not draw me against him, but rather lifted me up so my feet were safely out of the ever-drifting snow. Bearing me thus, he carried me through the garden and on into the shelter of the castle.

Something in his strength shocked me. For whatever reason, I had not thought to equate his unnatural form with unnatural might, but he lifted me as if I weighed nothing, and while I was slender enough, I was also tall and well built, and certainly should have constituted something of a burden to a man of normal strength. But Theran was certainly not normal...and most would not call him a man.

He set me down once we were inside and closed the door to the garden behind us. "Better?"

I nodded, although it was scarcely warmer inside than it had been outside. "I s-suppose that is enough fresh air for now."

"I believe so...and I also believe Sar will not be happy when she learns how thoroughly you've been chilled. Look," he added, and pointed at the hem of my gown, which was sodden with snow. My boots likewise had been soaked through. "You must go upstairs and warm yourself at once."

What I really wanted was to go up to his chambers, to warm myself in front of his fire. But although I had been bold enough to put my arms around him, I didn't quite have the courage yet to make such a suggestion.

"Very well," I said. "May I come to you at dinnertime?"

"Of course."

At least he hadn't hesitated. That was something.

"Until then," I told him, as I took care to keep my tone light. Then I hurried away from him and up the stairs, for truly, my feet felt as if they were still standing in the snow, so soaked had my boots and stockings become.

Through great good luck Sar was nowhere to be seen when I regained my chambers, and so I was able to slip off my sodden footwear and set it before the fire. After that I drew on fresh hose and my good indoor shoes, as I had only the one pair of boots.

Some hours remained, of course, until I could go up to Theran's suite, and oddly enough I had no great inclination to pick up my paintbrush. Perhaps it was only that memories from a dream could not match the reality of the Dragon Lord's arms around me, the heat of his body against mine. The stranger's portrait would have to wait.

Restless, I moved from room to room, stopping now and then to gaze out the windows. The storm had struck in earnest, and I could see nothing but a wall of whirling grey-white. Even down in Lirinsholme people must be sheltering indoors, waiting for the blizzard to pass. Oh, we were used to storms here in the north, but this one was fierce, especially for so early in the year.

*Something else killed them, Rhianne, and you need to find out what it was.*

"Easier said than done," I remarked irritably to the air. "I am somewhat limited in my resources, you know."

A knock came at the door then, and Melynne stepped in with my lunch tray. I thanked her absently, and was about to sit down and begin eating when a thought struck me. "Melynne."

She paused, one hand resting on the door latch. "My lady?"

I regarded her carefully, considering. True, she was young, around my age, and so couldn't have been in service when the previous Bride lived here. The servant girl had to have heard something from the more senior retainers in the castle, though. Back in Lirinsholme, my family kept only the one servant, but even she gossiped with the other scullery maids and pot boys up and down our street whenever she had the opportunity.

"The other Brides," I began, feeling my way toward the question. "Did they all live in these chambers? Or are there other places in the castle where they had their rooms?"

Melynne's eyebrows lifted. "Are the rooms not to your liking, my lady? Perhaps Sar—"

"No—no. My rooms are fine. I was just curious."

"I wasn't here for any of them, my lady."

"No, Melynne, I know that. But perhaps one of the other servants has mentioned something?"

Her hesitation was obvious, but I guessed that Melynne did not have the strength of will to avoid answering a direct question put to her by the lady of the castle. My guess was borne out when she replied, "I—I've heard that there were two other suites used by the Brides. One was in the same tower as his lordship's suite, only two floors below. And the other is in the east tower, at the very top. No one's stayed there for years, though, my lady."

"I expect it's because these rooms are so much more comfortable," I suggested with a smile. No need for her to start wondering why I should be inquiring after such things. "Thank you, Melynne."

She accepted the dismissal gratefully and made her escape. I sat down in front of the fire with the cold meat pie she'd brought and began pondering my options. Attempting to inspect the rooms in Theran's tower would be difficult, since I had no idea how often he came and went from his own suite, or whether he roamed that part of the castle when he was not reading or working on his little devices. It seemed the rooms in the east tower were the place for me to look first.

"Look for what, precisely?" I asked myself, in scornful tones that would have done my sister Therella proud. Surely the place had to have been cleaned out and swept from top to bottom before it was closed up. At least, that is what my mother would have done if she had the largesse to lock up an entire suite of rooms because they were no longer needed.

Still, better to start there, on the opposite side of the castle from Theran's chambers. Luckily, I was not much disturbed during the hours between luncheon and supper, as Sar tended to assume—correctly, most of the time—that I was busy painting.

The paints would have to wait today, although I did stop in the alcove and take a quick peek down at the painting in its corner hiding place. The stranger's aquamarine gaze seemed almost disappointed this time, as if he very much wanted me to make just a little more progress today.

*Tomorrow*, I promised him, and then shook my head at myself. What on earth difference did it make to the painting whether it was finished at the end of this week or two months hence?

*Because two months hence you might not be here to complete it*, said that spiteful voice in my head, the one that sounded a little too much like my sister.

"All the more reason to do some investigating," I told the room, as I wrapped a woolen scarf around my throat as some protection from the chill I knew I would encounter in the corridors. Questions might be asked if I went forth in my cloak, but no one would question the scarf.

As I left I set the tray with its dirty dishes on the floor outside the door. I had done that in the past when I was working and did not want to be disturbed. It seemed the safest way to keep either Sar or Melynne from entering my rooms while I was gone.

I had never been in the east tower; there had been no reason. However, I knew to get there I must descend the steps from my suite all the way to the great corridor that bisected the ground floor of the castle. I had spied the steps leading up to that other tower on more than one occasion, and because of that I knew they were not locked off or otherwise inaccessible. It might be a little tricky to go all the way down and all the way back up without being seen, but I would have to trust that everyone in the castle would be occupied elsewhere. Certainly if I were one of the servants I'd be doing everything in my power to keep at tasks that required close proximity to one of the keep's numerous hearths.

The air that greeted me as I left my rooms was so icy I wondered at the wisdom of my errand. But I had decided up on my course of action, and so I would not let mere discomfort dissuade me from it. Wrapping the scarf more tightly about my throat, I hurried down the stairs, trying to ignore the little puffs of white vapor that rose from my mouth and nose in the chill air.

As I had guessed—and hoped—no one was about. I made it to the base of the stairs without incident and then sprinted down the corridor to the east tower's stairwell. After giving a quick, furtive glance about, I hastened up the stairs.

Of course the abandoned suite had to be located at the very top of the tower. Then again, the exertion helped to keep me warm. This part of the castle clearly had not been lived in for some time—although it was clean enough, and relatively free of cobwebs, I saw no tapestries or paintings, and even the sconces on the walls were bare of candles. I would have to be quick. Getting caught up here in the early dusk of late autumn did not seem very appealing.

At length I reached a landing outside a pair of double doors. Here was a window that let in some wan daylight, along with several icy drafts around its poorly caulked edges. No matter, as I did not intend to linger here.

I put my hand on the door handle, halfway expecting it to be locked. But it gave way easily enough, opening with a slow creak into a space dimly lit by several narrow casements. Like the steps leading to it, the place seemed clean enough, although it smelled faintly of dust and mildew.

Something about the stillness of the place made me want to hold my breath, to tiptoe through it. The furnishings were all covered in some sort of heavy green cloth, but the layout seemed similar to my own chambers—a front room with a divan and several tables, a bedchamber with a large canopied monstrosity and a few more small tables and chairs.

The main difference that I could see was a pair of large bookcases in the front room, built into the wall itself on either side of the hearth. Unlike the bookshelves in Theran's rooms, these were sparsely populated, with only a few lonely volumes left on the lengths of polished oak. I wondered at that, for I would have thought all the books would be collected and brought to the lord of the castle's chambers. Certainly they seemed too valuable to be left here, moldering. No doubt they were the source of the mildew smell.

Despite that, I found myself drawn to them. I moved closer to the shelf on the right and found nothing more ominous than a history of Farendon, along with a tome on the lives of the kings of the realm, and a geography of the continent.

"No wonder they were left here," I murmured, as I replaced the geography—complete with mouse-eaten bindings—back on its shelf.

The left-hand shelf had a collection of slender volumes, and I found myself hoping that perhaps they were diaries. Surely something so personal would have been removed long ago, though. It turned out I was right, as the thin little books proved to be collections of poetry, and a single bound volume of *Mardrake & Evlyn*, a drama Lindell had once said was quite popular in the capital, although Lirinsholme hosted the traveling players who performed such things only once in my memory, and my parents had forbidden me to go.

Well, they weren't here to forbid me now. I grasped the volume and pulled it from the shelf, intending to take it back with me so I could see for myself what was so scandalous about it.

But when I touched the binding, a sensation of such anguish, of such bleak despair, rose from it that I cried aloud and dropped the book. And as I did so, a small piece of paper folded over many times fell out from within its leaves.

Without thinking, I reached for it. As my fingers closed around the paper, more waves of agony seemed to rise from it to ripple up my arm. I gasped, but somehow I could not let go, and instead found myself opening the paper and reading its contents.

Just five words, repeated over and over, in letters so scrawling I had a hard time at first even making them out.

*It has all turned black.*

*It has all turned black.*

*It has all turned black.*

The cold seemed to hit me in a great crashing wave, as if I had been flung into the deepest snowbank in the garden. Then the paper fell from fingers too stiff to hold it, and it dropped onto the stone floor with a rustle like that of a dead leaf. I backed away, gasping, seeing my breath rise as great clouds of grey, an echo of the stormy skies outside.

I didn't know then if the voice I heard came from without, or simply within my head.

*Get out. Get out now!*

No stopping to think. I turned on my heel and fled as if the dread wolves of legend had chased me from the chamber, pounding my way down the stairs until I was safely in the castle's main corridor. Even then I didn't pause, but ran toward the safety, however spurious, of my own chambers. Again, no one was around to question my mad dash through the castle, though the tray was gone when I did finally reach my suite. I flung myself inside and shut the door, then went to the hearth and sank down on the rug in front of it, trembling. I was sure I would never be warm again.

Little by little, though, the fire worked its magic, bringing the feeling back to my numb fingers, to my trembling legs. Just the cheerful crackle of the flames and the soft hiss of a log as it split apart seemed to guide me back to myself. I was back in my rooms. I was safe.

Or was I?

I got to my feet and unwrapped the scarf from my throat. With it gone, I seemed to breathe a little easier.

Had that all been a vision, some kind of waking dream? Perhaps, but I had never experienced such a thing before, and it all seemed too clear to me, unlike my dreams. Even the true ones had a bit of fuzziness around the edges. But everything in that desolate room had been all too real, from the chill air leaking around the badly sealed windows to the mouse-chewed edges of the book bindings. The scent of mildew seemed to rise in the air and I choked, fleeing to my bedchamber so I could pour myself some water from the pitcher that always sat at my bedside.

What did it mean, "it has all turned black"? Had one of my predecessors written those words, seized by some dark madness I couldn't begin to comprehend?

To tell the truth, I could not understand any of it...and I somehow doubted illumination would come any time soon.

# Chapter Thirteen

As much as I had looked forward to seeing Theran again, climbing the stairs to his chambers after my exertions of that afternoon seemed to take every last ounce of strength I possessed. At least I had changed out of my dusty garments and brushed my hair. I knew I looked presentable enough, even though I felt as if I'd been dragged behind a pack of wild horses for several miles.

Theran seemed to notice at once; almost as soon as I had stepped into his suite he asked, "Are you sure you're feeling quite well?"

"Yes," I said automatically, although that was far from the truth.

"Then let me fetch you some hot wine."

That sounded good, for several reasons. I was chilled again, and I knew the warmth of the wine would help to dispel some of the icy sensations from my fingers and toes. Also, if I drank enough wine, perhaps I could forget that forlorn room, and the wave of black despair that had threatened to engulf me, although I knew it was not of my own making.

"Thank you," I told Theran, since it seemed he expected some response.

He went from me and busied himself with pouring a good measure of wine into a goblet. I noticed he had already prepared a glass for himself; it sat on the low table in front of the divan. When he handed the wine to me, I took it gratefully and swallowed perhaps more at once than was wise. It was warmer than I had thought, too, and I gasped a little as it went down.

"Slower, perhaps," he said. "There is plenty more."

"I am sorry. It is just so very cold..."

*Cold as night...cold as death...*

I blinked, wondering where that had come from, and said hurriedly, "That is, I suppose I am still not quite used to how cold a stone castle can be. Our house in town is made of wood."

"As is most of the town. Yes. I suppose it will take some getting used to. But you have a whole winter for that."

"I suppose I do."

He made no answer, but instead indicated the small chamber with its round dining table where we always took our meals together. I took my goblet and went to sit down.

In silence I watched as he ladled something that appeared to be venison stew onto my plate. What possessed me then, I could not say. Perhaps it was merely that I had collected yet another secret to keep from him, and the one evil seemed lesser than the other. I blurted out, "I found the graveyard."

No reply, although I thought I saw a tremor go through the hand holding the ladle before he replaced it in the tureen that dominated the center of the table. Then, "I know."

"You do? But Sar—"

"Yes, I suppose Sar told you that your secret was safe, and that I need never be told. I am the master here, Rhianne. Do you really believe I do not know when my wife goes afield and has to be fetched back by one of my servants?"

The words sounded calm enough, but I heard the flicker of anger along the edge of those smooth tones.

"I—I am sorry," I faltered, and he lifted a hand.

"Spare me your apologies. I have no need of them. It is unfortunate, I suppose, but you have a questing spirit, one that seeks answers. I would have been more surprised if you had not found it."

Unsure of what to say, I spooned a portion of venison stew into my mouth, though I confess I barely tasted it. After I had swallowed, I said, "I did not seek it out, Theran. Truly."

"I believe you. That doesn't change the fact that it is dangerous for you to venture forth alone. There are boars and bears in the forest, as well as hidden gorges and ravines. You could have been hurt. You will not do such a thing again."

"You—you care whether I am hurt?"

The hood shifted toward me. "Of course I care. I may be a monster, but I am not that much of one."

"I don't think you are a monster."

He seemed unable to reply to that, instead using his own spoon to shift the food around on his plate. At length he said, "You might think differently, if you knew the truth."

"What truth? The truth as you see it, or as I do? I came to you willingly enough this morning, did I not? Are those the actions of someone who believes her husband is a monster?"

"You were chilled—you did not know what you were doing."

"I knew exactly what I was doing," I said, and pushed back my chair. "And if you don't believe me, come here, and I shall show you all over again."

A chuckle, but even to me it sounded forced. "No need, Rhianne. Sit, and finish your dinner."

Always blocked, always denied somehow. I was not sure exactly how he did it, except that of course he'd had many years of practice. Was I the first of his wives to speak in such a way, to invite the intimacies a husband and wife should share? Surely that couldn't be true, and yet something in his manner seemed to speak of hesitancy, of not knowing the best way to respond to my sallies.

He was not the only one unsure of what to do next. I suppose it was foolish of me to believe he would drop everything and come and take me in his arms, and yet disappointment surged through me. Although my exertions of earlier in the day should have encouraged my appetite, I found myself pushing the food around on my plate in a listless manner that certainly would have earned me a rebuke if I had still been at home to receive it.

Not to say he didn't notice; I felt rather than saw his eyes on me, but he made no comment. I did force a mouthful down from time to time, more because I knew he expected it than because I wished to.

After what felt like an interminable silence, I asked, "Who puts the flowers on their graves?"

"What?"

"When I was in the—the clearing. Some of the graves had flowers on them. Who puts them there? Sar?"

"I do."

"You do?" Startled, I looked up from my plate at him, although of course I could see nothing but the low-dipping hood, the shadows where his face should be.

"You sound surprised."

"I—well, that is—" I floundered, struggling for the correct thing to say, and had to settle for, "That is to say, I did not think you ventured out of the castle all that often."

"I do...but not at a time of day when you would notice. I see very well in the dark."

There being no good reply I could think of for that, I made some sort of noncommittal sound and drank a little more of my spiced wine. By then it was hardly more than lukewarm.

"They deserve some sort of remembrance," he added, surprising me once more. I would have thought he'd let the subject go. "So few recall their names, or faces. It has been such a very long time."

A long time, indeed. If what Theran had told me was true—and I had no reason to believe it was not—some of those young women had been sleeping in that quiet ground for almost five hundred years. No one spoke of the Brides once they were gone from Lirinsholme, and if their families grieved, they did so in secret.

*As mine must be grieving now*, I thought, and swallowed. It had been so easy to get caught up in my life here, in that oddly compelling portrait which was even now hidden in my chambers, in my interactions with Theran and my conflicted feelings for him. Here all was new and different, but in Lirinsholme, my family would be going about their normal round of life, and so noting my absence far more keenly. I could only hope that time would begin to smooth over the wound, even though it could never heal completely.

"It is very kind of you—" I began, but Theran waved a hand.

"It is the least I can do, considering."

*Considering what?* I wanted to ask. Such avenues of questioning had been shut down before, and so I did not think I would have any more success this evening. Instead, I gave up picking at the food on my plate and stood, then moved toward the windows. Of course I could see nothing at this time of day, save the glint of a snowflake here and there as it touched the uneven panes of glass before melting quite away.

From the sound of wood scraping against stone, I could tell Theran had stood as well and come toward me, although he stopped a few paces away.

"What do you see?" he asked.

I didn't reply at first, but only stared out into the blackness. Was this what that unknown Bride had seen so many years ago—unending dark, with no hope of light or relief? What else could have driven her to write those same words over and over again?

*It has all gone black.*

"I see nothing," I said at length. "But I do feel a dreadful draft coming through your windows." And I turned away and went to him, again pressing myself into his warmth, wrapping my arms around his waist.

This time he did not seem quite as startled. He allowed me to stay there for a moment, and I felt his arms settle about me, the drift of heavy wool as it covered me from shoulder to toe. So much more comfortable that way, and in here, in the warmer air, I could smell something sweet and aromatic in the fabric.

"You are a forward little thing, aren't you?" he murmured, almost absently, as if he hadn't intended to speak the words aloud.

"I'm not, really," I remarked. "My sister Therella was the one who paid more attention than was seemly to young men. My mother quite scolded her for it. I suppose she might scold me for my behavior now, only since I am your wife, there is really nothing untoward about me coming to you like this."

"Save that I am the Dragon of Black's Keep."

"Well, save that, of course."

He actually laughed aloud, and I felt his breast move beneath my cheek as he did so. The arms encircling me tightened for a moment, but then he gently extricated himself from my embrace, holding me a handspan away from him, as if he wanted to see me more clearly.

"What is it that you want, Rhianne?"

That was a good question. I wanted to know what had happened to all his former wives…I wanted to know the source of the bottomless despair I'd felt when I read that pitiful scrap of paper…I wanted to sit down and talk all this over with Lilianth in real life, and not just in a dream. So many things I wanted, but I realized there was one thing I wanted more than all else. Something I could have that was real, and not just a memory from a dream.

"I want to kiss you," I told him.

"You cannot." The words were cold, implacable.

"Do you mean I cannot possibly want such a thing, or simply that you will not allow me to kiss you? You kissed me on our wedding day, if you will recall."

"That was different."

"True, in that I did not know you then, and did not welcome the kiss. But now it is some months later, and I know very well what I want."

"You cannot possibly know what you are asking. You have no idea what would be kissing you back."

A rough brush of skin, a mouth whose shape did not feel like any other mouth. These things I remembered clearly enough, and yet now they did not trouble me the way they had on that bright day back in Augeste, when I had feared I would die that same night. Now I knew that mouth belonged to someone who cared about my safety, who had given me the gift of time enough to paint, who had tried, in his own rather prickly and difficult way, to make me feel as if I had a home here. And all that put together, and all the time I had spent in his company and listened to his voice and come to understand what a quick mind hid under that hood...all that and so much more had brought me to where I stood now.

"I have some idea," I said stoutly. "The Dragon of Black's Keep. I know you are as no other man. And I am glad of that, because I would want you no other way."

He stood still, and I saw his gloved fingers knot themselves into the heavy wool of his robes, as if he were wrestling with himself, struggling for his next words. When he did speak, his tone was harsh.

"And is this some fancy you have conceived, that if you kiss the dread Dragon Lord, then the spell will be broken and the curse will fall away?"

I might not have put it in so many words, but perhaps somewhere in the back of my mind I had fostered a hope that such a thing would be true. After all, when one is already living a life that might have come out of a storybook, it is no great stretch to think such actions might be the only thing required to reverse some long-ago mage's fearsome spell.

But to say such things aloud seemed a sure way to invite Theran's ridicule, and so I said nothing, but only glanced away from him, as if doing so might shield me from any further comments on the subject. I should have known better.

"Let me disabuse you of that notion," he went on. "Even in your tale of Alende and Allaire, Alende was doomed to his deformity for the rest of his life. In his case at least that life was mercifully short, no greater than the span of a normal man. I have not that grace. Neither will a single kiss—even when bestowed by such a lovely young woman—relieve me of this torment. Were it that simple, the curse would have been broken years ago."

Each word seemed to be a death knell for the simple hope I had let bloom in my breast. And yet something in his words told me there was a solution...if only I could think of what it might be.

I lifted my chin so that I stared directly into his face—or at least where his face should be, could I but see it. "And what if I wanted to kiss you only because you are my husband, and I as your wife should have that right?"

"I would say that ours is not the first marriage made for reasons which have nothing to do with love...and it will not be the last."

That remark, in its casual cruelty, made tears sting at the back of my eyes. I blinked; I did not want him to see how he had hurt me. I took a breath, willing myself to stay calm. "And I would say, my lord, that although you have ruled this castle for five centuries and more, and I am only a woman with but two decades to her name, still I am wiser than you. At least I am willing to admit to the truth of what lies between us, even if you would deny it."

Then I truly knew I could not bear to be in his presence any longer, and I ran past him, out the door and down the steps, and finally back up the staircase that led to my own rooms. I rushed through the outer chamber and flung myself on the bed, weeping noisily, letting the tears flow until my pillowcase was quite damp with them. As if my own misery summoned it, a cloud of dark anguish seemed to descend upon me, choking me with its insufferable pressure, until I gasped and flung myself off the bed, going to the window and pressing my cheek against the icy panes. Something about that chill touch brought me back to myself, and I shook my head.

What was wrong with me? Had I, by going to those deserted chambers, unwittingly awakened some demon that would now haunt me with its despairing presence?

I didn't know. I only knew that although I should sleep, I could not bear to shut my eyes, in case I fell into darkness and never awoke again. Instead I went to my worktable and feverishly went about setting up my paints, and then used the single lit candle by my bedside to touch off all the others in all the sconces and candelabras around the room so it was illuminated as brightly as I could make it.

The sharp scent of the linseed oil also helped to clear my head, and with a jaw gritted in determination I pulled out the portrait and set it on its easel before I turned to freshen the pigments required. I still wasn't entirely satisfied with the set of his mouth, nor the tiniest etchings of laugh lines on either side of it. If I focused on such minutiae, perhaps I could forget Theran's cruel words, his refusal to allow any sort of intimacy between us.

But my hand trembled, and I forced myself to pause and take a few bracing breaths before permitting myself to daub any paint on the canvas. No point in making foolish mistakes simply because I hadn't allowed enough time to pass so I could calm myself sufficiently.

Whether there would ever be enough time for such a thing wasn't a concept I wished to contemplate at the moment.

*Do not think of that. Think only of that hint of a shadow at the corner of his mouth...darken the tint ever so slightly...not too much, or it will simply look dirty...*

And so on. It did help to distract me somewhat. However, after a time I began to think I should have focused on something less troubling, such as the collar of his doublet, because all that time spent staring at the stranger's mouth only led me to remember my odd dream, and how he had felt far too real... if only until I awoke.

Still, he had not been afraid to kiss me.

*Of course not*, I chided myself. *Because you have made him up completely out of your imagination. With all the time you've spent staring at this portrait, it would have been more surprising if you hadn't dreamt of him sooner or later.*

True enough, I supposed. I set down my paintbrush and tilted my head to one side, examining the changes I had just made. It did look better now, although I would have to inspect it in daylight—assuming there was much light when the sun rose again. The wind was howling in earnest now, wailing as it blew past my window.

Only that wasn't the wind. Oh, part of it, of course, but above that came the high, keening cry I had heard before, when the lord of the castle launched himself into the air in his changed form. That first time it had been my doing, and I feared it was the conflict between us which drove him forth now.

I put my hands up to my ears to blot out the sound, crying, "No, gods, no, please stop!"

Of course he could not hear me, far away as he was in the wind and the storm. I could not hope to work now, could do nothing but fling myself across the room and onto my bed, where I scrambled underneath the covers and clutched the pillows around my head.

Even that was not enough; the sound seemed to somehow pierce its way through to my very brain. All I could do was huddle there and hope it would stop. Eventually...hours or minutes later, I could not say...the keening seemed to move off and then die away completely. At first I did not stir, fearing that it might return, but as time wore on I realized he truly had gone. Only then did I slip out from the spurious shelter of my bed.

There could be no more thought of painting this night. I had learned my lesson not to leave the portrait or any of my paints sitting out, for fear of rousing suspicions. Yes, I had an innocuous painting of the bare gardens in progress so as to throw the casual observer off the scent, but that subterfuge would only work as long as no one inspected my palette too closely. It was clear that the pigments used in the garden painting differed greatly from the flesh tones I employed in my portrait of the stranger.

So I tidied things as best I could, and after I was done with that, moved about the room, blowing out the candles until only the one on my bedside table remained lit. Somehow I couldn't bear to extinguish that one. I didn't want to be left alone in the dark.

And as I prepared myself for bed, I tried not to think of those anguished cries in the night, and how it had to have been our confrontation that put him in such a desperate state. What else could it have been?

It seemed I had wept all that day's tears, however, and when I lay down at last I stared up into the dim canopy above my bed with curiously dry eyes. Was I to blame here, for reaching out to him, or was his misery no one's fault but his own?

I found I did not want to know.

Melynne came the next morning with my breakfast, looking more subdued than usual, despite the spurious cheer of a clear morning. The blanket of snow on the castle and the surrounding gardens sparkled so much it appeared to have been dusted with diamonds, and if it were not for the tumultuous night which had preceded it, I might have greeted so glittering a day with more enthusiasm than I was currently able to muster.

Whether the servant girl had picked up on my own dreary mood, or whether she looked so downcast because she, too, had her sleep disturbed by the Dragon's ragings, I had no way of knowing. Once or twice she appeared on the verge of saying something and then seemed to hold her tongue, as if thinking better of it.

At last, exasperated by her hovering—normally she would leave the tray and then come back for it later, instead of waiting for me to finish my meal—I snapped, "Well, what is it, Melynne? You have the look of someone who has something to say, so out with it."

She gave a furtive look around the room, almost as if she expected someone to be eavesdropping on our conversation.

"Well, my lady, we aren't supposed to speak of such things, but..."

"But what?" Was she going to mention Theran's raging of the night before? I somehow doubted it, but I had also begun to realize I knew very little of how other people's minds worked.

"It's...well, it's only that my cousin Nan spoke with Linnart the carter when he came up to Greyton day before last, when the weather was clear, and he said he had news of your family." Again she gave another one of those sidelong glances around the room. Perhaps she thought Sar had secreted herself within a fold of the draperies so she might overhear what we were saying.

I couldn't be bothered with that. News of my family? From Melynne's appearance, it couldn't be anything good. Perhaps my father had suffered a relapse, or my mother had caught a fever. And what of all the slips and falls and other accidents that might befall young girls who had a predilection for charging up and down the stairs like a herd of wild horses?

"What is it?" I demanded. "Are they well? What has happened?"

Obviously comprehending the path my thoughts had taken, Melynne replied at once, "Oh, no, my lady. Nothing like that. They are all well, as far as Linnart knew. Only he thought it was something amusing that Liat Marenson had been dangling after you, and now he's apparently gone and gotten engaged to your sister Therella!"

If meek little Melynne had slapped me across the face, I could not have been more surprised. For the space of a few breaths I could only sit there and stare at her, thinking I must have heard incorrectly. "Master Marenson, the wool merchant?" I managed at last.

"The same. The rumor is that the wedding is planned for Midwinter."

Less than a month away. He didn't waste time, did he? I reached for my cup of cider, hoping to wash some of the sick taste from my mouth. Therella was not quite eighteen. And they were going to marry her off to Liat Marenson, a man of forty-five? These things happened more often than they should, of course, but I had not thought my parents would subject Therella to such a marriage.

"Thank you, Melynne," I said faintly. "I think I would like to be alone now."

She dipped a curtsey, expression neutral, but I thought I saw the curiosity in her eyes. No doubt it was fairly obvious that I was less than pleased by her news. "Of course, my lady."

Once she had gone, I rose and went to stand in front of the fire, but its warmth did little to dispel the chill that seemed to have settled in my bones. Liat Marenson and Therella? Why in all the gods' names had my parents allowed such a thing to happen?

Surely the thousand gold crowns they'd been given in exchange for me couldn't have been spent so rapidly. It would take a household far more profligate than ours to run through such a sum in so short a span of time. There seemed to be only one other logical explanation, even if I didn't want to admit it.

My sister had wanted the match.

She had always been far more interested in young men—and, apparently, the not-so-young—and always talked of what it would be like once she set up her own household. While I used what little free time I had to sketch the streets around us or the people I saw from day to day, her hands were always busy with a needle, whether embroidering a pillowcase or tatting a length of lace to trim a chemise. All these bits and pieces she stored away against the day when she would be mistress of her own house.

I could almost picture it, even now. A chance meeting when she went to market, or an encounter at the home of an acquaintance. An apology for her sister's outlandish behavior, with the intimation that of course Therella herself would never have acted in such a way. Perhaps then a few carefully placed compliments, and Liat Marenson would have fallen into her hand like a ripe plum. I could not even allow her youth as a rebuttal against such behavior, as I'd seen such cunning in the past, during times when she managed to cajole even our father into agreeing to some scheme or another. Our mother, of course, saw through such duplicity, but I could not expect a man being flattered to have that sort of insight.

No, when I thought of it that way, I supposed it was no real surprise. Therella wanted comfort, and luxury if she could have it; a man more than twice her age was a good enough bargain, if by such an agreement she would be mistress of one of Lirinsholme's finest houses. Had she been glad, then, when I botched things so completely, and finished the job by giving myself over to the Dragon of Black's Keep?

Such a thought was perhaps uncharitable, but I knew my sister well enough that I did not put it past her. At least she would have a husband who wanted her, or thought he wanted her. Whereas I...

I leaned my head against the mantel, once again feeling myself perilously close to tears. This was ridiculous. Could I look forward to a winter where all I did was weep, and wring my hands over my situation?

"Oh, damnation," I said aloud, and pushed myself away from the fireplace. The day was clear, and the light was good. I should not waste it, but should go back to my painting.

By some effort of will I did return to my chamber, where the white morning light sent everything into clear relief. By its unforgiving glare I could see that I had been a bit too heavy-handed the evening before, and some of my work would have to be undone.

I did not precisely sigh, but I did feel my mouth tighten as I laid out my pigments and brushes once again. And as the light touched the stranger's painted eyes, it seemed almost as if they met mine with some sort of secret amusement, as though he were laughing at some joke unknown to me.

"If it's that amusing, I wish you would share," I remarked with some acerbity, dipping my paintbrush into the linseed oil so I might freshen the pigment I required for a flesh tone paler than the one I had used the previous night. "I think right now I could do with a good laugh."

But of course the painted mouth did not move, and nothing happened except I experienced that same sensation of creeping despair as the day before. This time, perhaps, it was subtly different, in that it was less amorphous, more an ache within, as I thought of Theran, and how he had rebuffed me.

It was the cry of a child, really, that plea of "but I love you!" These things were not always so simple. Love given was not always returned. A lesson I would rather not have learned, of course, but...

But nothing. It hit me then, cold and rough and painful as the winds that had buffeted me in the garden the day before. I loved him, but he did not love me.

And gods, the ache of that, the realization of how I wanted him— the need cramping my very limbs so the paintbrush fell from my nerveless fingers, and I dropped to my knees, doubled over as if someone had hit me in my midsection. I found myself hunched on the rug, body shaking with the sheer misery of it. What could I do, when he seemed so immovable? How could I go on in such a state?

I had no answers, and none came to me. After what might have been a few minutes or a few hours, the spell seemed to pass, and I wearily got to my knees, moving with a stiffness that spoke of someone four times my age.

The painting stared across the room at me, but I saw no compassion in those still, perfect features. Indeed, the slight tilt to his mouth seemed more a mockery, and I turned away, knowing I could not look at it a second longer.

I crossed to the door and slammed it, shutting the painting away.

If only I could do the same thing with my pain.

# Chapter Fourteen

I resolved from then on not to dine with Theran in his chambers. In the past we had quarreled and made up, but I saw no resolution to our current impasse. I did not have the steadiness of mind to sit down with him, knowing he could never give me what I wanted. And so I made excuses that sounded even feeble to me when Sar came by to ask if I would care to change for dinner.

Of course she knew the Dragon had circled overhead the night before, and so she also must know that all was far from well between us. To her credit, she did not press me, but said she agreed that I was looking pale, and that perhaps I should go back to bed for a while; she would send up a tray.

I seized on this opportunity for solitude and thanked her, and she went away soon enough. Whether she'd seen this particular little drama play out before, I had no idea. I didn't want to know.

Perhaps I was the only one foolish enough to develop feelings for the Dragon Lord. Perhaps all those other Brides had seen him for the monster he was. Monster within and without, unfeeling, incapable of love.

No, I could not believe that. I would not. We had had enough interactions that I had seen something of his quickness of wit, his appreciation for beauty, even if he believed he possessed none of his own. It was not his fault that I was not clever enough, or pretty enough, or interesting enough, to engage his affections. Who was I really, but a foolish girl from a simple family, a girl who fancied herself a painter but in actuality had done nothing but disgrace her kin?

Misery seemed the best company for me then, and I let it overtake me, falling into it like a swimmer diving into a deep, cold lake. I did not question it. How could I, when I knew I had done everything wrong since the moment I first stepped foot inside Black's Keep?

Days passed in a similar fashion, days in which I barely struggled out of bed to eat a few bites before crawling back under the covers like a wounded animal. This was not even like the time when I had spent so many hours asleep; at least then I had some recollection of time passing, although I spent much of it in slumber. Now, however, I seemed to drift in and out, barely aware of the world around me. I thought Melynne came in from time to time, and Sar, but I could hardly be certain. They seemed like something out of a dream, insubstantial as ghosts.

Once I thought I even heard *his* voice raised in question outside my door, but this time I did not answer, and he did not come in. And then perhaps an exchange with Sar that I only partially overhead, something about it being "far too soon." What was too soon, I had no idea.

At length, though, I roused myself from my torpor, fighting away the cobwebs within my mind as if they were physical things. My legs felt shaky and my head as light as the time when I was ten and had contracted a rare case of tertian fever. But I had won out against that, and I would not let this...whatever it was...get the better of me.

I tottered out of bed and gazed around my chamber as if I had never seen it before. All seemed more or less in order, and once again my instinct for self-preservation seemed to have won out, for the stranger's portrait had been safely stashed away in its hiding place. I had no clear recollection of doing so. The important thing was that at least I had remembered enough to put it away.

The water in the basin was almost freezing, but I splashed it on my face anyway, knowing that it would help to shock me into some semblance of alertness. Toothbrush, comb. I could not remember the last time I had used either one of them. They helped to make me feel a little more human, although what I really needed was a hot bath. Soon. I could have Sar call for one after I had eaten.

Stockings, chemise, gown...I struggled with all of it as if I had never dressed myself before, never tied a garter or struggled with the lacings on a dress. This one at least fastened up the sides and not the back, so I could get myself into it without having to ring for help.

Once I was more or less decently attired, I went to the outer chamber and pulled on the bell in the far corner. Usually I did not have to resort to these summons, as Melynne and Sar seemed to know instinctively when I needed assistance. Now, though, they had absented my chamber, almost as if they were fearful of catching some sort of dread disease from me. Perhaps I was ill, although I did not feel particularly unwell. Tired, and the darkness had only retreated to the corners of my mind and not disappeared entirely. But that was not the same thing as being physically sick.

Sar appeared within a few minutes, obviously surprised to see me up and about. She cleared her throat. "What is it you wish, my lady?"

"Some food, I think...and a bath before I retire this evening. What time is it?"

A quick, uncertain glance at the window, where the familiar grey snow light showed beyond the diamond-shaped panes. "Just past the third hour of the afternoon."

Too late for luncheon, and early for supper, but my stomach had turned into a ravenous beast, awake now that I had roused myself. I could not bend to convention. "Something solid, I think. No soup. And bread. I would like some bread."

"Of course, my lady."

I moved toward the casement and observed the familiar contours of the garden, all blanketed in snow. Then again, what had I expected to see? The snow seemed to have stopped for the moment, but the skies were so low it appeared they touched the tops of the towers, and I guessed snowflakes would begin to fall within the hour. "And what is the day?"

Her hesitation was obvious this time. "The second of Decevre, my lady."

Perhaps my sudden faintness could have been attributed to my hunger, as I had not eaten for longer than I could recall. I doubted it, though. The second of Decevre? Had I really spent the greater part of a fortnight drifting in and out of darkness, noting little of the world around me, eating and drinking only enough to keep myself from fading entirely away?

I had thought my gown felt a little loose, but so many of the gowns in my wardrobe did not fit me precisely, hand-me-downs that they were, that I hadn't thought anything of it. But if I had eaten little for the past two weeks, then it only stood to reason the dress would have enough slack in it that I would have to pull the laces so tight they almost overlapped.

Somehow I managed to gather myself and remark lightly, "No wonder I feel so ravenous I could eat a boar!"

"Then let me see to that at once, my lady. His lord—that is, there was smoked pheasant last night, and there is a goodly portion left over. I'll bring it up directly."

I thanked her and she left, clearly relieved to be given the errand. For myself, I still had a hard time believing her words, though of course she had no reason to give me anything but the truth. Two weeks? A fortnight gone, slipped by while I had drifted in and out of darkness, knowing nothing of the world.

A sudden impulse made me rush to the portrait and retrieve it from its hiding place. I touched the surface gingerly; it felt dry enough, with none of the tackiness of freshly laid pigments. Clearly I had not set paintbrush to the thing for quite some time.

"I'm so, so sorry," I murmured, though why I felt it necessary to apologize to the portrait, I couldn't say. Perhaps he had begun to appear a little too real to me, as if he deserved some sort of explanation for being neglected for so long. Certainly such a rationalization seemed no less illogical to me than anything else I had experienced lately. "I'll return to you this evening, just as soon as I've had something to eat." And I ran a finger along one edge of the canvas, as if in a caress, before I set it back in its hidey hole.

Sar appeared soon after, bearing a tray positively brimming with food. Not just the pheasant she'd promised, but whipped turnips with butter and cunning little rolls studded with currants, and spiced apple compote, and peas covered in more butter.

How I would ever eat it all, even in my current deprived state, I couldn't have begun to guess. It seemed a feast fit for Midwinter. When I sat down to eat, though, I found I was able to devour an alarming portion of the meal, so much so that all I left behind was a bit of the turnips and half a roll.

"Good," Sar said, and it appeared she was somewhat relieved to witness my ravenous appetite. "And you will sleep again now?" She sounded dubious, as if she did not want me to curl up in bed again so soon but knew she would be overstepping her role as my subordinate if she advised against it.

"I think not, actually." I dabbed my mouth with a napkin and set it down. "A bath, I believe, and then I plan to read by the fire." This was only a partial lie; I did desire a bath very much, but after that I planned to return to the painting. I could not make up for two weeks of neglect, of course. Still, a good evening's work would make me feel better about the whole situation.

"I'll have a bath sent up directly." And with that she gathered up the denuded plates and stacked them on the tray before whisking them away.

Knowing her efficiency, I guessed it would not be long before the bath arrived. They would not even have to pump water, but could gather fresh snow from the courtyard and melt that instead. So I did not return to the portrait, but instead drew a chair up to the window and gazed outside, considering.

Two weeks. What had happened during that time? All here at Black's Keep seemed very much as it always had been. Then again, it was a place cut off from the world, keeping much to itself. The weather only served to increase its isolation. Sar had not mentioned the Dragon Lord, and I had not asked. We'd parted on such bad terms, and yet I know it was his voice I had heard through the darkness. No one else had a voice like that, one which seemed to caress every syllable as it was spoken. So obviously he had cared enough to check on me, even if he had not come in to visit my bedside.

I wished I had the courage to go to him, although even if I had possessed such fortitude, I would have waited until the promised bath arrived and I was fit for company once again. But I found myself quailing at the thought of seeing him again, knowing I did not have the words to put right what was between us.

In the storybooks, the words "I love you" held a charm, could act as a cure for any misunderstanding, any slight. But they could not heal the rift between Theran Blackmoor and myself, not if I repeated them a hundred times. And how does one recover from such an admission? I could not take the words back. They would always linger, staining whatever relationship we might salvage after this.

Thankfully, I was saved from further brooding by the arrival of the bath. As wretched as I felt, I could not help but be a little revived by the touch of the warm water against my skin, the scent of the lavender oil reminding me of summer gardens and happier times. I stayed in the bath until the water turned lukewarm, and then reluctantly climbed out and dried myself off in front of the fire. The heat of the flames soothed my bare skin, and I wondered what it would be like to have the warmth of Theran's hands on my naked flesh, to have him touch me as a husband touches his wife.

That cramping need came again, and I clutched the linen towel against my body even as I grasped the mantel with my other hand, seeking to steady myself. I must stop reaching for things I could not have. It was foolish and would only upset the fragile calm I appeared to have reclaimed.

With those admonishments fresh in my mind, I went to the bedchamber and pulled on a clean chemise, followed by my heavy quilted dressing gown. I saw no point in putting on yet another dress when I only planned to stay here in my rooms and paint. My feet went into a pair of fur-lined slippers, and then I was quite ready, save for my hair.

I returned to the hearth and stood in front of the fire, combing out my damp locks, hoping the heat would dry them sufficiently so I could return to the painting soon. It was then that Sar came to check on me and have the bath removed. Once more I watched as the guarded expression on her face softened somewhat when I thanked her for the bath and told her of my plans to do some painting.

She told me that sounded like an excellent notion and went back out, now that the tub had been removed by the two burly servants whose sole job it seemed to be to move the thing from place to place within the castle. I found myself wondering then if Theran used the same tub...but no. That way only lay more tortured imaginings, and I had had quite enough of those.

Better to go into my bedchamber and retrieve the painting, now that I knew myself to be truly alone. The preparation took more time than it usually did, simply because all the pigments on my palette had quite cracked and dried, and I had to carefully measure out a good batch of new ones. Perhaps it was a blessing, for in doing so I had to focus on the task at hand and nothing else.

At length, however, they were ready, and I picked up my paintbrush, surveying the portrait with care. Truly, I had so very little left to do—enhance the shading of the fabric on his right shoulder, to evoke more of the velvet's nap, and perhaps the lightest touch at the crown of his head, to bring out the slightest hint of deep brown in those otherwise raven tresses. But I knew I must keep going until I was satisfied, until I thought the man's image was truly complete.

Even those small things took longer than I had thought, and I paused at one point to light all the candles in the room. Their flickering illumination was oddly comforting, as if the dancing flames were a series of delicate little companions, something to help me believe I was not quite so alone. With them to guide me, I returned to my work.

I did not note the hours passing, and no one came to look in on me. Finally, though, I stepped away from the painting, and realized I was done.

Nothing to add, nothing to change. Nothing to do but stand there and gaze at him, and have those painted eyes regard me in return.

What had I expected? I honestly did not know. My mind had been a stranger lately, slipping from one fancy to another, dwelling in darkness. Perhaps I had thought once the painting was done, the man within it would step forth to rescue me from my solitude.

Of course he did not.

I realized I still held the paintbrush clenched in my fist. Very gently I set it down on the worktable. I knew I should lift up the portrait, set it back in its hiding place, put myself to bed. It had to be very late, even though I had dined early.

I didn't know where the thought came from. It echoed in my mind, soft and insidious, oddly compelling.

*She will tell you what to do next.*

Perhaps once I might have paused to question it. However, in that moment, in my emptiness and despair, I knew where I must go.

Dark and silent the corridors of the castle, only a candle in its sconce from time to time to light my way. I slipped through the dim hallways, moving silent as a shadow, heading back to the place where I had thought I would never return.

Even colder now than it had been, my breath like shards of crystal here in the abandoned chambers. Of course these rooms had no candles, but a full moon poured its icy light through the tall, narrow windows. Somehow I knew where to go.

The book had several loose sheets tucked within its pages. They drifted to the ground like withered leaves, and I knelt to retrieve them. The same scrawling hand, although it seemed slightly clearer than in the note with its five words repeated over and over. More than five words here, too, at least as far as I could tell. I moved to the window, ignoring the chill air that seeped around the frame. I was far colder than that by now; my heart had turned to ice.

*There is only one way out. It seems so simple, now that I understand. A moment of pain, perhaps, but then I will be free of this place. I will fall, and drift on the wind.*

*I will be free of him.*

It seemed so clear to me then. I had finished my painting. What else did I have to hold me to this place? I could go, and there would be a new grave for the snow to drift upon, and then in five or seven years the Dragon would summon another Bride. My heart ached for her, but I knew I could not warn her. Whatever doom came upon her, it must be hers alone.

The latch was stiff, the wood swollen with damp and neglect. I felt a fingernail break upon it, and yet I still struggled with the stubborn piece, somehow telling myself that it must be here. It must be this window, for from here I would drop quickly, with nothing to break my fall. It must be here, for the tower was quite desolate, and no one would mark what I had planned to do until it was too late.

Finally the latch lifted out of its housing, and I tossed it away into a corner before pushing the window open. A rush of freezing night air blew in, lifting my hair away from my face, penetrating my dressing gown as if it were not there. Well, it did not matter. In a few minutes, I would feel nothing at all.

I grasped the casement with both hands, steeling myself for what would come next. As she had said, it would be only a moment of pain. Only a moment.

"Rhianne!"

His voice cut like a whip crack through the empty rooms.

No. I would not allow him to stop me.

Fingers tightening against the rough stone, I pushed myself outward, letting the night wind embrace me.

"No!"

His voice fell behind me, dropped away as I let myself drift into the cold air. White swirls of snowflakes followed me down, wrapping around me. Their touch was gentle, as if in welcome. Why, this would not hurt at all...

But then a rush of movement, the glint of gleaming scales beneath the harsh moon. Clawed hands reached out to grasp me, to pluck me from the wind's embrace and gather me into his own. I struggled, but those inhuman arms were too strong. He held me close to him, and I felt the heat of him go through me, heard the thudding of his heart as it echoed the beating of his mighty wings.

We came to rest in the snow-covered courtyard, and he set me down before the castle's front entrance. A shiver of those enormous wings, and then he was himself again, black robes forever hiding the evidence of his curse.

At another time, in another life, I might have still marveled at what it had felt like to be held in a dragon's embrace. At the moment, though, I only ached with thwarted fury. I should have been free. I had not asked for him to save me.

"Let me alone!" I cried, and ran up the steps into the keep.

What I was thinking precisely, I could not say, except that the one tortured Bride's tower was not the only one in the castle. My own rooms were quite high enough. They would serve.

I heard Theran's heavy boots behind me and knew he had not given up the pursuit. Very well. He was taller and stronger, but I was lighter of foot. And I guessed he did not have room in the narrow tower stairwell to safely change into his dragon form.

So I fled up the steps, taking some of them two at a time, nothing in me but the pounding fear that he might catch me and stop me again before the deed was done. Why he should care whether I ended it, I did not know, but I could not let such concerns slow me down. Not now.

I burst into the corridor only a pace or two ahead of him. It was enough. It would have to be enough. I grasped my door and flung it open, but that small pause proved disastrous, for then he was there, pulling me into his arms, holding me close even though I set my hands against his chest and pushed, attempting with all my strength to free myself from his grasp.

"No, Rhianne," he exclaimed, and his arms tightened around me. "Fight it. You must fight it, my darling."

Once I would have thrilled with joy to hear him address me thus. Now I could only whimper and push against him, writhing like a cornered cat. "You don't need me!" I cried. "You don't want me. Let me go. Let me be free of you!"

Whether he relaxed his hold slightly in shock at my words, or whether I had found just the right angle to slip out of his arms, I did not know, but somehow I found myself sliding away, running once more to my bedchamber, where the windows were set lower and I thought I might have a better chance at flinging myself from them before he could stop me.

But I had not counted on his speed, or perhaps his desperation. I had only gone a few paces before I felt his hands on me again. This time we both crashed to the floor, his weight almost fully on me. Still I pushed forward, crawling on my hands and knees. Not the most dignified way to go to one's doom, perhaps, but in my maddened state I was hardly thinking clearly. I dragged myself a few inches, and kicked backward, catching him in the midsection. He let out a muffled grunt of pain, and I took advantage of his momentary disability to push myself up to a standing position and stagger forward. Only a few more yards...

Behind me I heard him climb to his own feet, his breathing ragged and hoarse. I fully expected him to continue his pursuit, and so I continued to totter toward the window.

He did not, however. He stood rooted in place, staring at the portrait, which I in my unthinking haste had left exposed on its easel.

"Gods," he breathed.

Something in his tone penetrated the fog of madness in my brain. I stopped and turned toward him, watched as one gloved hand reached to his throat. The hood shook slightly, as if he could not believe the evidence of his own eyes.

He said, the words seeming to reverberate throughout the room, "She will see you as you truly are."

I did not know what the words meant, but something about them transfixed me, kept me from pursuing my headlong flight to destruction.

The tower trembled, as if some giant's blow had shaken it to its very core. I stumbled and put out a hand to grasp one of the bedposts, clung to it as the shuddering increased. Behind me I heard a tinkle of broken glass as the goblet on my bedside table crashed to the floor. Theran fell to his knees, hand still clutched at his throat. Even through the commotion I could hear his labored breaths.

Then he let out a wordless cry, piercing as the dragon's keening I had heard before, only this time somehow worse because it emanated from a human throat. At once the shaking eased, and all went still again. I remained clinging to the bedpost, unsure as to whether the earthquake or whatever it was would begin again.

Theran put out both hands on the rug beneath him, using them to force himself slowly upward. For a long moment he stood there, unmoving, and at last he reached up to push back the hood of his cloak.

I gasped then, and let go of the bedpost. Unwise, because my knees trembled so violently I wasn't sure I wasn't about to collapse to the ground myself. It wasn't possible. This had to be yet another vision from a fevered mind.

For the man who stared back at me was the stranger from the portrait.

# Chapter Fifteen

"It can't be," I breathed. "You aren't real."

"Oh, but I am. You have broken the curse, Rhianne."

I shook my head. This was all happening too fast. And yet, somehow as I gazed at him, I felt something within me shift, as if some alien presence removed its hand, allowing me to return to myself. That fog of madness, of delusion, seemed to be burning away, lifting like the morning's mist.

"Yes," he said, and stepped forward before pausing, as if unsure what my next reaction might be. Instead, he gestured toward the painting. "That was the stipulation the mage laid down, so many years ago. I would wear that dread form until the woman I married could see past it to the truth of my being. He did not seem overly concerned that such a thing would ever happen."

No, I supposed I could understand that. After all, the odds were not very good that any given Bride would have any artistic talent, let alone my odd true-seeing dreams. And I supposed that was what the portrait had turned out to be, as if some force had guided that strange gift of mine and channeled it all into the portrait. No wonder it had consumed me...

Seeing him like this, hearing the voice I so loved emerge from the face that had possessed me during the last few months...well, it was almost more than I could bear. I sat down on the bed abruptly, as if my legs could no longer support my weight.

"I know it must be a great deal to take in," he said, as he moved around so he faced me more or less directly. "It's a bit overwhelming for me as well." And he grasped one of the gloves and pulled it off, then stopped to stare down at his exposed fingers as if he had never seen them before.

Not in five hundred years, at least.

He was pale, very pale, as anyone would be whose flesh hadn't seen the sun in centuries. Otherwise, though, he looked exactly as he did in the painting. His hands were beautiful, too, with long, clever fingers. I thought I should very much like to sketch them.

*Later*, I told myself. At least, I supposed there would be a later. We were still husband and wife, even if he was no longer the Dragon.

I could not let myself be distracted, even though every movement, every shift in expression, revealed something of him that I had not yet painted. The portrait had not captured the true glint of his blue-green eyes, or the lift of his eyebrows. And I could not let myself focus too closely on his mouth...

"What happened to me?" I asked him. "Why was I behaving in such a way?"

If the questions surprised him, he did not show it. A slight tightening of his lips, perhaps, before he replied, "It was the curse, Rhianne. It was all the curse."

"Then perhaps you should tell me something of it. Or is that still forbidden?"

"No. All those constraints are gone now as well. I am free."

*Then I will be free...*

Only this was not the freedom that poor, doomed Bride had imagined, and not the freedom the curse had tried to impose on me. I shivered then, thinking of how close I had come to being yet another grave in that quiet, lonely cemetery.

"You are cold," Theran said, apparently noticing my shudder.

"No, I am fine." I realized then I faced him clad in my chemise and my dressing gown, which had come halfway undone during our struggles. To tighten it now would only draw more attention to my disarray, and so I did my best to ignore it. "Please, tell me what happened. I think I deserve to know."

"Of course you do." He turned away from me for a moment so he could fetch one of the side chairs from where it sat under a window, and positioned it so he could sit facing me. "Many years ago, not long after I had inherited Black's Keep, I went to visit Lystare. Like many other young men visiting the capital for the first time, I amused myself with the usual carousing and wild living. It was a chance to taste freedom, if only briefly—I knew at summer's end I must return home and choose a suitable wife from the candidates my father had chosen for me before he died. It was my duty, and I did not have any notion of shirking it. However, I met a young woman in Lystare."

Foolish as it was, I experienced a pang of jealousy at the thought of this unknown woman, even though I knew she must have passed away many years earlier.

Luckily, Theran appeared to notice no alteration in my expression, for he continued without pausing, "Like me, she was new to the capital, and somewhat swept away by the social whirl, one might say. One might also say that her father was rather lax in letting her roam the city so freely, attended by a maidservant only a few years older than she. At any rate, this young woman and I formed an attachment—one, it turns out, she took far more seriously than I. She spoke of her father being a scholar of some sort, but even I, fresh from the country, knew that meant he was a mage. Such a match would not have been suitable, of course, but she did not want to believe that. When it was time for me to return home to Black's Keep, she thought I would take her with me."

"But you did not," I said softly.

His expression darkened, and the heavy lashes swept over his eyes for a moment as he appeared to contemplate some long-ago, bitter memory. "No, I did not. Our parting was not pleasant, but I thought that would be the end of it. We had only known each other for a few months, a summer of idleness and diversions. I liked her, enjoyed her company, but I knew I could not marry her. And I, in my blindness, thought she understood how things were between us."

This time I said nothing, but only watched the fleeting emotions cross his features, and thought how different, and how unexpected, the reality of his face was, even though an hour earlier I could have sworn I knew it by heart.

His fingers clenched on his knees where they rested, the skin so shockingly pale against his dark garments. "I came to Black's Keep...and she followed, begging me to let her stay, to let her be my wife, that her reputation was now ruined because of me, that she feared her father, his reaction when he found out how she had behaved over the summer. I tried to be kind, but I would not allow myself to be cajoled in such a way. I bade her to return to her father in Lystare, beg his forgiveness, and think no more of me. She went away, cursing my name. And then..."

I hardly dared to breathe. I thought I might know what was coming next...or at least I guessed.

"She did not go to her father. Instead, she went forth from this place and into the woods, where she ate some of the toadstools growing there, and died in great agony. It was intentional; have no doubt of that. Her father had schooled her in herb lore, so she knew exactly what she was doing."

My heart ached for her, this unknown young woman who had thrown her life away in such a precipitous fashion. I could not even judge her, for I knew what the depths of despair could drive a person to. I was suddenly ashamed of my earlier jealousy.

Theran hesitated for a few seconds, as if halfway expecting me to say something. When I did not speak, he sighed and went on, "There was little we could do except bury her in the forest, and raise a stone to mark her name. And I sent word to her father in Lystare, so that he might know where his daughter lay, even if he could do nothing to save her."

"Would he not have known anyway?" I inquired. "After all, one would think that a mage of such powers would have some way of discovering his daughter's whereabouts."

Theran lifted his shoulders. "One would think...but he showed no evidence of knowing where she was or what she was doing that entire summer we spent together. He was a man buried in his studies, not seeming much connected with the world. And living now, you know only of legend and rumor, but back when the mages still wielded their powers, those powers were not always consistent. True, the small magics, the harmless ones, all of the mages could perform. But when it came to the greater powers, one man might be able to call down the lightning and storms, and also create terrible curses, while another could find anything that a person had lost, or strengthen a castle's walls so they were well-nigh impregnable. This was partly why at the time there was competition amongst the nobles, to secure a mage whose powers were most useful.

"At any rate, my reaching out to him was a mistake, but it was done out of kindness. I did not wish for the man to forever wonder what had happened to his daughter, even if he did not seem to keep a very good watch on her while she was alive. And then one day he came to Black's Keep."

I thought then of the mage who had cursed Alende, all those years ago, and whether the two men shared the same choleric temperament.

"He blamed me, of course, this Udell of Lystare. Said I had seduced his daughter, given her false promises, lured her away from his protection. None of that was true, but I could not protest too much, for I could see how much pain he was in. Perhaps it was the hurt of someone not knowing what he had until he lost it, but I could not blame him overmuch for that. And then..."

Theran went very still, his gaze looking somehow past me, as if into a dark day now centuries gone. "He laid upon me the curse, saying I should no longer have a form that would tempt young women, but which would instead earn their revulsion. And this form would be mine forever, until I somehow found a wife who could see past my hideous being and recognize my true self." Surprisingly, he smiled then, his expression warming as he looked on me. "He did not think that was something which would ever come to pass."

"But that was not all."

The smile faded at once. "No, it was not. He said also that I, who had avoided marriage, must take a Bride from among the townsfolk of Lirinsholme—"

"Rather rough luck on us, I should say," I interjected. "What did we have to do with it?"

"Only that Lirinsholme has always been under the protection of Black's Keep, and so I suppose he thought you should share my doom."

It still seemed grossly unfair, but I thought then that this unknown mage did not seem to be the most logical of men. I lifted my shoulders.

Theran appeared to take that as his signal to continue. "Having done his work, and taken from me my body, my person, he disappeared. I thought he had done his worst, and although it was dreadful beyond words, I thought I might someday come to live with it. Surely it could not be so difficult as it sounded to find a young woman who would learn to look past what the curse had wrought, to see the man I had once been. But then the first Bride came to Black's Keep."

His hesitation this time was so lengthy I began to wonder whether he intended to say any more. At last he said, "She feared me, of course, but she was treated well, and at first I thought we might be able to get along together well enough, even if she could not love me. Then she began to act oddly... stayed in bed for days at a time, would not speak to me, would not speak to anyone. And then one day, only three months or so after she had come to live in the castle, she flung herself from the tower."

I shut my eyes, trying to will away the image of the young woman's body hurtling from a window, gown fluttering in the air before she smashed into the pavement below. That could have been me.

It almost was.

Theran's voice went on, "I began to see then. I vowed I would not take another Bride. That resolve lasted a good seven or eight years. Then a mysterious wasting illness struck the population of Lirinsholme. I thought it only a coincidence. But immediately afterward the River Theer flooded its banks and devastated half the town. Out of desperation, I called for another young woman to be sent to me. And the illness faded away, and the river receded to its proper course. Obviously, the mage had foreseen I might avoid taking a new wife, and so made sure the consequences of doing so would be far worse than the death of a single woman."

His voice was calm, quiet, as if he were relating events that had happened to someone else. I opened my eyes and saw that his hands were knotted into fists, almost as though he still strained against his past impotence. Obviously his calm was but a surface thing.

"I thought I would be clever this time. This urge to suicide did not come suddenly, but crept in after weeks of malaise. And so when I saw the signs in my second wife, I made sure she was watched around the clock, and never left alone. When she attempted to drown herself while taking a bath, a servant was there to pull her out, and she was kept in her bed, restrained, so she might do herself no harm."

The corners of his mouth lifted in the slightest of smiles, but there was no humor in the expression, only a weary amusement at his naïveté. "That seemed to work for a time...until one of the servant girls slipped on the steps in this very tower and broke her neck. The next day, one of the grooms was thrown from a horse and trampled to death. My steward suffered a palsy and collapsed in the courtyard. And so I understood that here, too, was no refuge. If I prevented my Bride from taking her life, just as poor Lianna had taken hers, then everyone in my household would be made to suffer. Again, I could not sacrifice many lives just to save one. And so I removed the restraints from Elliane myself. The next night she broke the pitcher of water by her bedside and slashed her wrists."

I wanted to shut my eyes again, but I could not. I could not turn away from the agony naked on his face. "It seems a terrible sacrifice for simple heedlessness. You could not have known Lianna looked on your time with her as anything more than the casual amusement you thought it was."

"Perhaps. I was young and foolish, and knew little of young women. I should have taken more care. But even with that, the punishment was...severe. I can only think Udell wanted me to suffer as he had, for me to see a young woman cast herself away and know I could do nothing to stop it." He shook his head. "I cannot begin to understand his madness, and his vengeance. I only knew I was doomed to watch this horror repeat itself through the years, for in cursing me with a dragon's form, he had cursed me with a dragon's longevity as well. And so it went, for more years than I wished to count. Until..."

"Until?"

"Until you came here, Rhianne." Some warmth returned to his features, and the thin lines of his mouth softened. "You seemed different to me, but I tried to tell myself that was only a vain wish. I did not want to become close to you—I only wanted to make sure you were comfortable here until the inevitable time came."

No wonder he had done everything he could to keep some distance between us. He could not allow himself to care, not after so many years, so many deaths.... "I fear I did not take the hint."

"No, you did not, and may the gods bless you for that. I felt the first stirrings in my heart, the first glimmer of hope. And then when you seemed to slip away, when all seemed lost again...." He shook his head. "I could not bear it, and yet I knew I could do nothing."

"And yet you saved me."

"Yes. The gods only know what it was that sent me roaming the corridors this night, for it is not something I often do. But I saw your door ajar and set out to find you. I knew you had gone to Sirella's tower before—"

"And here I thought no one knew anything about that."

"I have my ways of keeping track of people's comings and goings within the keep."

I wondered at that, if it were a part of his dragonish powers, or something to do with all those ingenious little devices in his chambers. Perhaps one day he would tell me. At the moment all that mattered was that he had known where to find me.

"And now—" I began, then stopped, as I was not sure what I had meant to say.

"And now," he said heavily. The aquamarine eyes were fixed on me in an odd mixture of hope and dread. "The curse is broken, and you will always have my thanks for that. I fear you must stay here, for you are the lady of Black's Keep, but I will make sure you have everything you need, all the supplies—"

I stood then and placed my hands on my hips, and stared down at him. "What by all the gods are you going on about, Theran? You *fear* I must stay here? You do not want me?"

His lips parted, and he shook his head. "It is rather that I thought you would not want me. Not after you knew the truth—knew I had been the cause of so much misery and death."

Oh, how could he possibly have gotten it so muddled? I dropped to my knees before him and took his hands in mine. His fingers were cold now, the inhuman dragon heat long gone. I would have to do my best to warm him. "You were not the cause of anything, Theran, and your only guilt—if one could even call it that—was a certain heedlessness, which poor Lianna certainly shared. It was that mage Udell...and if his curse is any indication of the sorts of magic the mages used to perform, then no wonder they were all hunted down and killed! I will stay here, because I am your wife, and I love you. I loved you when I thought a monster was hidden under those robes, and I loved your face when I did not even know it was yours. I fear you are stuck with me, Theran Blackmoor."

The light breaking over his features was like the coming of dawn after a long, cold winter. He grasped my hands and pulled me upright, then gazed down into my face. "You are quite certain?"

"I have never been more certain of anything in my life."

And he took me in his arms, and kissed me, and it was like the kiss from my dreams, only so much better, because this was the real man holding me, the real Theran, everything so vivid and true, from the faint taste of wine on his lips to the sweet herbal scent of his robes.

It seemed the most natural thing in the world for my body to press itself against his, for him to fumble with the laces at the neck of my chemise, for the two of us to fall to the bed, our need bringing us together. I understood finally just what I had ached for, as Theran touched me, stroked me, made me cry out his name. And then we were no longer two halves, but a whole that could not be denied, a consummation all the more sweet because I had never dreamed it could truly be mine.

For the first time, I understood reality could be so much lovelier than dreams.

Midwinter was upon us, and Black's Keep had opened its doors to not just the residents of Greyton, but also those of Lirinsholme hardy enough to make the snowy ascent. My parents were there, and my sisters—Therella scowling quite a bit as she realized not only was I the lady of the castle, but also that the feared Dragon Lord had turned out to be young and handsome—and Lilianth and Adain and so many others of my friends and family.

"I told you the true Seeing would come in handy one day," my Granny Menyon told me with a wink, as she helped herself to yet another cup of mulled wine. "Proud I am, that my own granddaughter should be the one to break the curse!"

"It was luck more than anything—" I began, but she shook her head.

"Not luck. It was the gods' doing, knowing it was time for things to change."

As may be true. I somehow doubted the gods occupied themselves with such petty matters, but if that was what my grandmother wished to believe, I would not gainsay her. Who knows, really, why a certain combination of circumstances brings about a given conclusion? Chance, or luck...or the gods. I was not quite stubborn enough to say it couldn't be any one of those things, or perhaps all three.

All I knew was that I stood in the great feasting hall where once I had taken my first meal with Theran, and reflected that it could not be more different. Evergreen boughs were swagged from the mantel and from the great wrought-iron chandelier overhead, and even from the sconces along the walls. The air smelled of spiced wine and rich roasted meats, and everywhere I looked I saw smiles, albeit mixed with glances of wonderment. After all, no one save members of the castle's household had set foot in Black's Keep for five hundred years.

Well, that was changed now. We would have to make our own traditions, and forge our own path in the world. And I knew I could face the future without fear, for I would have Theran at my side.

I gazed across the room and saw him watching me. A rush of warmth went through me as I recalled the touch of his mouth on mine, the heat of his skin against me as I lay in bed next to him. We were now man and wife in every sense of the word, and again I marveled at how much I desired him. Even now, with the hall crowded around us, I recalled his touch, and a flush of desire went through my body once more. The celebration was grand, but I would be glad when we were alone once more, and could disappear into one another all over again.

As if our eyes meeting were a signal, he excused himself from the portly merchant with whom he had been speaking, and came to meet me.

"Do you like it?" he asked.

Most likely he referred to the gaiety of the Midwinter gathering around us, but in my mind his question meant so much more. "It's wonderful. More than I had ever dreamed it would be."

He didn't pretend to misunderstand me, instead taking me by the hand and leading me into a little side gallery, where a mullioned window looked down over the snow-covered gardens. "I invited all these people, thinking it would be a gesture of goodwill, but I confess now that I would much rather they were elsewhere."

Since I knew no one could see us, I stood on my tiptoes and kissed him soundly, my body thrilling as he folded me into his arms and deepened the kiss. I tasted mulled wine on his lips and tongue, as no doubt he tasted it on mine as well.

"A poor host," I said, after we had pulled apart. "And yet, I must be a poor hostess as well, for I confess I feel much the same way."

"Ah, well, we must console ourselves with the knowledge that there are many more nights to come after this."

"And mornings, and afternoons..."

He laughed then, the lines around his eyes crinkling with amusement. "Yes, and those, too. And you said you would teach me to paint—"

"And you would teach me to ride—"

"So I did. We have all these things to look forward to, but in the meantime, I suppose we should not shirk our duty as hosts."

"No, I suppose not." I kissed him again, quickly, a deposit against a future, more lengthy engagement. "Shall we go back in?"

He nodded, and took my arm, and led me back into the hall, where once again we were surrounded by well-wishers. Light and warmth filled the room, a bulwark against the cold winter night, and from a place of honor above the mantel the portrait of Theran looked down on all of us, that secret smile still touching the corner of his mouth.

Seeing it, I smiled as well.

www.ingramcontent.com/pod-product-compliance
Lightning Source LLC
LaVergne TN
LVHW091119080826
845145LV00008B/1976